on track ...
Billy Joel

every album, every song

Lisa Torem
Foreword by Liberty DeVitto

sonicbondpublishing.com

Sonicbond Publishing Limited
www.sonicbondpublishing.co.uk
Email: info@sonicbondpublishing.co.uk

First Published in the United Kingdom 2022
First Published in the United States 2022

British Library Cataloguing in Publication Data:
A Catalogue record for this book is available from the British Library

Copyright Lisa Torem 2022

ISBN 978-1-78952-183-2

Typeset in ITC Garamond & ITC Avant Garde
Printed and bound in England

Graphic design and typesetting: Full Moon Media

on track ...
Billy Joel

every album, every song

Lisa Torem
Foreword by Liberty DeVitto

sonicbondpublishing.com

Acknowledgements

Lisa Torem is grateful to musicians Felix Cavaliere, Rhys Clark, Liberty DeVitto, Dennis Dunaway, Howard Emerson, Anthony Gourdine and Elliott Murphy, producers Joe Nicolo and David Thoener, photographer Dawn Richter, publicist George Dassinger, publisher Rob Wallis, Hudson Music, editorial consultants John Clarkson and Christopher Torem.

Liberty DeVitto went above and beyond by composing a timely forward and offering his invaluable insights.

This project was possible because of publisher Stephen Lambe's foresight and patience.

Thanks to Madeline Torem for creative consultation and to Billy Joel for a discography that continues to inspire worldwide audiences.

Love to Emily, Allison and Stella and Viv and Phil.

on track ...

Billy Joel

Contents

Foreword

Lisa Torem delves headfirst into her analysis of Billy Joel's recordings. She sees his lyric not only as part of the song but as pure poetry – poetry that is connected to the music by the perfect melody, rhythm, chord structure, arrangement and production. This combination becomes the story.

With her explanation of each song, she will make the listener hear it as perhaps they have never heard it before. On *Turnstiles*, she makes the true Billy Joel fan go back and hear how Topper – which was comprised of myself, Russell Javors, Doug Stegmeyer and Howie Emerson, along with Richie Cannata – steered Billy's musical ship into new waters.

I have played drums for Billy both live and on the record for 30 years. In my book *Life, Billy, and the Pursuit of Happiness*, I write about how those songs were put together in the studio as if I am a spectator perched on the drum seat. I know these songs as performing on them.

Lisa writes how she, the listener, hears these songs. This book is written with the same passion that was first recorded on every song. In the end, she will leave you with knowing how Billy Joel became one of the biggest names in the world of music.

Liberty DeVitto (The Lords of 52nd Street, Slim Kings; sessions with Meat Loaf, Paul McCartney and so many more legends.)

Introduction

Over the course of merely a few days, I found Billy Joel's music everywhere: an American football team huddled on a high school field as 'Movin' Out' streamed from a tinny speaker. Soulful sounds courtesy of saxophonist Richie Cannata and bassist Doug Stegmeyer rose above the piano man's shatter-glass chords the following day.

On Saturday morning at minigolf, Joel belted out names of the 'We Didn't Start The Fire' movers and shakers. The sun drifted below a rotating windmill, but drummer Liberty DeVitto took us to higher ground on the pulsating 'You May Be Right.'

From bodegas, strip malls and airport terminals to king-size arenas, Joel's music intersects generations. Some discovered his talent via the 1988 animated Disney musical *Oliver & Company* – featuring 'Why Should I Worry?', the first recorded song Joel didn't scribe, but for which he supplied New York *savoir faire* and gave agency to the imaginary mutt Dodger based on Dickens' irascible pickpocket.

Joel's history with producers is a story in and of itself. At 15, he ventured into a Hicksville basement – the site of Dynamic Studios – where fellow Long Islander George 'Shadow' Morton held court. In 1987, Joel told *Q* magazine in the UK that 'Shadow' needed a keyboardist to demo 'Remember (Walkin' In The Sand') for The Shangri-Las in 1964 (and later, biker-anthem 'Leader Of The Pack.') 'Shadow' had a peculiar way of communicating: 'He's waving his arms in the air saying, 'Give me more purple,' and I'm sitting there kinda nervous.'

What did that phrase mean? Finally, a session guitarist leaned over. 'Uh, just play louder, kid,' he snapped. (Ironically, the co-producer was none other than promoter Artie Ripp.) Covers got Joel into the studio; his originals kept him captive.

'Shadow' also recorded Joel's CBS folk singer labelmate Janis Ian, with whom Joel performed at the Philadelphia Academy of Music on 25 November 1974, and where an excited Bruce Springsteen and mentor DJ Ed Sciakey taxied to catch the double bill. Ian had also supported Joel on 15 November at two consecutive concert dates at New York's Avery Fisher Hall. In her 2008 memoir *Society's Child*, Ian recalled that her *modus operandi* for the first eight months of touring in 1974 included 'opening for bigger acts whenever I could.' While some acts invariably trumped others, she extolled, 'My favorite by far was Billy Joel, who had a terrific band and was always down to earth and fun to be with.'

When contending with 'Shadow,' Ian was proactive, particularly when he buried his head in a newspaper during her audition. She told *pennyblackmusic.co.uk*:

He kept saying that he was going to leave the music business, and he wasn't even polite enough to look at me, and so I set the newspaper on fire. When the lawyer who brought me asked me to sing a third song, I went ahead and set the paper on fire. Well, for Shadow, he was so used to people just thinking,

'Oh, God, this is the great Shadow Morton,' and I thought, 'Man, you have no manners.'

With melodies that feed the souls of everyday people as they perform perfunctory tasks, Joel has become one of the biggest-selling artists in the US, yet he'll often dismiss his rock-star status. He's liable to shrug and shy away from the camera or look up at a king-size screen in disbelief. Still, his studio work speaks volumes.

'Rock and Roll, it saved my life; it's my religion,' Joel exclaimed to journalist Bryant Gumbel on YouTube.

The *Oxford Dictionary* defines eclectic as 'A person who derives ideas, style or taste from a broad and diverse range of sources.' Joel's eclecticism spans classical, reggae, jazz, blues, classic rock, new wave and punk. Did I mention bluegrass? These slices-of-life are peppered with people for whom he's felt empathy, but he has also drawn from Shakespeare, Blake, Thomas, Frost and war-centered novelists. To honor his muses, though, one needs to review the faces behind his rich catalogue. What I'm getting at is that Joel's determination to branch out musically from song to song and album to album from the inception of *Cold Spring Harbor* to *River of Dreams* and *Fantasies & Delusions,* has never been compromised.

Hardly a product of privilege, Joel began working at a young age. To make ends meet, he stamped typewriter ribbons, boxed in tournaments, pumped gas and fished from a Long Island Sound oyster boat at ungodly hours. The common denominator – his resilience – played a big role in the maintenance of his concert and recording career.

Fast-forward to March 2011 and *The Book of Joel*. Notable peers had penned memoirs, and fans were anxious to hear his story, but Joel surprised the publisher by asserting that his life would be better represented through his songs. Countless interviews and lyrics upheld that line of thought. His songs *should* tell the story. His *children* have endured growing pains, self-doubt, euphoria and trauma. Some developed early, and some will remain pubescent. Why not let *them* speak?

In 2002, choreographer Twyla Tharp directed the Broadway musical *Movin' Out*, which led to the songwriter's first Tony award. To carry out the theme, dancers enacted his vivid stories. 'One explanation for the dance piece's enormous appeal is the story of heartbreak and reconciliation that Tharp located in the semi-autobiographical material written by Joel during his 'still rock and roll to me' years,' observed theatermania.com. *They* spoke. To that end, Joel's songs remain in service.

This book is not a biography. The excellent books listed in the bibliography serve that purpose, yet the pathos and proactivism that Joel weaves into his canon are unique and do require backstory.

The singer-songwriter's family history was riddled with tension. Joel's grandparents Karl and Meta, fled from the Nazis in Nuremberg, Germany.

Fortuitously, they reconnected with their young son Howard (Helmut), who'd been attending school in Switzerland. Determined to escape and with limited choices, the family boarded a ship in England headed for Cuba in 1939. After the harbor master's clearance, they spent three years on the Caribbean island before relocating to New York City.

Howard met his future wife Rosalind Nyman at Gilbert and Sullivan's *The Pirates of Penzance*, in which the musical enthusiasts took part. But their lives, too, endured a drastic change. In 1943, Howard was drafted into World War II and sent back to Europe. While stationed in Germany, he came upon the ghosts of his ancestral past: in a jeep with other soldiers, he witnessed the remains of the family's overtaken, burned-out factory.

They married in 1946. Their newborn William Martin Joel took his first breath in the Bronx under Taurus skies three years later. Joel was raised in a musical home. Though his father made his living as an engineer, he enjoyed spending his free time playing concert-pianist material. Joel shared his father and paternal grandfather's high regard for classical music. That early exposure greatly influenced his melodic and often complex harmonic arrangements.

Joel took easily to the piano and possessed another gift which would influence his future writing. With Tori Amos, Mary J. Blige and Billie Eilish, Joel shares an extraordinary condition called synesthesia which enables him to actually see the colors of the music that he plays. In January 2020, Joel explained to *popdust.com* in the article, '15 Iconic Musicians with Synesthesia', 'When I think of different types of melodies which are slower or softer, I think in terms of blues or greens. When I see a particularly vivid color, it is usually a strong melodic, strong rhythmic pattern which emerges at the same time.'

After World War II, urban planners built affordable housing for veterans. As such, the family relocated to a cheaply-constructed development called Levittown in Hicksville, Long Island, when Joel turned one. Life in this sheltered enclave likely inspired *outsider* writing, but stereotypes about suburban youth had to be addressed. Joel told *Entertainment Tonight* in the 1980s: 'We are people. We had loves and hates and gangs and sex and all of those things. You don't have to come to the inner city to have something to say.'

As Joel acquired monetary success, he was value-judged by certain critics who questioned his integrity. Reminders of his blue-collar background helped dispel disparaging remarks. 'How do you think I got my money? I didn't inherit it. I worked very hard. Touring is hard. Writing is work. Doing interviews is work.'

Piano lessons began at four years old. Like many American students of his era, he would sight-read from the rosy-red covered John Thompson series. His early piece, 'Music Land' was perfectly designed for little fingers but monotonous. Dissatisfied with 'reading the dots,' he ad-libbed bass lines and ornamentation.

Joel loved hearing his father play classics, but his happiness was cut short when Howard returned to Europe four years later. Despite monthly support checks, the family struggled financially. To compound matters, social biases in the 1950s created divisions. Theirs was one of the few Jewish families in the neighborhood, and a stigma regarding divorced women also persisted. In hindsight, one could understand why Joel might have grown up feeling like an 'Angry Young Man.'

Yet, there were pluses. Some fathers reprimanded or physically abused their children. With an absentee parent, the youngster had no such concerns.

Joel developed a curious rapport with his suddenly-single mother. He has joked in interviews about keeping her at bay during practice. For instance, rather than reading note-for-note, he emulated a specific composer's style. This got him off the hook in one sense, but then again, he had to replicate that practice session the following day, and his memory couldn't always abide. Nevertheless, Joel kept up, even when logistics put him in harm's way. When word got out that 'Miss Frances' also taught ballet, Joel became a target for bullies. Fortunately, boxing lessons helped forestall further attacks. In fact, he won a high percentage of fights as a teen, developed inner confidence, and came away unscathed, save for a broken nose.

After plowing through 12 years of classical music, he fell in love with rock. The high school years caused his mother concern. Working in clubs put money in the coffers but left him exhausted. Though sharp academically, the lack of sleep made it difficult to keep up with the Hicksville High schedule. Because he skipped his final English exam, he didn't receive his diploma (until years later after completing essays). Still, he knew he'd devote his future to music, and as a voracious reader and history lover, education would always be within his grasp, even without a tassel and gown. In other words, there was no plan B. The foreseeable future entailed life as a gigging musician, not a concert pianist; the heirloom Lester piano shared by father and son got recycled as a garden planter.

Yet classical music continued to pique Joel's interest throughout his rock career. A turning point occurred after hearing the haunting 'Adagio For Strings' by Samuel Barber, which was played during the 1986 American film *Platoon*, and at Albert Einstein's funeral. Joel took stock: 'This is what I want to create. I hope, before I can't write anymore, that I can create music like that.' Some of Joel's most popular songs began life as instrumentals. 'The Longest Time' for example, was a Mozart-inspired variation on a theme, but ultimately became an *a cappella* vocal number on *An Innocent Man*. 'Lullaby (Goodnight My Angel)' also began as an instrumental,' Joel explained during a master class conducted at CW Post at Long Island University. But for his first daughter Alexa, he inserted reassuring words after she asked, 'What happens after we die?' Joel confirmed to Gumbel: 'I'm not a poet, I'm a lyricist, but first, I'm a musician': a thought best encapsulated in the 'Piano Man' line, 'We're all in the mood for a melody....'

Like many of his peers, Joel was captivated by The Beatles' first appearance on the American TV program *The Ed Sullivan Show* on 9 February 1964. He explained to Gumbel: 'When I saw The Beatles, it was like seeing friends of mine. They were just regular guys. They were just a bunch of wise guys. I said, 'It can be done.'' Joel was equally intrigued by these gifted, black-American vocalists and pianists: Ray Charles, Fats Domino, James Brown, Wilson Pickett, Otis Redding, and duo Sam and Dave.

On the BBC TV program *The Old Grey Whistle Test* – aired from 1971 to 1988 – Joel mimicked his heroes' styles. Blessed with an exceptional ear for vocal inflection, he expertly imitated his influences: sometimes unintentionally. But while he has been outspoken about his muses, his transparency has often backfired; certain critics have labeled his work 'derivative.' True, Joel modeled certain aspects of his work after specific artists, but who hasn't? The Beatles cited Chuck Berry and The Everly Brothers as instrumental and vocal influences. Their 1964 *Introducing The Beatles* included the covers 'Anna (Go to Him') by Arthur Alexander, 'Chains' by Gerry Goffin and Carole King, 'Boys' by Luther Dixon and Wes Farrell, and 'Twist And Shout' by Phil Medley and Bert Russell. The Rolling Stones cited Willie Dixon's 'Little Red Rooster,' among others, for their success, and Led Zeppelin's fourth album included Memphis Minnie's 1929 song 'When The Levee Breaks.'

One auspicious night, Joel set this burning issue to rest. The moment of truth occurred in 1999 after Ray Charles good-naturedly inducted Joel into Cleveland's Rock and Roll Hall of Fame. Firmly grasping his gold statuette at the podium, Joel rattled off names of significant shoulders on which he has stood. Then, peering out over stage lights, he asserted that every soul there was inspired by someone else; case closed.

Joel could hardly wait to play in a band. At 14, this happened when bassist Howie Blauvelt urged him to join The Echoes (then The Emeralds, and later The Lost Souls). Like many British Invasion bands, the guys coordinated outfits and balanced harmonies. At first, the bandmates thrived on covers. But to remain in the good graces of club owners, they wrote originals. Ultimately, being the most well-read, Joel took up the mantle and dreamed up a stanza or two.

When The Lost Souls got scooped up by Mercury Records, they became labelmates with the mellow-voiced Lesley Gore. The teen's one-off talent was not reflective of the mostly-pedestrian acts the company employed. They hadn't developed a brand; Mercury couldn't successfully market The Lost Souls' sound. They switched gears again, as their current name was already in use, but complained when the label suggested the militaristic moniker The Commandos. Yet these crucial decisions mattered little. The label lost interest and failed to release Lost Souls records.

Nevertheless, Joel experienced the thrill of writing, co-writing and hearing songs arranged by fellow musicians. Despite label ennui, the band kept up their spirits by performing at My House in Plainview, which was owned by the parents of their manager Irwin Mazur. (The original venue name was Danny Mazur's Cat and Fiddle. After losing his liquor license, Mazur catered to teens.)

Meanwhile, future Billy Joel drummer Liberty DeVitto was actively performing with The New Rock Workshop. The two admired one another's work and exchanged greetings, but a partnership would take a few years to solidify.

My House featured several nightly bands. Headliners included The Young Rascals (The Rascals) and The Four Tops. The blue-eyed soul band The Hassles featured charismatic frontman John Dizek, Harry Weber on keys, Rich McKenna on guitar, and drummer Jon Small. Their sterling reputation yielded a loyal following. With Mazur as the vigilant gatekeeper, the club was in good stead, and the band enjoyed a steady flow of fans. But their popularity couldn't camouflage internal issues. Weber's glue-sniffing habit – having gotten out of control – was affecting the band's performance and reputation. Having heard Joel audition for The Commandos, Small was impressed by the pianist's bluesy style and cool demeanor. His intent was to usher Joel into the fold. But Joel faced a tough decision: he had a deep sense of loyalty to his then-bandmates. (His loyalties would be tested in the future with Beatles producer George Martin.) The musicians reached a settlement when Joel brought Blauvelt onboard. Mazur, in turn, sweetened the deal by offering the keyboardist a Hammond B3, but other setbacks occurred.

The two albums produced for United Artists rarely saw the light of day, although the band's cover of the Isaac Hayes and David Porter-penned 'You Got Me Hummin'' – made famous by Sam and Dave, and retitled as 'You've Got Me Hummin'' – generated sales in 1967. (Joel re-released the song under its original title in 1983 as a live version on the B-side of 'Tell Her About It'.) The first song Joel wrote on behalf of The Hassles – 'Every Step I Take (Every Move I Make)' – appears on the 2005 album *My Lives*.

Joel hit it right. Manhattan had traditionally been the ultimate score card, but in 1967, Long Island was acquiring a reputation as a hotspot, offering unprecedented exposure and the possibility of getting signed. The Vanilla Fudge (formerly The Pigeons) cultivated a fan base. The scene was exploding. Long Island singer-songwriter Elliott Murphy (now residing in Paris) looked back at the era fondly in a 2021 interview with the author:

When I started playing professionally at 16 in the late-1960s, there was a big club scene. We had the Action House, where the great house band was The Vagrants featuring Leslie West. And the Long Island sound usually involved a Hammond B3 organ. And *they* were heavy as hell! Every band needed a van to carry around that organ and Leslie speaker cabinet and all the other gear. We would write the band name on the side of the van. So, you would see these little Econoline vans riding around on Long Island Expressway with band names on the side. Not only were there The Hassles and The Vagrants, but also The Rich Kids, The Illusions, The Good Rats, and my first band, *The King James Version*. We all shopped at Sam Ash Music in Hempstead. It was a great boot camp for the music business because we were professionals, but the real music scene in Manhattan was like a Land of Oz that we only dreamed of breaking into. A few of us – like Billy Joel, myself, Twisted Sister – finally did.

Initially, Joel commandeered the keys. Raspy-voiced Little John sang lead, but eventually, the keyboardist established a dynamic vocal presence.

Long Island musicians are a loyal bunch. Billy Joel inducted Murphy into the Long Island Hall of Fame in 2018. Both natives jump-started their musical careers early and kept in close contact. Murphy's discography has been enriched by Joel's musical contributions and vice versa. In a video interview with rockhistory.com, Murphy referred to Joel as 'another Long Island guy,' and recalled driving to a 'club in a snowstorm' to see his friend. Although Joel was not the lead singer, whatever he sang was 'note-for-note perfect.' Murphy left the club with this impression: 'He hears something; he can play it and he can sing it in that style too. He's an amazing chameleon.'

In an updated interview with the author on 20 October 2021, Murphy elaborated:

The first time I saw Billy Joel perform was at a club called My House in Plainview, Long Island, with his band The Hassles. They opened the show with a cover version of 'Gimme Some Lovin'' by The Spencer Davis Group, and it was phenomenal! I don't think there were more than 50 people in the audience, but Billy was so amazing that it was like a stadium show. He was the most naturally-gifted musician to come out of the Long Island music scene that I know.

Murphy relayed that he 'opened for Joel on many occasions in the 1970s' when both artists were at Columbia Records. Accordingly, Murphy mentioned that he observed fan reactions to classic songs: 'Captain Jack' and 'Allentown' always went over well, and of course 'Piano Man.' Joel's later hits 'Uptown Girl' and (my favorite) 'We Didn't Start the Fire', came later.'

As Joel's career progressed, Murphy developed a keen awareness of his friend's legacy:

He was always a great performer and very confident on stage, but perhaps he's grown as a bandleader. What's most amazing is that his song catalogue stands up so well. He hasn't released any new songs in decades, but the old ones still sound fresh when he performs them. And his voice hasn't deteriorated in the slightest. He's the Frank Sinatra/George Gershwin of my generation.

The Rascals (formerly The Young Rascals) inspired up and coming bands in the 1960s in the Long Island area and beyond. Singer, keyboardist, producer Felix Cavaliere kept up his friendship and professional relationship with Joel over the years and played keyboards on the 'Hey Girl' (Goffen, King) video. Cavaliere told pennyblackmusic on 14 March 2022:

We were one of the first American groups to come out during the British Invasion. Billy's a little younger than I am, and so he basically saw us as a milestone as to what could be done in music. He liked the group a lot. Billy's amazing and his main instrument was piano. At that time, my main instrument was organ. Billy's in a class by himself; there's no question about that.

But back to Joel's early days: the newly-minted group The Hassles' self-titled album did well locally. Follow-up *Hour of the Wolf* allowed the budding songwriter to hone his writing chops, but the project received little critical acclaim. The Hassles hadn't captured the psychedelic sound fans craved. They were losing momentum, so Small and Joel – determined to develop a new sound – paired up in earnest.

Attila – the stripped-down entity – featured Small manning the drums and Joel blending keys with aggressive vocals. Their main believer Irwin Mazur stayed on as manager. Epic Records picked them up, but the album flopped and they were panned by the press.

Joel's funds were diminishing, but his friendship with Jon Small was deepening, so he moved in with Small, his wife Elizabeth Weber and their young son Sean. This was the first of several entanglements to follow with the extended Weber clan. Joel and Elizabeth fell in love while all parties lived under the same roof. 'Jon and Elizabeth started to part. It became common knowledge that the marriage was going to go,' observed friend and musician Bruce Gentile in the Hank Bordowitz book *Billy Joel: The Life and Times of An Angry Young Man*. According to Joshua S. Duchan in *Billy Joel: America's Piano Man*, 'Eventually, she took off with Joel, her husband's best friend, who assumed – incorrectly – that she had already broken things off with her husband.' The two men were left alone to patch things up.

It was all too much. Devastated by the failure of Attila and the possibility of losing his romantic partner forever, Joel made two suicide attempts several weeks apart. For the second attempt, he drank furniture polish. After falling into a coma, Jon Small and Bruce Gentile discovered their friend in a 'cedar closet'. When he regained consciousness, Joel found himself in the Meadowbrook Hospital Psychiatric Ward for observation. 'Once you signed in, you had to stay for three weeks. It was a good slap in the face,' Joel confided to Gumbel. According to the Bordowitz book, Mazur executed a plan. Posing as a psychiatrist in lab attire, he finessed his way past authorities and guided his client to freedom. 'They wanted a shrink to release him, so I did a little impression of somebody who was an authority figure,' Mazur said.

After being released, Joel rejected show business. Certain that Elizabeth was through with him, he assured Mazur he'd make ends meet with odd jobs in the Midwest. But Mazur scowled at the defeatist remark and offered an ultimatum: he promised to secure a record deal within 30 days. The metronome was clicking...

Mazur's brother worked at Paramount Records and had connections. When the eager manager ran into Michael Lang, the former Woodstock impresario expressed curiosity about Mazur's time-sensitive project. Lang suggested that California-based promoter Artie Ripp could clinch the deal and agreed to hand Joel's demo over on an upcoming West Coast trip.

The demo contained future hits 'She's Always A Woman' and 'She's Got A Way,' which Elizabeth Weber inspired. She would become Joel's wife, and eventually, his manager: a decision which would dramatically affect the songwriter's destiny.

In 1971, Mazur cemented the deal with Artie Ripp's Family Productions label. Mazur had made good on his promise. But what about the deal? Ripp, a producer for Kama Sutra and Buddha Records, had signed The Lovin' Spoonful, who charted with 'Summer In The City.' He promoted the catchy genre known as bubblegum – a commercial godsend, as records were easy to churn out, inexpensive to produce and profitable for the labels, yet the genre was sometimes perceived by critics as vacuous. Case in point – the two-minute 'Yummy Yummy Yummy' – boasting the hook 'I've got love In my tummy' – by Ohio Express attracted young record buyers in 1968, but would this lightweight music continually chart? Could Ripp promote serious work?

Joel required a producer that could cultivate and expand on new ideas and respect his point of view regarding the final sound quality of instrumental and vocal tracks. A fair financial agreement would ice the cake. But according to Bordowitz, the contract was biased: 'It gave away all the things an artist lives on: publishing rights, copyrights and royalties.' Joel – like many of his peers – signed a contract that was relatively one-sided. He told Bordowitz: 'I didn't know anything about publishing or monies that were owed to me.'

In 1971, Joel released *Cold Spring Harbor* – the solo effort that emphasized his then-acute melodic sense. But the record suffered from cavalier mastering. The sped-up tape made the vocals sound like America's animated Alvin and the Chipmunks. (In the 1980s, Ripp remastered the album, but Joel also found fault with the updated version, for which he'd not been consulted.) On a positive note, the album yielded a tour that enhanced Joel's stage persona and gave him valuable experience working with other musicians on his own arrangements.

Ultimately, CBS executive Walter Yetnikoff reclaimed Joel's publishing rights; he discussed details during *The Last Play at Shea* documentary. Joel remained on the hook for ten albums in which the Family label logo would remain visible, and royalty points were allegedly divided unfairly. But with contractual issues resolved, Joel could pursue his dream of becoming a Columbia Records artist.

Joel's faith was renewed when 'Captain Jack' – a searing original taken from a live Philadelphia WMMR-FM broadcast – set forth a tsunami with college-aged students. Word spread quickly about the gritty-voiced performer and his envelope-pushing theme: a tale of a housing project drug dealer that Joel spied from his Oyster Bay apartment window. While the liberal college kids loved the song, conservatives misconstrued the meaning. Was Joel encouraging American youth to become drug addicts? After all, the hook was 'Captain Jack will get you high tonight.' Ironically, Joel intended 'Captain Jack' to be an 'antidrug' song. After all, he painted the protagonist as an unsavory character. But this wouldn't be the last time Joel would get thrown under the bus for his lyric writing. Nevertheless, critical cries were drowned out by the ballad's gyrating rhythms and passionate delivery. College crowds rallied for more. Finally, Joel's flexibility and fluency were being acknowledged. This chameleon could sound like Paul McCartney, Ray Charles, Tony Bennett or Joe Cocker, and more importantly, like the most natural version of himself.

Joel had exceeded his goal of simply creating demos for others. He was becoming virtuosic in his own right. *Mar y Sol* was an exceptional breeding ground for budding skills. After opening for The Beach Boys at the Miami Convention Center, Joel – with bassist Larry Russell, acoustic/electric guitarist Al Hertzberg and drummer Rhys Clark – flew to Puerto Rico the next morning to perform at the island's first international music festival in April 1972. In an updated interview with the author in December 2021, Clark recalled:

> There was no time for nerves, only excitement. We connected to a 10-seater commuter flight to Vega Baha Resort Casino. Two hours later, we hopped a 'copter to the fest site, where we hung out in a palm-thatched and plastic lean-to dressing room, with Billy's name scratched on a plank supporting a 'plastic' roof. We were scheduled for the 5 p.m. time slot on day two of the three-day, 32-act festival. We set up and had lines and mics checked. Then, it started to heavily rain. The fans – who were frolicking in the rain – were giving full attention to the act. We scrambled for cover, but at 6 p.m., the weather cleared and we rocked! The crowd of about 30,000 loved it. We ended the six-song set with 'Tomorrow Is Today', and to our surprise, they started yelling for more. We came out and launched into Billy's Joe Cocker version of The Box Tops' 'The Letter' (at the suggestion of Mazur). The crowd surged to the stage, thinking it really was Cocker, and yelled for more. (In an earlier YouTube interview, Clark depicted this event as, 'the most euphoric and frightening experience.') Billy got Elizabeth and Brian (Ruggles, the original sound mixer and road tech from 1971) up for background vocals, and then we rocked on The Rolling Stones' 'Jumpin' Jack Flash.' It was a highly magical set. I personally got an extra lift when Dave Brubeck's then-drummer Alan Dawson asked to use my drum set.

Although the band enhanced Joel's originals, Clark acknowledged, 'There was a lot of musicality in what was going on already.' Ironically, the disagreeable weather worked in the band's favor, as the act enjoyed increased encore time.

The *Mar y Sol* lineup included headliner Dave Brubeck. The pianist's unorthodox time signatures (5/4, 9/8) and progressive harmonies on *Time Out* had left a deep impression on Joel. Like Brubeck, he strove to defy convention. Joel told Mary Travis in 1975:

> Brubeck was my first inspiration to get into improvisation and style. When you don't have a bass player and your left hand is the bass, it's the wrong way to play. You're supposed to have left-hand chords and right-hand fooling around. I play left-hand bass and right-hand fooling around. Right-hand classical, left-hand boogie-woogie came from playing lounges.

Another headliner was the shock rock act The Alice Cooper Group. In a 7 October 2021 interview with the author, original bassist, co-songwriter and co-founder Dennis Dunaway commented on Joel's public status: 'Few knew who he was at that time.'

Although the band was raring to go, they had to readjust plans due to logistics: which, ironically, worked out in Joel's favor. Dunaway explains: 'Scheduled to play at 11 p.m., we were tuned up and ready to go, but the festival was running so far behind schedule that we didn't hit the stage until the following morning at sunrise.'

Rumors circulated that Columbia Records executive Clive Davis was present. Certainly, his scouts showed up, but according to his autobiography, Davis discovered Joel not at the fest but through a public-relations colleague. Davis, who had earned respect for signing Janis Joplin, Laura Nyro, Donovan and Pink Floyd, was on high alert after the fever that 'Captain Jack' and *Mar y Sol* induced.

So, with the security of the major label CBS (Columbia Records) behind him, Joel relocated to L.A. and gigged at the Executive Room as a piano bar entertainer. To maintain a low profile, he used the moniker Bill Martin (not really a stretch: Martin *was* his middle name.) By hiding out for a spell, he hoped that Ripp would move on if he couldn't locate his client; maybe he'd lose interest and loosen up on the ironclad demands.

In the meantime, Joel wrote the hummable signature ballad that would gild his career path moving forward (although, ironically, this commercial gem would not yet translate into major revenue for the 'piano man'.) Joel intuited early on that people had to strongly relate to a theme. To that end, he modeled 'Piano Man' after down-to-earth people and nuggets of casual, believable conversation. This pattern of noting everyday discourse and morphing it into a catchy lyric, would repeat over the course of his decades-long career.

On the romantic front, Joel exchanged vows with Elizabeth Weber Small in 1973. As a signed artist with income, he ceased couch surfing and offered his new wife and stepson a future. Weber in turn, as manager, assisted in jump-starting her spouse's career.

Joel has sold more than 150,000,000 records – according to his website billyjoel.com – since signing his initial recording contract in 1972. Twenty years later, he became a recipient of the Songwriter's Hall of Fame. In 2013, vocalist

Tony Bennett awarded Joel the 36th Annual Kennedy Center Honor. There, Joel heard choice arrangements of his originals by Don Henley, Garth Brooks and Rufus Wainwright, among others.

At Madison Square Garden – where Joel first played in 2014 – he has continued the monthly tradition, although the Covid-19 pandemic altered dates. To commemorate all concert dates, a Billy Joel banner waves in homage.

Known for his philanthropy, Joel performed at The Concert for Sandy Relief in December 2012; many other causes followed.

Billy Joel – a veritable craftsman and one-man orchestra – has performed with legions of others yet is equally on-target as a lone wolf; well, not completely alone: he is, after all, in constant communication with 88 keys.

At the Rock and Roll Hall of Fame induction – along with Paul McCartney, Dusty Springfield, George Martin and others – Joel came full circle. When Ray Charles presented the award, Joel shook his head in disbelief. 'Can you believe this?,' he quipped, gazing at the gleaming trophy: 'That's the Washington monument.'

What's included and what's not included

We'll amble through Joel's extensive discography: every album, every song, every single, compilation and live concert recording. I won't dwell on demos, videos or concerts, but will cite stories and anecdotes relative to the songs at hand.

Our studio album journey begins with *Cold Spring Harbor* (1971) and concludes with *Fantasies and Delusions* (2001). I'll balance out opinions with other journalists and *I-was-there* testimonials from drummers Rhys Clark and Liberty DeVitto, guitarist Howard Emerson, bassist Dennis Dunaway, singer Anthony Gourdine, singer-songwriter Elliott Murphy, and studio producers David Thoener and Joe Nicolo.

Whether you're a superfan or a browser, we'll hopefully reach common ground when reviewing Joel's distinctive oeuvre. I have invariably provided more information on some tracks than others and varied the lengths of my album introductions over the course of this document. As author, I reserve the right to make considerations based on criteria such as back story or musical style, but rest assured that I have given attention to every album, every song.

That said, let's get started. American singer-songwriter Billy Joel has procured worldwide fame for over five decades. How has he sustained that level of success? Let's shine a light on his uniquely New York state of mind with his debut album.

Cold Spring Harbor (1971)

Personnel:

Billy Joel: acoustic piano, Hammond organ, harpsichord, harmonica, vocals

Rhys Clark: drums on 'Everybody Loves You Now' (1971 mix), 'Falling Of The Rain,' 'Turn Around' (1971) and 'Tomorrow Is Today' (1971); cymbals on 'She's Got A Way'

Sal DiTroia: guitar

Don Evans: guitar

Jimmie Haskell: arrangements

Sneaky Pete Kleinow: pedal steel on 'Turn Around'

Larry Knechtel: bass

Artie Ripp: arrangements, conductor

Denny Siewell: drums on 'Everybody Loves You Now' and 'You Look So Good To Me'

Mike McGee: drums on 'Everybody Loves You Now' and 'Turn Around' (1983 remix)

Al Campbell: keys on 'Turn Around' (1983 remix)

L. D. Dixon: Fender Rhodes on 'Turn Around' (1983 remix)

Production:

Artie Ripp: producer, engineer, remix, editing, direction

Irwin Mazur: executive producer, art director

Larry Elliott: engineer, remixing, editing

John Bradley: engineer

Michael D. Stone: second engineer

Gordon Watanabe: assistant engineer

Bob Hughes: mastering

Doug Sax: mastering (1987)

Joseph Palmaccio, remastering (1998 CD)

Ted Jensen: remastering (2011 CD)

Produced in July 1971 at Record Plant West, Los Angeles, California; July 1971 at Ultra-sonic Recording Studios, Hempstead, NY by Artie Ripp ('Why Judy Why' and 'You Look So Good to Me')

Label: Family Productions/Columbia

Release dates: 1 November, 1971 (UK, US)

Chart positions: (1984) UK: (OCC) 95, USA: 158, Japan (Oricon): 44

Length: 33:07 (Original), 29:53 (Remix and remaster)

Cold Spring Harbor was the sole record not distributed on Columbia, the label Joel dreamed about getting signed to when in high school. The album featured strong, melodic songs. Joel has stated in interviews that melody comes first whenever he sits down to write. At times, he has downplayed his lyrics, regarding some as casual afterthoughts. But many fans and critics consider his lyrics to be as expressive as his melodies. His nods to colloquialism, pop culture, American and world history set him apart from many of his peers.

Even at this early stage, Joel's vocal quality and storytelling had the potential to please fans as much as his instrumental ideas. 1971 was an excellent time in which to showcase original material, as singer-songwriters were in demand. These cost-efficient studio angels eliminated the need to negotiate permissions issues.

Joel had an enviable spot in the queue – John Prine's self-titled epic was launched in January, followed by Carole King's *Tapestry* in February. Leonard Cohen's third album *Songs of Love and Hate* and James Taylor's *Mud Slide Slim and the Blue Horizon* were released in March. Joel idol John Lennon released *Imagine* in October. Era-wise, Joel was on a golden path with a delivery date in November, and even if *Cold Spring Harbor* lacked the thematic focus he'd later create, his passion for storytelling was clear. With strongly-structured songs packed with genuine emotion, Joel's future held promise; in years to come, he would articulate more persuasive riffs and experiment confidently with theme, production effects and attitude.

Moving forward, Joel enjoyed imitating his vocal heroes on studio projects. He deliberately did so on *An Innocent Man*. With 'Uptown Girl,' he resurrected the Frankie Valli and the Four Seasons' 1960s flavor; on *The Nylon Curtain*, he eerily echoed Lennon but wasn't aware of the phenomenon until colleagues pointed that distinction out. But on *Cold Spring Harbor*, Joel seemed most excited about performing in a variety of styles.

The studio musicians came from diverse backgrounds. New Zealand drummer Rhys Clark also contributed to *Piano Man*. In an interview with the author in December 2021, Clark described himself as a 'groove/pocket-player' influenced by numerous rock, pop, blues, Latin, soul, gospel, swing masters: British and American. Clark – who recorded in L.A. and New York – recounts session protocol here:

My first handshake with Billy was at Record Plant Studio, L.A., studio A. Each song was basically complete. Songs to cut were pre-selected: 'Let's shoot for three songs in three hours.' Don Evans, guitar, Larry Knechtel, bass, Jimmy Haskell, arranger, Billy, and myself were basic-trackers on the whole album. We would tweak/embellish with solos, and determine when to come in, leave out, end the song or fade, and do a take, while always striving for a great live performance, lead vocally too. Somewhere between the first and third take, we would have the successful track.

Clark described Billy Joel's studio persona as 'always confident and good-natured. He gives everyone a warm space, occasionally chews his fingertips, has a cigarette, and just plays and sings intricate, complex, melodious, sweet, tender tunes to ferocious rock and funk feels in endless moods and flavors!'

Clark was the drummer on the WMMR-FM broadcast in April 1972 that took place at Philadelphia's Sigma Sound Studio, and he played at the Mar y Sol Festival in Manati, Puerto Rico, two weeks earlier. He toured with Joel between

1971 and early-1975. According to *YouTube, The Truth About Music*, Clark acquired firsthand knowledge of Joel's work after hearing a seven-song demo:

> He (Artie Ripp) brought the fellow out to L.A. to sign the deal with his label, and I got selected to be the drummer. Don Evans got elected to play guitar. Billy wrote the songs. We got together as the rhythm section to record the rhythm track. Haskell (Jimmie) made the arrangements from us already doing the songs.

Haskell proceeded to create horn and string charts, although the songs that Joel brought into the studio were essentially self-contained. Clark confirmed: 'It was all Billy. There was little else to do but to play.' In a YouTube interview, Clark commented on a missing promotional link: 'Billy was making wonderful fans who were eager to buy the album and they can't buy them. The albums were not readily available at record stores.'

Cold Spring Harbor did poorly commercially, but Joel made inroads live. Contracted for 35-minute opening sets, he set the stage for The J. Geils Band, The Beach Boys and Robin Trower, among others. Clark observed that Joel 'used wit and improvisation to connect with audiences.'

The *Mar y Sol* Fest performance boosted visibility and created a bidding war between Atlantic and Columbia record executives.

American drummer Denny Siewell (co-originator of Paul McCartney's Wings) played on two tracks; parts were replaced on the 1980s remix by Ripp.

Guitarist Sal DiTroia was a much-in-demand session player. That same year, DiTroia recorded with Mary Travers – lead vocalist of the folk trio Peter, Paul and Mary – on her self-titled album, *Mary*, Melanie's *Gather Me* and Dion's *Sanctuary*.

Guitarist Don Evans reappeared on *Streetlife Serenade, Billy Joel's Greatest Hits, Vol. 1 & 2* and *Billy Joel: Complete Hits Collection* 1974-1997. He strummed on the Jamaica-set 'Montego Bay.' (Clark's work would *also* grace subsequent Joel collaborations.)

Bassist and multi-instrumentalist Larry Knechtel played piano on Simon & Garfunkel's 'Bridge Over Troubled Water,' Elvis Presley's self-titled 1968 album and The Beach Boys' award-winning *Pet Sounds*. He was a leading member of the Los Angeles-based Wrecking Crew: hired guns who enhanced recordings from the 1960s to the 1970s.

Steel guitarist Sneaky Pete Kleinow joined in after a stint with Joe Cocker and Joni Mitchell. Kleinow first came to North American fame with the Flying Burrito Brothers as one of the first steel players to achieve acclaim in a rock band. Preferring 'atypical tunings,' Kleinow's work ultimately influenced future country rock acts such as Jerry Garcia. After *Cold Spring Harbor*, Kleinow accompanied – among others – Harry Nilsson, Stevie Wonder and Leonard Cohen.

Before coming aboard, Jimmie Haskell garnered Grammy awards for arrangements of Bobby Gentry's 1967 hit 'Ode To Billie Joe', Simon & Garfunkel's 'Bridge Over Troubled Water' and 'If You Leave Me Now' by the horn-centric Chicago.

Cold Spring Harbor included a lineup of top-notch musicians, with Joel providing lead vocals, ballads and detailed instrumentation. So why didn't the project achieve immediate success? The Achilles heel pointed to production snafus and promotional negligence. As previously mentioned, songs mastered at an incorrect speed, shortened their lengths and stretched-thin Joel's vocals. The higher-than-normal pitch influenced the overall quality and influenced critics.

On *Cold Spring Harbor*, one could foresee the songwriter Joel would become given the right personnel, promotion and incubation time. Perhaps he was puzzling out his persona, as some vocals sounded forced and others tentative, but he conveyed a spectrum of moods and a raw innocence.

When Artie Ripp and a host of engineers and session musicians remixed and remastered *Cold Spring Harbor* in 1983, they left out the original (but brief) orchestration. Rhys Clark recalled: 'My drum parts on 'You Can Make Me Free' and 'Turn Around', survived. Artie's producing style was to extract every last emotion from the performer *and* musician he believes in.'

Remix: In 1983, Artie Ripp with engineer Larry Elliot remixed and remastered the album to adjust Billy Joel's lead vocals. The following session musicians also assisted: drummer Mike McGee, synth player Al Campbell, and Fender Rhodes player L. D. Dixon. The trio created alternative rhythms for 'Everybody Loves You Now' and 'Turn Around.' Ripp eliminated the fade on 'You Can Make Me Free,' cutting out about three minutes. 'Tomorrow Is Today' was also altered. Ultimately, *Cold Spring Harbor* reached 202 on the *Billboard* Bubbling Under The Tops LPS chart in 1972.

Album Art

A prominent *Cold Spring Harbor* thoroughfare is the backdrop on the simple black and white cover. In the foreground, the mustachioed songwriter looks lost in thought. The title refers to the surrounding region – originally a prosperous whaling community, relaxed into a popular resort town, and finally, a bedroom community. A plaque at Cold Spring Harbor Park commemorates Joel's success.

'She's Got A Way' (Billy Joel)

B/w 'Everybody Loves You Now' and released as a single in 1971, 'The Ballad of Billy The Kid' in 1981 and on Songs in the Attic, Peak: U.S. *Billboard* Hot 100: 23, U.S. *Billboard* Adult Contemporary: 4, U.S., Canada RPM Adult Contemporary: 2
This opener features simple gospel voicings and resounding, related bass notes on the piano. During the first verses, lead vocals are especially sonorous. Joel purrs 'mmm' between phrases: a paralinguistic flourish that reappears in future songs.

Many artists over-saturated their tracks with backing singers to create melodic variety, but during this period, Joel relied primarily on his own voice to keep up the momentum.

'She's Got A Way' is dreamy and romantic. Joel's desire to write this way would be short-lived, as he would eventually tire of airing personal thoughts to the world at large, and would focus on aggressive rock, punk or socially conscious themes relayed in the third person. That said, these time capsules find Joel wearing his heart on his sleeve. There's a genuine beauty in these gentle lyrics and hymnal progressions. Not feeling rushed as a listener is a pleasurable experience; even wordless utterances are moving.

It's relatively easy to hear the influence singer/pianist Ray Charles had on Joel's vocals and piano voicings. In fact, on a March-1978 performance on the BBC's *Old Grey Whistle Test* – where Joel performed ten numbers – his vocals on 'New York State Of Mind' imperceptibly mirror the texture of this idol. Both men possessed the ability to bring out the soul of a given song and create a natural flow. Cadences end on an altered chord, creating a moment of tension, but with a burst of shimmering strings, tensions dissipate.

Joel has stated in interviews that he had mixed feelings about the lyrics; he feared they would be construed as trite, but ultimately, he grew into the emotion that he hoped to evoke. There's not a trace of insincerity in his recorded performance.

The song was a single from the live album *Songs in the Attic* (1981), and achieved the status of reaching 23 on the *Billboard* Hot 100 in 1982.

'You Can Make Me Free' (Billy Joel)
The ballad contains a short, spare piano intro. On beginning verses, soothing lead vocals are directed toward the love interest. The melody is pumped up by simple chording and the occasional 'mmm.' Cadences end on a tense chord, but again, quickly resolve. The bass line – clearly competing with swirling electric guitar – gradually opens up the sonic landscape. Drummer Denny Siewell (former Wings member) serves up a light touch.

At the bridge, the story evokes more emotion. But with the definitive, simple accompaniment set in stone, the voice and tear-stained story win the listener over. The modulation provides a safety hatch from the emotional landscape. 'You can make me free', the lover croons, then adding, 'You can make me cry.' There's an underlying sadness, even desperation; he's pleading with his partner to fix him. He's a loosening thread; a sparrow with a clipped wing: Joel at his most vulnerable.

Drummer Rhys Clark told the author in December 2021 that he also played on this 'seminal jam track,' which ends on a fade.

On later songs, Joel would demonstrate more romantic confidence and take further ownership of his feelings within a relationship.

'Everybody Loves You Now' (Billy Joel)
In her 'prime,' the subject has come 'of age.' Joel laments the vagaries of fame, and his cynicism is clear. The subject is new and shiny and on top of the world, but one day the dream will topple; the hot white star will crash and burn.

Perhaps the bitterness Joel endured moving his own career along, is at the root of the biting lyric. Joel takes chances: a tender croon morphs into a Harry Chapin-like grumble. Piano chords move along at a fierce clip; the subject remains passionate about his thesis. At the bridge, Joel sneers, 'Nothing's going to touch you anymore,' and name-checks the Staten Island Ferry in the same breath. He'll use landmarks again in the future to designate pride in his roots or to indicate dissatisfaction in a specific locale (particularly on *Turnstiles*, i.e., 'Say Goodbye To Hollywood' and 'New York State Of Mind'), but here, the landmark is a slight: an inference that, with fame, the subject will disregard humble beginnings.

Percussion on recurring verses heighten and come off like the thrash of a thousand Irish step dancers on a caving hardwood floor: a powerful and functional choice.

'Why Judy Why' (Billy Joel)
Here, Joel confides to a female friend that his romance is flailing. The groove is driven by acoustic guitar and evokes a folk appeal: dissimilar to the other tracks. On the bridge, Joel summarizes the reasons for distress. Finally, he questions his place in the relationship: he's feeling old, although he's not. 'My dreams did not last, so I'll live in the past,' he submits.

In reality, Judy was the name of Joel's cousin. When his maternal aunt died, Judy moved to Joel's home, becoming an older-sister figure and confidante.

'Falling Of The Rain' (Billy Joel)
Against a series of constantly rolling chords, Joel conveys the poetic storyline in the third person. Three distinctive characters are drawn – 'a man who painted nature scenes,' 'a girl who put her hair in braids' and 'a boy with his eyes on the ground.' Each one reacts differently to the inclement weather while undergoing daily rituals. At the bridge, the narrator bypasses these characters and speaks directly to his love interest, assuring her of his affections: 'And I don't want to see another rainy day without you lying next to me.' His longing is conveyed within a span of only 2:38. This gentle, meditative piece harkened back to Scottish troubadour Donovan's poetic 1960s folk songs.

On future albums, Joel fleshes out specific sections to expand recordings. He rebelled against restrictive time limits when narratives required depth and an emotional payoff was at stake.

'Turn Around' (Billy Joel)
Drummer Rhys Clark secures empty spaces with airtight fills. There's a pronounced Americana feel here that's fresh and exciting. Sneaky Pete Kleinow's pedal steel adds to the authenticity.

'You make believe the past was just a dream'. The phrases have a flow that recall early James Taylor tunes. Emotions come to a head when Joel points out, 'You've been gone too long,' followed by soaring dynamics.

Joel's ephemeral country period will give way to a mainstream rock and pop sensibility, although the Hendrix-inspired 'Shameless,' unexpectedly became a crossover hit.

'You Look So Good To Me' (Billy Joel)
The band swings, perhaps because of drummer Denny Siewell's (Wings, Janis Joplin, James Brown) seasoned influence. The chords are in a constant state of flux. The arrival of that flaming hot Hammond B3 is a delightful surprise. Joel's voice is airy. In contrast, blues harp cuts against the chords, and drum beats judiciously follow that confident lead.

'Tomorrow Is Today' (Billy Joel)
Joel heavily accents the piano chords. The melody is strong and deliberate. He wrote this ballad in the depth of a major depression; in fact, on his suicide note, he scribbled the three significant words which comprise the title. Thus the lyrics point to that crisis: 'People tell me life is sweeter,' he declares, 'but I don't hear what they say.' Chords faithfully follow words. His youthful vulnerability and sincerity, shine through the dark. When Joel's voice grows aggressive at the bridge, the abrupt change is startling, but the saving grace is that genuine tone.

'Nocturne' (Billy Joel)
Well under three minutes, this classically inspired instrumental is fragile, and at times, carried out in a whisper. Joel chooses lilting arpeggios as his currency until the bridge, where the chorale structure is more pronounced.

'Nocturne' is divided into three distinctive parts. In the first, Joel introduces the touching, simple melody while playing spare broken chords with the left hand. For the next section, he boosts dynamics and tempo and embellishes the chords on the upper register. Finally, when he returns to the A section, he restores a sense of calm.

'Nocturne' proved prophetic. Moving forward, Joel would demonstrate a strong attachment to his classical roots by composing a complex interlude for inclusion in a pop song or by specifically referencing a classical melody – as he did in 'This Night' from *An Innocent Man*, where the chorus borrows from the second movement of Ludwig van Beethoven's 'Sonata Pathetique.' At a Fenway Park performance on 30 August 2017, Joel preceded 'My Life' with an introductory 'Ode To Joy': another Beethoven brainstorm.

Worldwide, Joel has frequently accompanied tenor Mike Delguidice on the aria 'Nessun Dorma' (Written by Giacomo Puccini for the finale of the opera *Turandot)*. A lucky Frankfurt audience on 9 March 2016 heard Joel seamlessly launch into 'Scenes From An Italian Restaurant' after this emotional solo. Like Joel, Delguidice has a flexible instrument. He has also fronted the Billy Joel cover band Big Shot for over 15 years.

But Joel didn't start the fire of penning pop songs that incorporated classical themes – Chopin's, 'Fantaisie-Impromptu' (Op. 66) published posthumously in 1855, supplied the melody for lyricist Joseph McCarthy and composer Harry Carroll's 'I'm Always Chasing Rainbows.' Future labelmate Barry Manilow – with lyricist Adrienne Anderson – pinched Chopin's 'Prelude in C Minor,' Opus 28, Number 20 as an introduction for 'Could It Be Magic' in 1973 and also supplied all the chorus chords. Three years later, Walter Murphy and The Big Apple Band lit up the disco floor with the blasphemous single 'A Fifth Of Beethoven.' (See *Fantasies and Delusions* for more classical insights.)

'Got To Begin Again' (Billy Joel)

'I try to begin again, but it's hard,' Joel confesses, fleshing out frustrations with conviction. Using falsetto sparingly makes his performance feel genuine too, and will forge a signature sound in his tribute to Motown and more: *An Innocent Man*.

Rhys Clark recalled that Joel wrote the song overnight after Ripp suggested an uplifting song to balance out darker themes.

Piano Man (1973)

Personnel:
Billy Joel: acoustic piano, organ, electric piano, harmonica, vocals
Michael Omartian: accordion, arrangements (tracks 1-4, 6-10)
Jimmie Haskell: arrangements (track 5)
Richard Bennett, Larry Carlton, Dean Parks: guitars
Eric Weissberg: banjo, pedal steel
Fred Heilbrun: banjo
Wilton Felder, Emory Gordy Jr.: bass
Ron Tutt: drums (tracks 1-9)
Rhys Clark: drums (track 10)
Billy Armstrong: violin
Laura Creamer, Mark Creamer, Susan Steward: backing vocals
Producer: Michael Stewart
Produced at Devonshire Sound Studios, Los Angeles, California, September 1973
Label: Family Productions/Columbia
Release date: 9 November, 1973
Chart positions: UK Albums (OCC): 98, USA: US *Billboard* 200: 27, Australian
Albums (Kent Music Report): 3, Canadian Albums (RPM): 26, Year-End (1974) US
Billboard Pop Albums: 56, Australian Albums Chart: 16
Length: 42:51

Live at Sigma Sound Studios, 15 April 1972
Billy Joel: piano, harmonica, vocals
Al Hertzberg: acoustic and electric guitars
Larry Russell: bass
Rhys Clark: drums
Dennis Wilen: producer
Michael Stewart: producer
Ron Malo: engineer
Ted Jensen: remastering
Beverly Parker: design
Bill Imhofe: illustration

Piano Man: Legacy Edition

Release date: 8 November 2011 (Japan)
CD 1: Original album; CD 2: Live For WMMR recordings, introduction by DJ Ed
Sciaky, plus track introductions by Billy Joel.
Recorded: Sigma Sound Studios, Philadelphia, Pennsylvania, 15 April 1972
Label: Import, Sony Legacy, Columbia
Includes previously unreleased tracks: 'Turnaround,' 'Long, Long Time,'
'Josephine' and 'Rosalinda.'

Piano Man was certified gold by the RIAA (Recording Industry Association of
America). Joel was finally achieving critical acclaim. *Rolling Stone* wrote that

this breakthrough 'represents a new seriousness and flexibility.' *Billboard* acknowledged that the songwriter had a 'fine shot at establishing himself as a consistent quality AM artist with large scale songs and dynamic performing range.'

Brandishing a panoply of styles, Joel proclaimed himself a versatile writer, arranger and interpreter. Not yet ready to create political or ideological fare, he relied on well-constructed material and a merging of ideas with a musician and producer; *Piano Man* was the first of two projects with Michael Stewart.

Piano Man included exciting personnel choices – Eric Weissberg's bluegrass-based instrumental 'Dueling Banjos' had become popular via the American film *Deliverance*. Michael Omartian co-arranged nine of the ten tracks but would be mostly remembered for adding the celebratory accordion part to the title track. The jazz rock and pliable guitarist Larry Carlton had been a sideman for diverse acts, including Lani Hall, Johnny Rivers, Peggy Lee, Henry Mancini and Albert Hammond.

Accomplished drummer Ron Tutt had been a longtime member of the Elvis Presley touring band: TCB Band ('Taking Care of Business'). For *Piano Man*, Tutt put his stamp on every cut but 'Captain Jack', and was welcomed back for *Streetlife Serenade*. Billy Armstrong played percussion on 'Ezy Rider' by Jimi Hendrix, and fiddle with Buck Owens and his Buckaroos before contributing violin and fiddle to the *Piano Man* camp. His work would continue to make waves on *Piano Man: The Very Best of Billy Joel* in 2004.

Bassist Wilton Felder brought an early-1970s Motown influence to the studio. In high school, he performed with The Jazz Crusaders. With feet solidly planted in both genres, he added expertise to *Piano Man* and *Streetlife Serenade*.

Texan Dean Parks enjoyed work as a sideman for, among others, Johnny Rivers, Marvin Gaye and Helen Reddy prior to customizing his guitar arrangements for *Piano Man*.

With these handpicked players, Joel had at his disposal a plethora of talent, who brought jazz, bluegrass, country, soul and folk to the mixing board. Perhaps *Piano Man* was not as focused as future albums would be in terms of genre categorization, but during that era, adhering to a strict sound was relatively unimportant. Record-hungry youth wanted music that reflected their feelings and dreams, regardless of genre.

Back in the mid-1960s, Bob Dylan pulled a seemingly scathing about-face by going electric at the Newport Jazz Festival after accruing a devout fan base as an acoustic guitarist. Joel would create ripples of controversy, too, given time, but at this point, he was busy defining himself.

Album Art

Bill Imhofe had completed the album design for the Columbia recording artist Sweathog a few years prior to tackling Joel's album cover, as well as a few projects for other labels.

The front-facing portrait of Joel reveals penetrating eyes, pronounced features and untamed shocks of black hair. It's honestly like looking at the

Mona Lisa: those luminous eyes follow the viewer across the room. At the top, Joel's name and the album title are written in white script.

'Travelin' Prayer' (Billy Joel)
B/w 'Ain't No Crime', released as a single in 1974 and reached its peak on the US Hot 100 at 77.

This upbeat Americana-flavored ballad includes a host of instruments: some widely associated with the bluegrass genre. First up is the cool sound of brushes on a snare, followed by an effervescent bass line.

Joel spits the 16th-note phrases out in the first verse (and in the other three verses thereafter) and repeats the initial verse again at the end. The lyrics are of a spiritual nature, including requests to the almighty to guide his dear friend on her first trip abroad. The words are articulated quickly and can be difficult to decipher, but Joel's mastery of the meter is so thrilling, that even if you can't completely catch the gist, you'll enjoy the performance.

By the third verse, Weissberg's intricate banjo part is at full tilt. Freewheeling, honky-tonk piano is trailed by serious fiddle and a mouth harp excursion. Two high-energy instrumental breaks weave together this loquacious jamboree.

The imaginative 'Travelin' Prayer' crossed over into country when covered by The Earl Scruggs Revue (*Rockin' Cross the Country*, 1973) and Dolly Parton. The latter garnered a Grammy award nomination for Best Female Country Vocal Performance for 1999's *The Grass is Blue*. ,

'Piano Man' (Billy Joel)
B/w 'You're My Home,' released as a single, 2 November, 1973 and reached its peak: US *Billboard* Hot 100: 25; Adult Contemporary Singles: 4

Like a seasoned novelist, Joel packs a lot of subplot into each line. 'Son, can you play me a memory?' requests an older patron who addresses the 'piano man' respectfully. He doesn't quite remember 'how it goes.' Yet, he's in a safe space, where everyone in attendance is there for a similar reason: 'sharing a drink they call loneliness.'

Whether single, divorced or widowed, patrons count on the piano man to show them a good time and heal their wounds. Joel created an intriguing tableau for the flesh-and-blood characters that streamed through the now-defunct Executive Room in Los Angeles. The use of a five-line limerick structure also helped create a warm and welcoming world.

As for 'John at the bar' – a big spender who is 'quick with a joke' – we're led to believe that it's all an act because 'there's someplace that he'd rather be.' In fact, he daydreams about becoming a cinema star 'if I could get out of this place.' 'And the waitress is practicing politics' refers to Elizabeth Weber, who hawked drinks while Joel tickled the ivories.

Against this vestibule of dashed dreams and fresh connections, Joel even refers back to himself as a character. In some ways, this iconic ballad is one of Joel's most ironic. Although the rollicking accompaniment, singsong melody and playful words in the refrain suggest the makings of an all-inclusive party, he masterfully underscores the despair beneath the banter. Each character makes the best of a current situation while struggling to shake out ghosts.

It's the dichotomy that makes 'Piano Man' a classic. Insidious mountains of lyrical tension are set against a cheerful melody and a carefree waltz tempo. You get to laugh *or* cry. Like a Charles Bukowski short story, there are no wasted words – the dreaded phenomenon decent English teachers warned us about – and every character has a palpable function. It's jam-packed with similes: a piano that 'sounds like a carnival' and a microphone that 'smells like a beer.' The surprise ending occurs when the patrons who customarily put 'bread' in the piano man's jar, say 'Man, what are you doin' here?'

Joel's simple harmonica solo adds an old-school integrity that folks of any age can enjoy. When played live, Joel generally hands the chorus over to the fans, who cheerfully abide.

With so few – if any – piano bars left, younger people may have a different understanding of the song. What they might not know is that traditional piano bar players boast an incredible recall of hundreds of pop songs, and can transpose easily for the random drunk who wants to sing off-key to a Broadway tune or the fledgling music student who just turned 21. Many have photographic memories and can improvise on a dime. Many can glance at a simple lead sheet and turn it into a masterpiece by using substitute chords, sophisticated runs and modulations. In that sense, 'Piano Man' is a valuable anachronism; a treasure of a time capsule for those who've only inhabited sports bars or watched MTV.

The length of the ballad is another important factor. At 5:38, we get to luxuriate and allow the pressure of a workday to drain from our faces. We ease into a vinyl horseshoe booth during happy hour. We get to hear several verses, a refrain, a full chorus and outro. It wouldn't be a stretch to believe that this fictional but totally relatable place will never close. One would think that Joel spent years in the Executive Room on Wilshire Boulevard, yet he only spent about six months in the establishment: six months that would set up the career that could put his future kids through college.

The inherent sadness threading through the theme, cements the song's authenticity. When Joel first came to L.A., he was enthralled with the climate and palm trees, but the glamor quickly wore thin. Postcards sent home of the famed Tropicana may have impressed friends and family, but he hungered for his hometown. I believe much of that homesickness bleeds through 'Piano Man.' Ironically, it's one of Joel's least favorite songs, and it was certainly not a moneymaker at the time of the recording. In fact, in interviews, he has referred to the song as a 'turntable hit,' rather than a commercial entity.

The chordal structure is fairly simplistic compared to what he created with later works, but the walking bass moves along at an impressive clip, and the slick turnaround also sustains us. In this well-developed story, he stays with conventional voicings and simple chords: with the exception, of course, of the bluesy introduction. Thematically, one might feel sated when the four verses of this bittersweet cocktail come to a close, but Joel graciously offers one for the road. He ends this ballad with a sprightly outro.

According to a 2017 Library of Congress interview, Joel 'came up with a melody' and 'filled in the characters and the scenario' over the course of a few weeks. His description follows: 'It's a story song, and those tend to have a longer life. A lot of people at the time thought that it was Harry Chapin because he was such a story-song writer.' Rumors circulated that the wordsmiths were competitors, but Joel cleared the air by confirming admiration for his Long Island neighbor, on the 2020 Chapin documentary *Harry Chapin: When In Doubt, Do Something.*

'Ain't No Crime' (Billy Joel)
Joel springs eternal with a rousing, blues-inflected piano introduction. The backing singers – in their first brief appearance – spice up this rowdy Dr. John-like arrangement generously afterwards. The bass line – so pronounced in early verses – gets drowned out by a mélange of organ, sax and electric guitar.

In the unifying lyric, Joel cites examples of less-than-stellar behavior in the first verse: 'Did a lot of drinkin' come home stinkin''; in the second, he consoles a lover confused about romantic commitment: 'You may love 'em forever/But you won't like 'em all of the time.' In other words, life happens: chill.

'You're My Home' (Billy Joel)
The acoustic finger-style guitar section at the beginning – and which continues throughout – is relaxing and inviting. 'When you look into my eyes and you see the crazy gypsy in my soul,' Joel sings plaintively. He's not apologizing for his nomadic tendencies; he's merely hopeful that he and his love interest can coexist under the circumstances: very emblematic of the era.

Pedal steel adds a satisfying flair but will be short-lived on future studio work.

'Home could be the Pennsylvania turnpike,' spikes off a litany of place references, but regardless of where this lover goes, he will always value his partner. Joel allegedly wrote the ballad for his first wife, Elizabeth Weber.

'The Ballad Of Billy The Kid' (Billy Joel)
B/w 'If I Only Had the Words (To Tell You)' and released as a single in April 1974 in the UK
It's kitschy to begin this ballad with clanky horse clops, but also a comical contrast to the surrounding balladry. Joel loves studying American history but took poetic license with the storyline. So, the song won't withstand a fact check, but this blend of folk tale and American western nostalgia is a charmer. A hybrid of blues harp, electric guitars and playful rhythms, the ballad puts predictable spaghetti western theme songs out to pasture. Aaron Copland's *Billy the Kid* ballet from 1938 and movie soundtracks by Ennio Morricone, were inspirations.

'Worse Comes To Worst' (Billy Joel)
B/w 'Somewhere Along The Line' and released as the second single in 1974, Peak: US Hot 100: 80

Definitely a contrast from the rest, 'Worse Comes To Worst' features blips and bleeps, strident guitar and a driving reggae beat. At the bridge, the tempo slows considerably, and the choral singers supply warm textures. The steel drum sound is ephemeral but fun.

'Stop In Nevada' (Billy Joel)
Mournful pedal steel and Joel's deliberate chording make this arrangement pop. He relays the story of a three-dimensional woman rather than some quickly conceptualized stereotype.

'She tried so hard to be a good wife,' Joel sings with utmost sincerity. 'With some money in her pocket, she's a rocket on the fourth of July.' When the love interest leaves, it is clearly not without regrets. She reaches out again, but she's rebuffed.

This is an unusual goodbye song in that the dynamics constantly shift. Many other songs with this theme cruise down a more tranquil pike.

'If I Only Had The Words (To Tell You)' (Billy Joel)
Similar to a John Philip Sousa anthem, this track is well-structured but somewhat predictable melodically. But when the harmony changes in the bridge, the emotion escalates.

The organ rises up against the lead vocal toward the end, enhancing the emotion. The narrator seems unsettled in regard to expressing his love – the words suggest – yet the mature vocal performance in the final verse suggests he'll do just fine.

'Somewhere Along The Line' (Billy Joel)
The keyboard parts are exciting, and the vocals match in intensity. The line 'You'll pay for your satisfaction somewhere along the line,' sounds preachy but works because it's part of a well-conceptualized story, not simply a veiled threat.

This song is embellished with country-style pedal steel, which, as we've seen, made a frequent appearance in *Cold Spring Harbor*.

'Captain Jack' (Billy Joel)
Joel composed 'Captain Jack' in Oyster Bay, New York, but like Ringo Starr, he got by 'with a little help from' his friends. Ed Sciaky at station WMMR went above and beyond to promote 'Captain Jack' on Philadelphia airwaves. Joel would later say about the popular DJ: 'He's always stuck by me.' The song first created a buzz during an hour-long mini-concert at Sigma Sound Studios held before the official release. In a December 2021 interview with the author, Rhys Clark remembered:

Two weeks after Mar y Sol, the band performed the Sigma concert. Setlists were discussed based on previous audience reactions (kind of organically as to which song worked where and continuity flowed to the peak song of the show), so of course, 'Captain Jack' became this set's seminal standout, despite a nanosecond mistake by me due to nervous excitement. This song, on that live show, set the college fans on a rampage and request cycle that made Columbia Records take note. Eighteen months later, we recorded it onto the *Piano Man* album.

Sciaky developed a reputation for promoting lesser-known tracks by ambitious American recording artists. His promotional efforts increased Joel's chances of gaining national exposure; he'd done the same for Joel's Asbury Park pal Bruce Springsteen.

'Captain Jack' also attracted the attention of Columbia Records executive Clive Davis, who worked at the label from 1967-1973. In his memoir *The Soundtrack of My Life* – co-written by rock journalist Anthony DeCurtis in 2012 – Davis explained that Billy Joel came onto his radar when Columbia Records promotion man Herb 'The Babe' Gordon urged the CEO to check out 'one of the (Philadelphia) station's most requested songs': 'Captain Jack.'

At producer Artie Ripp's insistence, Davis saw Joel perform at a local club, where he 'tore the place apart.' At this point in time, Joel had moved on from his debut *Cold Spring Harbor*, and was performing 'songs that would eventually be on *Piano Man*, his first Columbia release.'

Some critics and religious entities accused Joel of being pro-drug-use because of certain phrases, i.e., 'Captain Jack will get you high tonight,' yet that was never his intention. He deliberately depicted the drug-pusher subject as a loser, yet this song and others would be the subject of controversy many times over.

Elliott Murphy – Joel's singer-songwriter compadre from Long Island – told *Newsweek* that Joel 'makes melody of the psychological side effects of urban sprawl' and that "'Captain Jack' is a portrait of the kids Joel grew up with: so bored all they know how to do is get high.'

Musically, Joel's voice is spot-on; his street cred flanked with steroids. Words are to-the-point and thrillingly urban. Plus, drummer Rhys Clark returns, and his percussive energy is palpable. Clark explains how he constructed his drum part: 'I just followed Billy's dynamics and vocal/lyrical seriousness in the verses to that huge release and high in the choruses. Performing that song will just never get old.'

Streetlife Serenade (1974)

Personnel:
Billy Joel: vocals, keyboards, Moog synthesizer, arrangements
William 'Smitty' Smith: organ
Richard Bennett, Gary Dalton, Mike Deasy, Don Evans, Al Hertzberg, Art Munson, Raj Rathor: guitar
Michael Stewart: guitar, arrangements
Tom Whitehorse: banjo, pedal steel
Wilton Felder, Emory Gordy Jr., Larry Knechtel: bass
Ron Tutt: drums
Joe Clayton: congas, percussion
Michael Stewart: producer
Ron Malo: engineer
Joseph M. Palmaccio: 1998 digital remastering
John Naatjes: tape research
Ron Coro: art direction, design
Brian Hagiwara: cover painting
Peter Cunningham: photography
Jim Marshall: photography
Produced at Devonshire Sound Studios, North Hollywood, California, 1974
Label: Family Productions/Columbia
Release date: 1974
Chart positions: UK: did not chart, US: *Billboard* 200, 35, AUS: 85, CAN: 16
Length: 37:41

As was the protocol, Joel was under pressure to complete a follow-up album. But after *Piano Man*, he faced a frenetic touring schedule. It was challenging to find time to create new, dynamic material. According to *YouTube, The Truth About Music*, Rhys Clark observed that Joel 'basically wasn't in control' during this stage of his studio life.

On the musical front, he featured two instrumentals: 'Root Beer Rag' and 'The Mexican Connection.' He'd demonstrated a preference for writing music and often struggled with lyrics, so composing a couple of instrumentals solved half of the immediate problem.

Songs in the Attic – Joel's first live effort – featured the songs 'Streetlight Serenader' and 'Los Angelinos.' In 2006, 'The Entertainer' appeared on *12 Gardens Live*. Both 'Souvenir' (despite its brevity) and the rambunctious 'Root Beer Rag' satisfied fan requests during 1970s concerts.

Multiple repeat players were present in the studio, but new hires were especially influential. Percussionist Joe Clayton added an illustrious layer of sound. Virtuosic Canadian organist William 'Smitty' Smith (session work with Tracy Chapman, Richie Havens, Etta James and The Chain Gang) had a U.S. hit with the Canadian group Motherlode's 'When I Die.' There were eight guitarists onboard, including guitarist/producer Michael Stewart.

Technological industry advances resulted in the album being released in a quadraphonic mix in 1974.

Producer Stewart's brother was a member of the folk-oriented Kingston Trio. Stewart helmed a folk ensemble too. The quintet – We Five – charted with 'You Were On My Mind.' Stewart's embrace of the folk idiom begged this question: Was he inclined to support Joel's transition to a hardscrabble sound? Joel explained to rollingstone.com: 'I had a band together that had been on the road for two years, and he didn't want me to use them on the recordings. That's when I parted ways with Michael Stewart.' Nevertheless, the relationship remained amicable. In the future, additional producers would test Joel's allegiance to existing band members.

One factor that made this album stand out was that Joel demonstrated an almost insatiable zeal for the Moog synthesizer: an unusually high-pitched part that gave 'The Entertainer' a unique veneer. Not everyone embraced these iterations. *Rolling Stone* writer Stephen Holden rated the album 'unfavorable' in December 1974: 'Billy Joel's pop schmaltz occupies a stylistic no man's land where musical and lyric truisms borrowed from disparate sources, are forced together.'

Critics continually drew comparisons between the piano-playing of Elton John and Billy Joel, although their approaches to melody and rhythm were markedly different. Holden also hinted that songwriter Harry Chapin – renowned for the bittersweet 'Taxi' – had been an influence, and although that may have been meant as complimentary, the comparison was dismissive of Joel's own progress and growth as a storyteller. Surprisingly, some critics didn't just comment on Joel's work; they aimed for the jugular. And although these reviews wore at Joel, he moved forward and created narratives that definitively set him apart from his peers.

Holden – while despairing of the songwriting – conceded that Joel was 'a talented keyboardist.' Similarly, *Cashbox* took note of innate skills by awarding Joel as 'Best new male vocalist of 1974.'

Joel yearned to choose his own personnel without reliance on producer contacts. He needed sufficient time in his schedule to expand the scope of his writing. Fortunately, some of these objectives would materialize on his subsequent studio project.

Album Art

The cover was the first to showcase a painting rather than a photographic image. According to an email interview from 2013 (conducted by the writer of popspotnyc.com), the graphic artist Brian Hagiwara based this rendering on a building in 'old San Pedro, California,' located at 615 South Centre Street. In that same interview, Hagiwara recalled that Billy Joel wanted an 'Edward Hopper-like, Midwestern scene.'

On the back cover, Joel is far from the happiest camper, having had his wisdom teeth extracted several days earlier. He was probably still in pain.

Donning a red plaid shirt and faded blue jeans, the barefoot songwriter sits spread-eagle on a yellow, wooden, backwards-facing chair. If scowls could speak, Joel's would likely scream. But you can't blame Jim Marshall – the world-class American photographer – whose luminous Leica lens caught the slightly sour expression. At the end of the day, Marshall walked away with a well-lit, natural portrait shot. Keep in mind that Marshall covered Woodstock and The Beatles' final live performance at San Francisco's Candlestick Park. The man knew his F-stops, and perhaps shooting Joel's swollen skin was not as thrilling as capturing Hendrix setting his guitar on fire at the Monterey Pop Festival, but that's a whole other rock 'n' roll story. American photographer Peter Cunningham assisted with stellar portraits as well.

'Streetlife Serenader' (Billy Joel)
Joel sets the tone with a snappy eight-bar introduction on the acoustic piano. The narrative is simple: about a musician that's making do. 'Never sang on stages/Needs no orchestration.' The melody has an easygoing vibe. When the band joins in, Joel's voice sounds richer and more confident. He plays another full verse featuring acoustic piano with accented beats. The drum fills grow more intricate as the lead voice escalates.

When singing 'Working hard for wages,' Joel slows the vocal down considerably. A darker piano passage follows, then the introduction of a searing electric guitar. The drumming is solid.

With 'I am a child of Eisenhower,' he sets this beauty in real time – Dwight D. Eisenhower, while not president during Joel's birth year, came into office in the formative years.

'Los Angelinos' (Billy Joel)
After Joel leads off with well-articulated keyboard chops, the band kicks in. There's definitive organ and electric keys, and an exceptionally funky bass line throughout to sustain interest. The live version on *Songs in the Attic* (which was taped in 1980 in New Haven, Connecticut's Toad's Place) is even more fearless.

In April 2014, Joel told Howard Stern, SiriusXM host, during a Stern's Town Hall session at New York's Cutting Room, that he wrote the offbeat tune with frontman Rod Stewart in mind: 'I always thought he had one of the great rock voices: that raspy thing. I liked Rod Stewart's voice.'

The narrative originates with a pedestrian observation: 'Los Angelinos all come from somewhere.' Los Angeles – a sprawling cosmopolitan city – is a fascinating mix of cultures, glittery facades and Pacific beaches, but Joel's message focused on socio-economic imbalances. As such, 'Los Angelinos' is riddled with disdain for the pampered elite: 'electric babies, blue-jeaned and jaded/Going into garages for exotic massages.' The chorus is catchy, and the polish includes Willie Smith's screaming organ and Tutt's fills on the outro.

'The Great Suburban Showdown' (Billy Joel)

'Sit around with the folks/Say the same old tired jokes,' Joel chides with an Americana twang. 'The place hasn't changed/That's why I'm gonna feel so strange.' Tutt lays back most of the way, yet is sensitive to Joel's dynamics as needed. This is truly a vehicle for Joel's compositional fluency, which will be followed up by virtuosic works like 'Goodnight Saigon.'

Arguably, Joel shows compassion for those in the music industry who work hard but achieve little acclaim. The short but emphatic electric guitar solo is followed by Joel's foray into a beautiful explosion of pianistic harmonies.

'Root Beer Rag' (Billy Joel)

This clever, quickly-moving instrumental is built around roving 4ths, 5ths and octaves, with a steadily moving bass line. Joel plays at lightning speed with slapstick humor and ornamented notes thrown in for a dazzling effect. At the B-section, he tears it up in double-time. This fun piece was imbued with the spirit of ragtime pianist Scott Joplin. In 1973, *The Sting* resurrected and revived this exuberant style for multitudes of moviegoers. This often-neglected genre brightly ushered in jazz.

'Roberta' (Billy Joel)

The castanets come in on the solo after the confession, 'And I'm in a bad way and I want to make love to you.' The theme is relatively transparent – the singer is falling hard for a call girl, but the lyrics are pure, nonjudgmental and understated. If she weren't in this trade, maybe there would be a future for them both. 'I know you're working, but you must get lonely.'

We know little else about this Roberta character – how she looks, the timber of her voice, or how she feels about this man – which lends a sense of intrigue, but at the same time, I would love to see 'Roberta' more vividly defined.

'The Entertainer' (Billy Joel)

B/w 'The Mexican Connection' and released as a single in 1974, Peak: U.S. *Billboard* Hot 100: 34

'The Entertainer' was the only single released from this album. The title might make one believe it's a 'Piano Man' doppelganger, but it's not. For 'Piano Man,' Joel chronicled the mates and miscreants at the bar with a self-effacing humility, and it is one of his most personal songs. In 'The Entertainer,' Joel puts the subject on a pedestal and keeps a cool distance: 'Today I am the champion/I may have won your hearts'. But since he has stated in interviews that he doesn't buy into the 'rock star' thing, the pumped-up qualifiers come off more like fiction.

Mandolin and Moog synthesizer make outstanding entrances, and the latter stays the course. Joel seems obsessed with the mysterious Moog sound and uses it liberally to connect the verses and underscore lyrics. Stegmeyer's bass line remains steadfast and potent against Joel's power-drill execution.

Employing a playful pentameter, Joel rattles off the lyrics in a loose-lipped manner, like the patron who gulps down one too many espressos at Starbucks and can't find his tongue. 'I'd love to stay, but there's bills to pay and I just don't have the time,' Joel complains, keeping up an infectious rhythmic flow.

He cuts to the chase with an acerbic comment about songs getting shortened in order to be radio-friendly: 'It was a beautiful song, but it ran too long.'

There are a lot of reasons to like 'The Entertainer,' but the union of electronics and emphatic vocals put it over the top.

'Last Of The Big Time Spenders' (Billy Joel)

There's a bluesy patter – 'If money makes a rich man, I might never make the grade' – played with an old-time gospel feel. Joel's vocals are nuanced. The next section reveals more introspection: 'Though it seems like the days are wasted and the nights are overdue.' Billy mirrors his vocal with rhythmic piano riffs, followed by a mourning pedal steel solo. 'You can call me the great pretender/In a way, it might be true,' he sings, perhaps hoping to be challenged.

The narrator comes clean on this verse; he's got nothing to hide. The song ends as it began: with a tasty blues lick and a shimmering echo.

'Weekend Song' (Billy Joel)

This ballad is similar in spirit to 'It Ain't No Crime' from *Piano Man*. The first instrumental break makes an emphatic statement. The words are straight from the blues idiom: 'Got some money to spend tonight.' Finally, the organ in the outro screeches with excitement.

'Souvenir' (Billy Joel)

The syncopated rhythms against the octaves in the four-bar intro give this short song, symmetry. The stately chords bring to mind Beethoven: one of Joel's greatest influences. From 'a picture postcard' to 'a program of the play,' Joel whisks us off to another world, where 'every year a souvenir slowly fades away.'

With his sonorous voice, Joel packs great emotion into this two-minute cocktail which he later used as a powerful encore on too many shows to list. I would love to see an expanded version of this pretty, nostalgic song which easily gets lost in the mix due to its brevity.

'The Mexican Connection' (Instrumental) (Billy Joel)

Traces of 'Los Angelinos' appear but with a riveting ostinato. A similar feel will be detected on 'Don't Ask Me Why,' where a Latin bass line and rhythm merge without apologies.

Joel included two instrumentals on this album to complete contractual obligations. Melody and harmony have traditionally given the songwriter less of a migraine than lyrics, but he gave the label more than its money's worth.

Related albums

The 50th Anniversary homage, *Billy Joel: The Vinyl Collection, vol. 1* includes *Billy Joel, Live at the Great American Music Hall, 1975.*

Turnstiles (1976)

Personnel:
Billy Joel: vocals, acoustic piano, electric piano, Moog synthesizer, clavinet, organ,
Howie Emerson, Russell Javors: electric and acoustic guitars
James Smith: acoustic guitar
Doug Stegmeyer: bass
Liberty DeVitto: drums
Mingo Lewis: percussion
Richie Cannata: saxophones, clarinet
Ken Ascher: orchestral arrangement
Jerry Abramowitz: cover photography
John Berg: cover design
Bruce Botnick: mixing
John Bradley: engineer, project supervisor
Billy Joel: producer
Don Puluse: engineer
Brian Ruggles: basic track consultant
Lou Waxman: tape engineer
Produced at Ultra Sonic Recording Studios, Hempstead, New York; Columbia
Recording Studios, New York City, New York; Caribou Ranch, Nederland Colorado,
January 1976
Label: Family Productions/CBS
Release date: 19 May 1976
Chart positions: UK: Did not chart, USA: *Billboard* 200: 122, AUS: 12
Length: 36:22

Turnstiles is to New York City what The Paul Butterfield Blues Band's self-titled 1965 debut is to Chicago, in that the project exemplified the guts, brawn, beauty and despair of the subject city without hyperbole. Like Broadway's traditional ball-drop on New Year's Eve, the album also broadcast New York's historical culture; the bustling Astor Place subway and colorful characters on the cover hinted at the content and diversity inside.

But outside the cloistered studio walls, New York City stood in a state of havoc. 'Ford to City: Drop Dead' was the alarming headline in a 1975 edition of the *New York Daily News*, although the then-president later denied making the statement. But regardless of who said what, when mayor Abe Beame begged the federal government for assistance, Gerald Ford took a hard line. With his hometown facing a crisis, Joel was anxious to offer support. As such, saying 'goodbye to Hollywood' was easy. Joel told friends, 'If New York's going down the tubes, I'm there.' The loyal Long Islander voiced the same opinion when facing New York City tragedies well into the future; that awareness shines throughout these tracks.

Turnstiles was a stellar accomplishment material-wise, although not a commercial success. Yet Liberty DeVitto, Russell Javers, Doug Stegmeyer and Billy Joel would ultimately perform more tracks from *Turnstiles* than from any of Joel's subsequent studio projects. DeVitto was especially aware that a sea change for Joel was imminent because up until that point, Joel 'had used studio musicians for the recording, and different guys out on the road.'

Allmusic observed: 'No matter how much stylistic ground Joel covers, he's kept on track by his backing group.' The remark about covering so much 'stylistic ground' is spot-on, but the critic missed the mark with the phrase, 'backing group.' In essence, these musicians deserved a more respectable title, as they gradually became cheerleaders, co-arrangers and critical thinkers behind the glass and beyond.

By ushering in members of the already-established group Topper, Joel acquired top-notch innovators and a cohesive, mature-sounding board for his original music. Doug Stegmeyer was the first musician from Topper to forge an ongoing professional relationship with Joel. The bassist – who had met Joel through soundman Brian Ruggles – had been hired for the *Streetlife Serenade* promotional tour. Joel conveyed to Stegmeyer that he was anxious to return home and establish a dual-purpose band; a united front. Stegmeyer knew all the right folks.

In an interview with the author on 25 January 2022, lead guitarist Howard Emerson talked about working with Joel from January 1976 to June 1977. He explained that he and rhythm guitarist Russell Javors worked as a duo, primarily doing Javors' songs before exploring Joel originals.

Howard Emerson:

Certainly, nobody can speak for Doug [Doug Stegmeyer died in 1995]. He was Russell's roommate in college or art school. He was like Russell's shadow. They worked on songs and recordings for thousands of hours down in the basement; certainly Liberty too.

One of Topper's great claims to fame was doing reggae during the disco era. I swear to God, none of the bars wanted to hear it. I can vaguely recall – and this was Topper – the four of us were playing, I believe, 'Born To Run.' The funny thing was that Liberty was in a band called Blue Hair. They were a very popular cover band back then.

They called me in. I did the guitar tracks and they immediately started asking me to join the band. I refused at first. Then I said, if you really want me to join the band, you have to take Russell. They only wanted one guitar player. Billy was really not a guitar-oriented player. I don't feel Billy felt comfortable with guitar players behind him at that point. Certainly when he got David Brown – who is one of my favorite players, coupled with Phil Ramone's oversight or overview – I think it opened up Billy's realm.

I certainly did not have *carte blanche* during the Ultrasonic sessions. Some overdubs and percussion by Mingo Lewis were done at Caribou Ranch, where we rehearsed for our first tour.

When we were playing out, right from the get-go, I got a lot of feedback: 'Could you play it a little bit more like the other guitar player?' who I didn't even know. I had no idea who he was or how he played.

But there was always a comparison to the last guy, which is ironic because one little thing that I put on 'Miami 2017,' – that one particular chord – every one of their guitar players ever since, plays the same thing. I'll never forget, when I first played it, Billy said, 'Yeah, I like that.' So they've all had to suffer the way I had to suffer: 'Do it like the other guy did it.'

I had no clue that Billy would be successful in the long run, but if you'd have taken me aside and said, 'I don't care about the music, but do you think this guy's going to be famous?,' I probably would have said yeah. He was such a hard worker. He had such a natural, natural energy and talent as a performer and as a piano player; every bit the player. I have such great respect for him now. At that time, I didn't think, 'That guy's going to be huge.' I purposely got myself fired so I could get unemployment.

The new lineup offered an opportunity to move on from the *sturm und drang* before the theoretical calm. Joel and Columbia hadn't seen eye-to-eye on production issues. Columbia wanted Jim Guercio – the producer of the brass-based Chicago – to control the *Turnstiles* reins. He owned Caribou Ranch in Boulder, Colorado, where Elton John had recently recorded. The British pop star had fired drummer Nigel Olsson and bassist Dee Murray, so Guercio hastily hired the downsized rhythm section as session players for Joel's latest project. This arrangement, while logistically apropos, failed to curry favor with Joel, who was adamant about creating his own sound with a 'New York-style drummer.' Besides, having been compared to Elton John *ad nauseum* over the years, why would he knowingly enter the ring to record with John's colleagues?

All stars pointed to Topper's Liberty DeVitto becoming the preferable percussive choice. In 1968, the Long Island professional had toured intensively with Mitch Ryder and the Detroit Wheels on a city bus for six weeks. In addition, DeVitto had spent a couple of years with a versatile wedding band, learning to infuse exciting Latin tempos into standard arrangements. Working constantly, with rare nights off, his demanding schedule recalled the 10,000 hours The Beatles accrued in Hamburg, Germany, in the early-1960s. Like Joel, DeVitto was acclaimed for using his physicality to express musical ideas.

DeVitto had surplus street cred but was not a sight-reader. Could he interpret studio charts? Luckily, he had developed a unique set of strategies. In an interview with the author in 2021, he explained:

The drummer mind is insane. As you know, I'm a lyric guy. I love words, but I saw The Beatles on TV and said, 'I want to do that.' I asked my father later why he bought me drums, and he said, 'Because they didn't make Prozac when I was a kid.' I wanted to be Paul McCartney. I loved the drums, but I loved music more. I was self-taught. I would listen to a record, and play where I was in a song and learn the lyrics and sing along with the song. I found that if you can play and sing along at the same time, you're probably playing the right part for the song. So, a lot of the ideas came from working with Billy because we'd be in the studio and I would get his lyrics while the other guys were writing out chords.

Here, DeVitto elaborates on the sequence of events which led to the seminal lineup:

Doug recommended me because Billy was looking for a New York-type drummer, aggressive and hard-hitting, and the rest is history. The three of us recorded the basic tracks for *Turnstiles,* and we both recommended Russell Javors and Howie Emerson, who played guitars in Topper, and with the addition of Richie Cannata on saxophone, the Billy Joel band was born.

Unbeknownst to Joel, Stegmeyer had slipped DeVitto a demo of new Billy Joel material so that when DeVitto arrived at the audition – having already done his homework – he would exhibit supreme confidence.

With this group of energetic professionals, Joel expanded his songwriting repertoire. Disregarding the label's push, Joel dismissed Guerico, and self-produced *Turnstiles*, with assistance from longtime sound engineer Brian Ruggles and Bruce Botnick (brainchild behind studio works of The Doors). As a result, the revised album smacks of originality, although Joel readily admitted he lacked the production skills he'd later obtain.

But like his tri-city peer Bruce Springsteen – who had recently released *Born to Run* – Joel was developing a lyric style with which fans could immediately identify.

The addition of the airtight Topper was a godsend; they'd developed telepathy with one another, and Joel fit right into their groove. With this united front, acclaim was imminent. *AllMusic* exclaimed that 'the key to the record's success is variety…' *Classicrockreview.com* later acknowledged the accomplishments of Joel's latest venture, proclaiming, 'It is the most reflective and nostalgic album that he would ever make.' Keep in mind that 1983's *An Innocent Man* would warrant similar reactions.

Album Art

Using the New York City Transit as a focal point, photographer Jerry Abramowitz and John Berg – who also designed album covers for Bob Dylan and Bruce Springsteen – captured a surreal moment in time in which Joel (in a long-sleeved white shirt, striped tie and trousers) leans in and looks out with a withered look on his face. His suit jacket is nowhere to be seen; maybe it's smashed up in a briefcase? The 20-yard stare gives the impression that he's coming home, not leaving for work.

The eight additional people gathered around the subway turnstile (with young Sean Weber closest to Joel) are modeled after characters profiled in the songs – 'James' carries a book; 'All I Wanna Do Is Dance' is exemplified by a girl with headphones; the apocalyptic 'Miami 2017' grandparent and grandchild are also close at hand.

'Say Goodbye to Hollywood' (Billy Joel)

B/w 'I've Loved These Days,' (A-side), 'Stop in Nevada,' (B-side) and released as a single in 1976, 1981, Peak: U.S. *Billboard* Hot 100: 17, U.S. *Billboard* Top Tracks: 11

'Say Goodbye to Hollywood' has an easygoing, sensuous vibe, but achieving that quality required patience and ingenuity. DeVitto explained in his biography that he 'overdubbed a snare drum in the bridge because the hi-hat was recorded too loud on the basic track.' In addition, he 'overdubbed tambourine and castanets.'

To make this ballad pop, perhaps DeVitto channeled his inner-Hal Blaine, the L.A. Wrecking Crew drummer who created the iconic introduction to 'Be My Baby,' featuring the stirring vocal stylings of Spanish Harlem's Ronnie Spector and The Ronettes. DeVitto's performance smacked of originality but paralleled Blaine's intensity.

The track was also a fitting homage to producer Phil Spector's wall of sound – a technique best described as a 1960s production formula in which multiple instruments created double or triple parts that – when mixed together – formed a singular unit of sound. Javors and Emerson contributed generously to the *sis-boom-bah* soundscape. It was easy to imagine Ronnie Spector's iconic vibrato resounding from the mixing board. In fact, Ms. Spector was so taken with this uplifting confection that she covered the song in 1977 with the E-Street band.

As far as lyrical content, Joel paints another superficial L.A. scene, reminiscent of 'Los Angelinos.' Coming from Long Island – a community with stealthy roots – it was easy to understand why he felt rudderless in this largely transient coastal city. The third-person verses revolve around 'Bobby,' who cruises nightly down Sunset Boulevard, and 'Johnny,' whose 'style is so right for troubadours.' We know little more about them; neither does the protagonist, but as the song moves into first-person, we get to the heart of the matter: 'So many faces in and out of my life.'

Despite the lively feel, there's an underlying sense of loneliness and a lack of connection that the swaying sugar palms and sandy beaches couldn't assuage. It was time to come home.

'Summer, Highland Falls' (Billy Joel)

According to songfacts.com, 'Joel wrote the music to reflect the highs and lows of manic depression.' He used the left hand to convey depression; the right, the hyper. 'I have seen that sad surrender in my lover's eyes,' he sings; one of many sobering lines. Joel will revisit this sense of isolation on future albums.

Joel did actually write the ballad while living in the Highland Falls section of New York State. Unlike most of his other material, there's no chorus or bridge, just a repeated verse, but this strophic style works well; the lyrics deserve complete attention. By structuring the song this way, the listener gets to focus entirely on the context. This gripping song about enduring transitions, is enlivened by Joel's sensitive piano treatment and Cannata's harmonizing clarinet.

'All You Wanna Do Is Dance' (Billy Joel)

The initially-light percussion incrementally ramps up. Joel references The Beatles and includes backing harmonies that recall their earliest tunes. The vocals are remarkably soft for a dance song, but that curious choice makes the instrumental aspects stand out.

Javors and Emerson jointly drove home the reggae-influenced riffs in this Jimmy Cliff hang with Ben E. King, but the track also bears a similarity to the Kinks classic 'Come Dancing,' which came somewhat later.

'New York State Of Mind' (Billy Joel)

Joel had definitive arranging ideas for this ballad; he knew he wanted a sax solo. Doug Stegmeyer's brother knew just the guy, which prompted Stegmeyer and DeVitto to scout out Richie Cannata at the club Cloud Nine. According to DeVitto, Cannata was flustered when he first walked into the studio. The band was working out the highly charged 'Angry Young Man,' but Cannata relaxed when he heard the smooth track he'd been hired to play. His solo here is dreamy, yet immaculately structured.

'New York State Of Mind' – an unarguable Billy Joel classic – begins with a laid-back, bluesy, piano solo that slowly picks up steam from the gang. In the first verse – after an instrumental piano breakdown – Joel comments on other New Yorkers unlike himself, who choose to 'take a holiday from the neighborhood.' Those folks prefer to fly south or west, but the singer stresses how much he prefers to remain homebound by 'taking a Greyhound on the Hudson River Line.'

On the second verse, he details why other parts of the U.S. didn't do the trick, alluding to the 'limousines' in L.A. and 'the Rockies' and 'the Evergreens' in the West.

Finally, Joel instills a sense of urgency about his decision to return: 'I don't want to waste more time.' Cannata, to his credit, robustly punctuates these yearnings, while keeping the ballad's warm character in mind. At the bridge, Joel admits that while he survived life elsewhere, he sorely missed his hometown connection: 'It was so easy livin' day by day.' Estrangement resulted. He felt 'Out of touch with the rhythm and blues.' Moreover, he longed to reinvest in everyday rituals: regarding 'The New York Times/The Daily News.'

In the third verse, Joel liberally name-checks the famous locales Chinatown and Riverside, which exist at opposite ends of the island. By doing so, he conveys a sense of personal pride to which any homesick traveler can relate. An intricate sax solo follows.

The story is so well-established that there's little more to add. So, after it's been told, we can simply enjoy the remaining verses and repeated bridge, while taking note of the vocal and instrumental nuances and cascading background strings. On the outro, Joel's pause after the words 'New York' ushers in a big cabaret ending.

Ken Ascher – a well-established, award-winning professional in his own right – artfully arranged this ballad for orchestra. To his credit, he achieved a superb balance. Joel's stride piano served as an essential element, and fortunately, he had no competition from strings.

'New York State Of Mind' is a singer's song (not all are!) comprised of short, conversational phrases. In between each one, a vocalist can leisurely grab a breath. In addition, the song is crammed with visual markers. It follows that, because of these factors, the ballad has been picked up universally. Singers as far afield as the big apple and Korea, have won awards for their renditions. On the North American front, the likes of Barbra Streisand, Tony Bennett and Frank Sinatra – three superstars – have put their own signatures on the ballad. The list is endless.

'New York State Of Mind' deserves equal footing with Alicia Keys' collaboration with Jay – Z 'Empire State Of Mind', and Kander and Ebb's, 'New York, New York': recorded passionately by Frank Sinatra, among others. Over time, Bennett and Joel impressed audiences by trading verses performing it as a duet.

Harmonically, Joel outdid himself here. The bones reveal simple chords, but Joel interjected additional chords in between the tonic and the relative minor chord (I to vi) of the first verse, and inserts dominant 7ths between more simple chords on subsequent progressions, yielding a sophisticated jazz-spiked texture.

'James' (Billy Joel)
Released as the second single in 1976
On the surface, the theme centers around the relationship between Joel and an ambitious high-school friend, who veers from his original career path. Initially, Joel simply states the obvious: 'and we had to go our separate ways.' But soon, he takes a firm line: 'When will you write your masterpiece?' His friend has been a hard worker, but perhaps not truthful with himself. 'Will you always stay someone else's dream of what you are?' That query is followed by an instrumental release of tension by way of Cannata's breezy soprano sax solo.

In interviews, Joel has explained that 'James' is a composite of several friends, although Echoes band member Jim Bosse was rumored to be the main reference. Along those same lines, Joel returned to high school for 'Scenes From An Italian Restaurant.' Whether symptomatic of mere nostalgia or a midlife crisis, it's a human phenomenon to look back on earlier days with judgment and/or affection.

So 'James' *is* reflective, yet not as lyrically impactful as neighboring material. Instrumentally, Joel noodles with the melody on the upper register of the Fender Rhodes; DeVitto complies with light, airy brushing. Sporadic harmonies favor a slight R&B feel. For the outro, Joel stretches out a baroque-style instrumental verse; Stegmeyer aptly accentuates on electric bass.

'Prelude/Angry Young Man' (Billy Joel)

While 'Say Goodbye To Hollywood' was a topical opening track, 'Prelude' would've been an exhilarating contender. It was a successful concert opener for years. Joel modeled the instrumental portion – which unpacks into three disparate parts – after a Bach invention. This complex jigsaw is riddled with major and minor 7ths, dotted rhythms, tricky drum fills and satisfying resolutions. In opposition to the harpsichord-driven Johann Sebastian Bach, brash Moog synth illuminates the mix. Live, Javors would often echo the constantly moving melody with a wailing blues harp.

But foremost, is the establishment of that opening piano motif. YouTube videos show Joel's alternating hands as they jackhammer middle C. With both hands moving quickly, they resemble slicing blades, as they blur contact with the keys. With his right hand, Joel inserts a series of syncopated thirds. Soon, the band joins in with a bottom-friendly driving rhythm. This call-and-response circles back to the original motif, but the zenith is Joel's frantic buildup at the 'Angry Young Man' chorus.

DeVitto chimes in at the height of the expected places, adding the full explosive heft of the kit, while expanding the beats under Joel's vocals. The arrangement demands full concentration from all, and the band knocks it out of the park. In essence, DeVitto sustains a defibrillating rhythm; Javors and Emerson rock maniacally, and Stegmeyer performs at his usual fever pitch. Howard Emerson:

> There was tons of guitar. The drum part that you hear during the verse? That's my stomach. They kept on trying to find the sound. Liberty must have been hamboning* it on his leg, or maybe he tried it on his stomach. I just remember laying down on two folding chairs. They put a mic on it, and that is what they used.

(*'a series of rhythmic slaps and pats on the body to create music' (*urbandictionary.com*))

Written about a disgruntled road manager, the song is chock-full of imagery and physical directives, which Joel exaggerates with gruff vocals. Live, he's been prone to thrust a fist into the ionosphere and thump on his chest like a Neanderthal, knocking out heated descriptors about the recalcitrant subject: 'He refuses to bend, he refuses to crawl.' At the chorus, he eases into a wordless euphoria. At the interlude, measured Moog ramps up the stakes.

The philosophy at the bridge, cottons to a conflicting belief system and a casting aside of impetuous behavior. This reflective character sings, 'I believe I've passed the age of consciousness and righteous rage.'

I enjoyed the juxtaposition of the characters. The peacenik and rebellious avatars show little regard for each other, yet both voices are strident. After they have their say, the song circles back to 'Prelude.'

Joel's rhythm was inspired by The Surfaris' 'Wipe Out,' yet the complex 'Angry Young Man' easily surpasses the bandwidth of that street-smart garage-band tune. The symbiotic drum and piano accents recalled 'Azrael Revisited' by The Nice in 1968: a fearless example of early prog rock. Keith Emerson left to form Emerson, Lake & Palmer, and further explored the genre.

Prog rock gave Joel goose bumps. In a 1975 interview with Mary Travers, Joel exclaimed, 'Yes is the best band in the whole world', and singled out 'And You And I' as 'one of the greatest songs ever written.' He admired the eclecticism: 'They're doing things like Stravinsky and Charles Ives. They look like a rock band, but they're not.' The four-part arrangement of 'And You And I' commences with a series of harmonics. Keyboardist Rick Wakeman switches from celestial mellotron and machine-like Minimoog to funky Hammond organ amid stunning orchestral hits.

Here, the band ignites a similar virtuosic flame. And if you love hearing DeVitto and Joel spar like *Mad Max* gladiators, you've entered the right arena.

'I've Loved These Days' (Billy Joel)
The inner rhymes and soaring melody uphold the tender lyric: 'We light our lights for atmosphere and hang our hopes on chandeliers.' This song rethreads the 'Piano Man' line, 'when I wore a younger man's clothes,' as Joel reflects back wistfully on a simpler time. Despite its brevity, it's profound.

DeVitto's passion for the story is clearly evident in his laid-back performance – a true professional, he can always be counted on to allow space for sensitive lyrics while keeping up the momentum. Cannata's horn solo adds a melancholic sweet spot.

'Miami 2017 (Seen The Lights Go Out On Broadway)' (Billy Joel)
This apocalyptic theme – brought to life with blistering synth, sirens and thrashing cymbals – is told through the perspective of an elder, looking back decades later at a destroyed New York City which lay abandoned after severe neglect. 'They turned our power down and drove us underground,' Joel seethes at the crescendo. The descriptive lyric and the tone – which dances between anger and resignation – reflect the real-life hurt that New Yorkers felt during the time of this recording.

In the article, 'The Legacy of the 1970s Fiscal Crisis,' 16 April 2013, Kim Phillips-Fenn wrote: 'People occupied firehouses to keep them open, organized massive campaigns to save college campuses and threw their trash into the middle of the street to protest the mass layoffs of sanitation workers and resulting slowdown in garbage collections.' Clearly, many lives had been turned upside down and those affected saw no end in sight.

Like an elegy, near the end, Joel gasps, 'They say a handful still survive.' And finally, he salutes survivor resilience against gripping piano chords. What stands out is the mature songwriting and strict adhesion to dynamics. In fact, DeVitto classified this song as one in which 'it's like running a race.' He had the challenging task of maintaining constant control of his kit.

'True music must repeat the thoughts and inspirations of the people and the time,' said New York composer George Gershwin. Joel – who won the Gershwin Award in 2014 – did just that.

Howard Emerson:

Downstairs in my storage closet, I still have the basic tracks – drums, bass, piano – and I'm pretty sure there is a vocal of 'New York State Of Mind' and a few other tracks. Maybe Billy redid the piano. I don't know. I really had no clue if the music would be a hit. At my age, I can listen to any music of any style and you can ask me – if it hasn't been released – what do you think of it in terms of its quality for what it is, and with the knowledge that I gleaned over the years, I could give you an objective answer.

The Stranger (1977)

Personnel:
Billy Joel: vocals, acoustic piano, keyboards, synthesizers, Fender Rhodes
Richie Cannata: organ, tenor saxophone, soprano saxophone, clarinet, flute, tuba
Dominic Cortese: accordion (4,5)
Richard Tee: organ (9)
Hiram Bullock: electric guitar
Steve Khan: 6 and 12-string guitars, acoustic rhythm guitar, high-string guitar
Hugh McCracken: acoustic guitar (3,4,7,8,9)
Steve Burgh: acoustic guitar (3, 7), electric guitar (4)
Doug Stegmeyer: bass
Liberty DeVitto: drums
Ralph MacDonald: percussion (2, 3, 8, 9)
Phil Woods: alto saxophone (3)
Patrick Williams: orchestration
Patti Austin, Lani Groves, Gwen Guthrie, Phoebe Snow: backing vocals (9)
Producer: Phil Ramone
Jim Boyer: engineer
Ted Jensen: mastering at Sterling Sound (New York)
Kathy Kurs: production assistant
Jim Houghton: photography
Release date: 29 September 1977
Recorded: July-August 1977, A&R Recording Inc., New York City; Columbia Records
Producer: Phil Ramone
Chart positions: UK: Albums (OCC): 24, US: *Billboard* 200: 2, Canadian Albums
(RPM): 2, Australian Albums (Kent Music Report): 3
Length: 42:34
The Stranger '30th Anniversary Edition' was released in July 2008

Turnstiles had done poorly on the commercial charts, so Joel faced the risk of being dropped by the Columbia label if his next project *The Stranger* didn't make the grade. That Joel ended up in this vulnerable spot was a shame. *Turnstiles* was an impressive work of art, but Joel's fan base was still evolving. It would take another studio record before commercial sales would indicate a substantial change.

Still, *Turnstiles* played an integral role in Billy Joel's career because this is where the Billy Joel Band came into being. In *Making Records*, producer Phil Ramone described *Turnstiles* as Billy Joel's 'anti-formality', and that the studio project 'was one of his most brilliant albums.' Consequently, *The Stranger* gave DeVitto, Cannata and Stegmeyer another opportunity to unleash their raw, unpretentious ideas. Joel had finally realized his dream of working with a steady group of dedicated artists. On this, their sophomore project, they could soar.

Joel continued to use session guitarists in the studio for the most part, but Steve Kahn – later of Steely Dan fame – stood out as a virtuoso. Steely

Dan was helmed by Donald Fagen and Walter Becker. Their trademark style included wide use of minor 7ths and jagged, jazzy rhythms. Considered studio perfectionists, they often demanded countless retakes. Only the strong tended to survive, but the multitalented Kahn rose to the challenge.

The accordion added flavor to multiple tracks. Currying popularity in the mid-1950s, this outsider instrument went in and out of style thereafter, particularly with the advent of guitar-driven rock 'n' roll. But 'Squeeze Box' by The Who in 1975, and Bruce Springsteen's '4th Of July, Asbury Park (Sandy)' with a solo by Danny Federici, led to a renaissance.

Phil Ramone hadn't been Joel's first choice for producer. A longtime Beatles fan, Joel first solicited the services of British wunderkind George Martin: well known for implementing wizardry into multiple Beatles projects. Ironically, Martin began his career in the 1950s by recording comedy and novelty records. But under the influence of The Beatles, he expanded his scope. He encouraged the usage of tape loops, altered time by playing tracks backwards, and used surreal sound effects. When Joel told his bandmates about the proposed plan, they were excited. But that sense of delight turned to disappointment when Martin – similar to Guercio – expressed interest in working with Joel but sans the band. Once again, Joel found himself with a conundrum. Martin's studio expertise and creativity could not be understated; working with this renowned professional would be a boost to the songwriter's career. Martin was in high demand; the offer was time-sensitive. On the other hand, Joel took great pride in working with this dream band. They admired his originality, made serious efforts to round out his ideas, and gave him the extra push he needed when the creative well ran dry. These hard-core musicians would be difficult to replace. Furthermore, Joel had been in a similarly precarious position before with Stewart, who also put Joel's loyalty to the test, yet Joel had walked away with a do-it-yourself confidence.

Moving forward, Joel struck gold when meeting Phil Ramone: the New York-based producer who had overseen Paul Simon's *Still Crazy After All These Years* and Bob Dylan's *Blood on the Tracks* (1976: Grammy Album of the Year), among others. In addition, Ramone garnered awards and accolades for scoring films, including *Midnight Cowboy* – where Harry Nilsson's 1968 cover of 'Everybody's Talkin'' had elevated the film's success. Still, could Joel have predicted that in 1979, Ramone would garner a *Record of the Year* Grammy for producing 'Just The Way You Are'? Working with a new producer involved a leap of faith, but the Julliard violinist and rock producer had a solid reputation and an open mind.

Ramone first set his eyes on Joel and the band at a Columbia Records convention in Toronto in 1976, when his wife urged him to witness a 30-minute evening encore. Once seated, Ramone caught on to the electrifying interaction that took place between the band and their leader. Several months later, Columbia executives Mickey Eichner and Don DeVito announced that Joel was seeking a changing-of-the guard. They invited Ramone to hear Joel perform at Carnegie Hall, where he had a triple-night spot.

Lunch at Fontana di Trevi – a popular eatery across from Carnegie Hall – was an ideal meeting place (not to be mistaken for Long Island's Christiano's: the actual setting for 'Scenes From An Italian Restaurant'). When the topic of studio production came up, Ramone exclaimed that he was impressed with how well the band members complemented Joel's music live. He assured Joel that a similar alchemy would take place in the studio if he were hired: 'I realized that these guys were completely self-contained in their own mountain, so to speak; the band was there, surrounding ideas,' Ramone said in a 1998 YouTube video in which he chatted with engineer Rob Prisament about his role on *The Stranger*.

Joel refused to barter or compromise. George Martin had an impressive resume but had reservations; Ramone knew in his heart that Billy Joel 'was 100 per cent tied to a band.' The two got along like lifelong friends, which Ramone attributed to their New York commonalities. He saw Joel as multidimensional, often referring to him as 'a street kid with an intellect.' Having been through classical training himself, Ramone was acutely aware of Joel's influences, which he assumed were inspired by the entertainer's strict father.

As their professional and personal relationship blossomed, Ramone became better able to discern the deeper aspects of Joel's songwriting process: 'He has chordal things that he really feels intellectual about, but they're all about feel,' Ramone also confided to Prisament.

The Stranger presented challenges, as only about nine songs – which were in various stages of completion – existed before the team entered the studio. Yet Ramone remained undaunted. His years of experience in the recording field often yielded groundbreaking ideas. This time, his *less-is-more* suggestion was to bookend the wispy whistling which jump-started the title song. (Ironically, Joel had never intended the whistling to be part of the arrangement. He'd whistled merely to illustrate the melody he had in his head, but Ramone insisted on keeping it.) Subsequently, Ramone sweetened the signature ballad, by recapitulating and lengthening that memorable sonic, and adding 'a hint of strings' at the end. This technique was reminiscent of successful Broadway soundtracks.

The success of *The Stranger* may hinge in part on Ramone's choice to under-produce Joel's songs. By avoiding gratuitous orchestration in an 'anti-Spector' approach, the team accentuated the lyrical content and basic chordal structures. By giving credence to playing live, as opposed to using excessive overdubbing, Ramone created a 'you are there' phenomenon.

In addition, Ramone staged the musicians in an order that made communication accessible. He was well aware that intensive studio work could bring on tension: which visual lines of communication could dispel. For example, he observed that Joel would get flustered when playing alongside guitarists. On the other hand, when bassist Doug Stegmeyer framed songs with roots and 5ths, his proximity to Joel was a blessing. Certainly, headphone use enabled Joel to catch indescrepencies that could be ironed out in the mix, but

Ramone's staging ideas addressed more emotional issues; Joel seemingly felt comfortable having certain musicians (especially DeVitto) within his sightlines. By working together so intensively, they'd developed a telepathy that went beyond simply sustaining the rhythm and enacting sonic stories.

Even before the Ramone era, Rhys Clark noted about Joel: 'He always left the space for anybody to have an idea.' In that regard, Ramone and Joel were kindred souls. Due to the producer's experience in professional management, Ramone gained a reputation as a pro. who could expediently resolve group tensions, allowing each craftsman to glisten. Ramone noted that band members would prod Joel to complete his material. At times, the pressure was intense: 'It was like target practice. They'd say, 'Where's the song?' They would guilt him.'

Sometimes Joel took the teasing to heart. But every situation was different. Some songs came in dressed and ready to go, like 'Only The Good Die Young.' But others – like 'Everybody Has A Dream' – were developed in-house.

Ramone's genius followed many subtle forms. First of all, he balanced work and time off. He knew that nights off were as beneficial as nights spent drilling details. Using tough-love tactics, he allowed the scent of take-out food to tempt the musicians but instructed them to cut a complete track before digging in.

Secondly, Ramone took the time to get to know his colleagues. Traveling in tandem enabled him to understand their idiosyncratic behaviors, as well as their career aspirations. Overall, he was open-minded, but at the same time, remained cognizant of label deadlines and financial pressures. As such, *The Stranger* was completed in – excuse the pun – *record time*. With Ramone setting definitive goals, and under his judicious lead, *The Stranger* was wrapped in three weeks.

Ramone took great pains to honor his clients' vocals. In another account from *Making Records*, he revealed, 'I lavish generous attention on the selection and placement of microphones ... getting a clean vocal is my number-one concern. The voice is a superb instrument with infinite color, and there are many variables that go into choosing the right microphone for a vocalist.'

Ramone cited Joel as a client who possessed 'a lot of dynamic range', and who 'can go from a whisper to a shout in an instant.' That said, Ramone used a Beyer M160 dynamic ribbon because it 'helped keep most of the piano and drums out of his vocal track' and 'gave Billy a big smooth sound without a trace of distortion.'

The album received praise from prestigious outlets. *Rolling Stone* observed: 'This is the first Billy Joel album in some time that has significantly expanded his repertoire.' *The Stranger* waltzed away with Song of the Year and Album of the Year at the Grammy Awards and was designated one of the 500 Greatest Albums of All Time by *Rolling Stone*.

The album was heavily promoted. Between September 1977 and July 1978, the following singles were released: 'Movin' Out,' 'Just The Way You Are,' 'The Stranger,' 'Only The Good Die Young' and 'She's Always A Woman.'

Album Art

In the front cover photo by Jerry Abramovitz, Joel – fully suited – sits on the edge of a bed, gazing at a white harlequin mask. A set of black boxing gloves hang to his side, a reminder of his short-lived training. While the white mask is open to interpretation, I believe Joel wanted to illustrate how people often modify their behavior according to the expectations of those around them.

The back cover was photographed by Jim Houghton, and features producer Phil Ramone and the band members Liberty DeVitto, Richie Cannata, Doug Stegmeyer and Billy Joel posing around a table at the now-defunct Guido's – otherwise known as the Supreme Macaroni Company, which was once housed in a five-storey building on 9th Avenue. Guido's was a popular Italian eatery based in Manhattan and frequented by many pop stars. The setting is familiar to New Yorkers and tourists alike, as New York City is famous for its family-run Italian restaurants that retain the traditional red-and-white checked tablecloths, linen napkins, silver cutlery and walls decorated with signed glossies of bygone legends.

'Movin' Out (Anthony's Song)' (Billy Joel)

B/w 'She's Always A Woman' and released as a single on 1 November 1977. Peak: UK: 35, US *Billboard* Hot 100: 17US Cashbox Top 100: 14

Joel hammers out the introductory piano chords, while humming softly. This juxtaposition continues throughout, as Joel moves from sotto voce to rough-hewn at key moments.

His first subject in this multipart song is the restless Anthony, whose 'Mama Leone' warns, that if he doesn't 'move out to the country,' he'll get a heart attack. Using Joel-speak, the songwriter dramatizes the fatal disease by accentuating and repeating the syllable 'ack-ack-ack.' Joel illustrates the futility of 'movin' up' with this description of the grocery-store employee, who is 'savin' his pennies for someday.'

In the second verse, Joel recycles the previous rhythmic device when referencing Sergeant O'Leary, the officer who upgrades his Chevy for a 'Cadillac' (ack-ack-ack). In the final verse, however, Joel catches us off guard by drawing out the soft, initial consonant sound of the word 'mind,' which mimics the soft murmurings in the introduction.

Joel points out O'Leary's efforts to 'move up,' but not 'out' with this humorous line: 'And if he can't drive with a broken back, at least he can polish the fenders.'

The characters Anthony and Mister Cacciatore grew out of improvisations the band members developed when lounging around a hotel swimming pool. 'We'd pretend we were visiting Billy, who had moved to the suburbs like we and our families did on Long Island,' Liberty DeVitto explained in his memoir. In that same book, DeVitto explained how the team created the organic sound effects that appear at the end: 'We took a cheap Panasonic cassette player and taped the microphone to the bumper of the car right around the exhaust pipe. This is what you hear at the end.'

Ramone recalled that Joel kept track of various melodies, riffs and lyrics that he could refer to if he needed a new idea. He coined these fragments 'spare parts.' George Martin judiciously encouraged The Beatles to make use of their leftover phrases and melodies too. This efficient, creative strategy was a surefire way to deal with paralyzing writer's block.

Rhythmic changes were also encouraged. Ramone encouraged DeVitto to play quarter notes on the bass and snare drums to create more definition. Ramone asserted, 'This is what people will remember.'

DeVitto explained to Kevin Curtain on the YouTube podcast *Curtain Call*: episode 12 that Joel scrapped the original melody after the drummer pointed out: 'That's 'Laughter In The Rain' by Neil Sedaka.'

Although Joel expressed frustration about this *faux pas*, he didn't trash the song. DeVitto elaborated: 'he loved the lyrics so much that he changed the melody.' Joel also heeded DeVitto's advice to create a short piano motif to add color at the end.

'The Stranger' (Billy Joel)
B/w 'Movin' Out (Anthony's Song)' and released as a single, Japan, 21 May 1978. Peak: Japan (Oricon Singles Chart): 2, New Zealand (RIANZ): 8
Joel wrote the introduction and closing section after recording the middle section. This serpentine song starts out saturated with soulful piano, bass and drums; the piano then takes the lead, but 'The Stranger' has become largely recognizable for its leitmotif, where Joel hauntingly whistles the melody and recapitulates it at the outro. But between those parameters, the pace increases as suddenly as a flash flood, and 'The Stranger' morphs into an unarguably assertive beast. At the verse, Joel's voice sounds clipped and hurried, almost like he's channeling Dr. John. But at the bridge, he settles into a reflective groove.

Steve Kahn and Hiram Bullock provide intense guitar work. Joel noodles around at the piano towards the end, with a salute to late-night lounge artists: the ones who refuse requests but make a handful of notes sparkle. The band took full advantage of the five-plus minute slot, as there's not a moment of slack.

'Just The Way You Are' (Billy Joel)
B/w 'Get It Right the First Time/Vienna and released as the lead single, September 1977. Peak: UK Singles (OCC): 19, US *Billboard* Hot 100: 3, US Adult Contemporary (*Billboard*): 1, US Cash Box Top 100: 2
On a YouTube video, Liberty DeVitto talked about creating his distinctive drum part using 'a brush in the right hand and a stick in the left hand.' When playing with a wedding band in his youth, DeVitto had picked up riveting Latin rhythms. His sultry bossa nova rhythm contemporized the original version.

Initially, the band members considered the ballad to be saccharine, but that was before they received feedback from notable music industry women.

According to pitchfork.com, Linda Ronstadt told Joel: 'That's one of the greatest songs I've ever heard.' Ronstadt and Phoebe Snow pleaded with Joel to record the song when they heard the playback at A&R Studios. They seemed to intuit that the ballad would become one of Joel's greatest hits.

This song covers all the bases. The instrumental hooks are simple but memorable. These are the words that everyone in a romantic relationship longs to hear, and Joel sounds completely sincere when relaying them. The words are complementary and unconditional. Except, when Joel asks, 'What will it take 'til you believe in me?' at the bridge, a few cracks in the area of trust are revealed.

Phil Wood's alto sax solos hit the spot and helped boost this ballad into the great American songbook. Woods came highly recommended – producer Phil Ramone had worked with the Charlie Parker aficionado during the recording of 'Have A Good Time' on Paul Simon's 1975 album *Still Crazy After All These Years*, and on the Steely Dan tune 'Doctor Wu' that same year. Highly-trained American composer Pat Williams – responsible for writing multiple American TV show theme songs – carefully arranged the parts.

The track was simply produced with synth, electric piano and no overt orchestral parts.

'Just The Way You Are' beat the Bee Gees' 'Stayin' Alive' (from *Saturday Night Fever*) for *Song of the Year* and *Record of the Year* at the 21st Grammy Awards: no small feat given the disco genre's domino effect.

'Scenes From An Italian Restaurant' (Billy Joel)

Because the band rehearsed sections on the road, DeVitto confirmed that it only took 'a couple of tracks' to get 'Scenes' recorded. With a more than seven-minute canvas, this seamed-together story song could comfortably be divided into three distinctive parts: 'The Italian Restaurant Song,' 'Things Are Okay In Oyster Bay' and 'The Ballad Of Brenda And Eddie,' with the frenetic latter section depicting flirtatious high school sweethearts. But there's no fairy-tale ending: 'Money got tight and they just didn't count on the tears.'

'Then the king and the queen went back to the green,' Joel sings breathlessly, referring to the town square: the Parkway Green in Hicksville.

Brenda and Eddie may have originated as simplistic flashbacks of hot secondary-school couples, but over time the twosome have morphed into cultural tropes, like McCartney's 'Lady Madonna' and 'Eleanor Rigby' or Simon & Garfunkel's 'Mrs. Robinson.' Fans can revisit this legacy and ponder, *Who was I in high school? How have I grown since then?* At the end of the day, Joel comes full circle by confirming that 'you can never go back there again.' Still, the fated couple *do* go a long way back towards creating a sense of nostalgia.

There is, too, the question of pure musicality. In an author interview, DeVitto recalls: 'People always ask me about this song. It sounds so hard to play, but it's easy to play because it has different sections. 'Scenes' has a beginning, and then there's the 'Brenda and Eddie' part and 'you're okay with me these days.''

(DeVitto reacted similarly to queries about 'Angry Young Man', which also contained multiple sections.)

Horns and cymbal swells were overdubbed. Accordionist Dominic Cortese finessed an old-world feel that craftily check-marks eras in which accordion was a kingpin.

Since its inception, the catchy 'Brenda and Eddie' part has become so popular in concert that the second Joel gestures to the audience, they cheerfully drown out all else, and sing along. So, even if Joel suffers from a sudden memory lapse, he's fully covered by crowd insurance.

'Vienna' (Billy Joel)
B/w 'Just The Way You Are' and released as a single in 1977

This moving ballad was written in the key of B flat. The stylized eight-bar piano introduction includes a slow succession of descending bass tones, balanced out with triplets, dotted notes and broken chords in the treble clef.

With the opening phrase, 'Slow down, you crazy child/Take the phone off the hook,' Joel preaches positively about appreciating life; recognizing what is and what isn't crucial. 'Vienna' was inspired in part by a relatively simple scenario. On a trip to Europe, when Joel reconnected with his father and met his half-brother Alexander (an established pianist and conductor), he watched an elderly woman sweep the sidewalk. (In 1972, when Joel and his father connected initially, he found out that his father had remarried and had a seven-year-old.) Joel was troubled by this act. Why was this senior citizen expected to do manual labor. But Howard Joel viewed this activity through a contrasting lens. From his vantage point, the perfunctory task gave the woman a sense of purpose within the community, whereas seniors in the United States often feel expendable. As such, 'Vienna' is a beautiful testimony to time. Joel gently reminds us that we won't get it back and should never take it for granted, whatever our age. It's a poignant epiphany about honoring one's past with grace and maturity.

On the other hand, 'Vienna' doesn't provide the longer clear-cut narrative that Joel may have labored over when constructing other ballads, yet that's part and parcel of what makes this work: 'Vienna' is refreshingly spacious. This deep inhalation of country air creates an exhilarating rush that makes one feel that little else matters at that very moment. Yet, it's not a vehicle for the sightseer as is 'New York State Of Mind,' where notable geographic spots are vehemently toasted. Ironically, this story could take place anywhere.

The progression is complex, as Joel begins with the G-minor chord, built on the 6th scale-tone of the key. From there, he rushes back to the tonic chord of B flat, then to the chord built from the 5th scale degree of the key, F major. But the unexpected bluesy effect comes to full force when Joel pivots to A flat and E flat before resolving to the tonic B flat. Finally, he makes a bright detour using the relatively predictable chords of C Major and D Major. Through the constant shifting of harmonies alone, Joel swells interest.

This B-side to 'Just The Way You Are' revolves around a slightly off-kilter, ornamented and gorgeous motif. Joel's voice remains evocative from beginning to end. Similar to 'The Stranger,' there's a wraparound ending courtesy of Dominic Cortese, who stays consistently in fine form.

'Only The Good Die Young' (Billy Joel)
Released as a single, May 1978.
A Catholic university radio station boycotted this upbeat single. The action backfired and young people clamored to hear the very thing their parents feared they'd hear.

'The church ended up selling a lot of records for us,' DeVitto explained in interviews. Joel did his best to avoid the controversy by pointing out on performingsongwriter.com and other outlets that the song wasn't meant to be an anti-Catholic treatise, it was really more 'pro-lust.' More specifically, Joel gets the opportunity to re-examine the flushed feelings he felt for his Long Island crush Virginia Callahan, who only began to take notice of her classmate when he started performing in clubs: 'So come on Virginia, show me a sign.'

Constructed around a series of simple chords, Joel's vocal swagger is the major payoff, but the follow-the-bouncing-ball riff that underlines the vocal is also an absolute monster. Only a body encased in embalming fluid could resist its come-on-and-dance allure.

Drummer DeVitto shared in his memoir that his contagious 'brush swing feel' was inspired by Mitch Miller: the drummer on the Jimi Hendrix track 'Up From The Skies.' Producer Phil Ramone also favored the contagious, truculent shuffle rhythm.

'She's Always A Woman' (Billy Joel)
B/w 'Movin Out (Anthony's Song)' and released as a single, 1977, Peak: UK Singles Chart: 29 in 1986: UK: 53 released as a double A-side with 'Just the Way You Are, U.S. *Billboard* Hot 100: 17, US *Billboard* Easy Listening: 2
Joel dedicated this July 1978 single to ex-wife and early manager Elizabeth Weber. Although he wrote the ballad in Weber's defense, proclaiming that she had to be a tough dealmaker in the predominantly male music industry of the time, his intentions were sometimes misconstrued and viewed as sexist, with detractors whining, 'You mean, she's *just* a woman?'

Bob Dylan wrote 'Just Like a Woman' (*Blonde on Blonde)* in 1966. He began a verse with 'You fake just like a woman', and ended with 'But you break just like a little girl.' The Canadian band The Guess Who released 'American Woman' from the album of the same name in 1970. In that case, the American woman is a metaphor for the then-raging Vietnam war. But in contrast, Joel doesn't condescend as Dylan does by qualifying the woman's behavior as that of a 'little girl'; nor does he exploit gender to underscore a loaded topic; he merely describes his love interest's behavior from his male perspective.

That said, the lyrics are complementary and hard-edged but authentic. After all, Joel's describing a human, and every human has flaws: 'She can kill with a smile/She can wound with her eyes,' he states in the first verse. 'But she'll bring out the best and the worst you can be,' he continues in verse three.

Joel's vocal feels genuine, especially in the bridge, so that when he describes his lover's more toxic characteristics, he doesn't do so with avarice. Instead, he appears to be viewing her from a distance like a fact-checking novelist; identifying her behavior, but not necessarily judging it or condoning it, just fully experiencing it. Thematically, he focuses on the subject's fierce independence. The lines: 'Oh, she takes care of herself' and 'She's ahead of her time' belie unfair misogynist accusations.

Joel uses block chords on the verse and tumbling chords on the chorus. This contrast allows him to catch a break. At the chorus, Richie Cannata uses his flute to gently harmonize with Joel's keyboard progression. Joel's toasty hum leads to a soft ending.

'Get It Right The First Time' (Billy Joel)
This is the obvious oddball song on the album. Initially, it's hard to find the samba-like rhythm and relax into it, but once you do, you'll discover that it's a viable bulwark for Joel's flexible voice. It's also the rare Billy Joel song in which you'll find a flute lead and mini-solo.

Moreover, it's an intelligent precursor to the closing track, which is conventional in structure, so in that way, it's a contrast and a treat. Phil Ramone once described it like this: 'It's almost like a showbiz thing.'

This is about making first impressions count. It's a reminder of how much anxiety dating can cause; one might never get a second chance. Joel grimaces: 'Just let me pull myself together,' as he swirls us into a vortex of self-effacing youthfulness.

'Everybody Has A Dream' (Billy Joel)
This gospel-tinged song is, as the title suggests, full of wisdom, longing and optimism. The passionate choral parts, clean piano and blasts of earnest organ, keep it real. Joel's vocal inflection affectionately recalls that of his longtime hero Ray Charles. A quartet of female backing singers included contralto Phoebe Snow, who charted with her original ballad 'Poetry Man' in 1975 and sang backing vocals on Paul Simon's '50 Ways To Leave Your Lover.' Lani Groves, Patti Austin and Gwen Guthrie were commendable harmonizers.

The problem is that the song almost gets lost on the album, as it so sharply deviates from the others, being the singular gospel selection. But if you shunt aside the orphan status, you'll derive pleasure from the penultimate track.

'So, let me lie and let me go on sleeping,' Joel urges mid-song. Thereafter, the chorus and Joel explode with emotion. Joel told *USA Today* on 9 July 2008 that originally, 'It was written as a folk song,' but eventually turned into a 'Joe Cocker gospel thing,' and that he composed the song way before recording *The Stranger*.

'The Stranger' (Billy Joel)

B/w 'Movin' Out (Anthony's Song) and released as a single, 21 May 1978 (Japan), also on Greatest Hits – Volume 1 & 11, Peak: Japan (Oricon Singles Chart): 2, New Zealand (RIANZ): 8

The album ends with an instrumental version of the title song, resurrecting that haunting and melancholy motif – now embellished with strings, a pronounced bass line, and down to the wire of that distinctive, stark whistle.

52nd Street (1978)

Personnel:
Billy Joel: acoustic piano, Yamaha CP-70 electric grand piano, Fender Rhodes, synthesizer, vocals
Richie Cannata: organ, saxophones, clarinet
Steve Khan: electric guitar, acoustic guitar, backing vocals
David Spinozza: acoustic guitar (2)
David Brown: electric guitar (3)
Russell Javors: acoustic guitar (3)
Hugh McCracken: nylon string guitar (6,8)
Eric Gale: electric guitar (7)
Doug Stegmeyer: bass, backing vocals
Liberty DeVitto: drums
Mike Mainieri: vibraphone and marimbas (4,6)
Ralph MacDonald: percussion (6,7)
David Freidman: orchestral chimes and percussion (8)
Freddie Hubbard: flugelhorn and trumpet (4)
George Marge: sopranino recorder (6)
Robert Freedman: horn and string orchestration (2,8)
Dave Grusin: horn orchestration (7)
David Nadien: concertmaster (2,7,8)
Peter Cetera: backing vocals (3)
Donnie Dacus: backing vocals (3)
Frank Floyd: backing vocals (7)
Babi Floyd: backing vocals (7)
Milt Grayson: backing vocals (7)
Zack Sanders: backing vocals (7)
Ray Simpson: backing vocals (7)
Producer: Phil Ramone
Recorded: July-August 1978, A&R Recording, Inc. 799 7th Avenue at 52nd Street, New York City
Label: Family Productions/Columbia
Kathy Kurs, Carol Peters: associate producers
Jim Boyer: engineer, mixing
David Martone: assistant engineer
Ted Jensen: mastering at Sterling Sound (New York City)
John Berg: cover design
Jim Houghton: photography
Release date: 11 October 1978
Chart positions: UK: 10, US: 1, Canada: 1, Australia: 1
Length: 40:26

For his sixth studio album, Joel took a sharp, stylistic detour. *52nd Street* is a celebration of American jazz which required the services of outstanding session players. With guitarists Steve Kahn and David Brown onboard, Joel wasn't under the gun to construct as many piano solos.

The album's moniker harkens back to the historically rich epicenter of New York City that embraced jazz in the 1930s-1950s, and where the recording took place.

With Joel looking forward to performances in arenas, he had to up his game as far as penning material that could excite exceptionally large crowds. He rose to the occasion by penning expansive hits with penetrating lyrics and thrilling tempo and harmonic changes.

This album was heavily promoted. Between 28 October 1978 and May 1979, the following singles were released: 'My Life,' 'Big Shot,' 'Until The Night' and 'Honesty.' *52nd Street* honored New York's illustrious past but allowed room for a future of open-minded fans. 'Zanzibar' satisfied the public's demand for a unique dance number, with disco dominating the charts.

The album enjoyed a seven-time platinum run, topped the *Billboard* 200, and was awarded two Grammys: Album of the Year and Best Pop Vocal Performance – Male. 'Honesty' was nominated for Song of the Year but lost to The Doobie Brothers' 'What A Fool Believes.'

Jazz artist and in-demand trumpeter Freddie Hubbard was handpicked for the dynamic 'Zanzibar,' but there were, in essence, a bounty of textures at any given turn.

Evening Magazine reported on Joel's interview that year for W10Q in Philadelphia. Among other questions, the rock star was asked about his wardrobe because it was unusual then for a youthful American musician to dress so formally. Joel said, 'The jacket and tie became my trademark. It's kind of a sign of respect.' These days, Joel can often be spotted wearing a similar suit with a pair of casual sneakers or in press photos wearing a baseball hat, a casual t-shirt and jeans with tennis shoes, but his onstage wardrobe of 5 November 2021 at Madison Square Garden marked a return to more conventional attire.

The album was well-received. *sputnikmusic.com* said: 'The reason why this album was so successful, is that nearly all the songs on here are just fantastic all the time and bring out most of Billy's talent and music.' *Allmusic. com's* Stephen Thomas Erlewine observed. '*52nd Street* is probably the most aggressive Billy Joel album to this point, and it is a solid listen.' Erlewine goes on to cite 'Ramone's seamless production and Joel's melodic craftsmanship' as contributing factors.

Album Art

Astonishingly, photographer Jim Houghton took the cool cover shot with a Polaroid camera. Joel, wearing a blue suit, leans against a white brick wall, gripping a trumpet against his chest with both hands. His tie is loosely fitted, leaving the impression that he's had a rough night. He's wearing a white pair of sneakers, but he's certainly no frat boy; the soul on his right foot is facing up, almost in an act of defiance. We see the bones of a service elevator on the left-hand side, which musicians used, to get to the now-demolished recording studio. The album title appears in white, on a black-framed window. There's litter on the ground. We're eons away from suburban, manicured lawns, in the thick of one of the busiest cities in the world. Houghton's natural snapshot captured that dynamic.

According to billyjoel.com, the rumor had been circulating that the trumpet Joel holds was Freddie Hubbard's – the jazz giant that played the solos on 'Zanzibar' – but Joel put the pesky rumor to rest: 'That was an old horn that Phil Ramone had laying around.'

'Big Shot' (Billy Joel)
B/w 'Root Beer Rag,' 'Half a Mile Away' and released as the second single in January 1979. Peak: U.S. *Billboard* Hot 100: 14, U.S. Cash Box Top 100: 13
Joel punches out the lyrics, a litany of slights directed towards society's most elite – except on the bridge, where he descends into 'woah oh oh' and Cannata takes the lead. Stylistically, Joel's voice goes gruff, yet remains playful in his phrasing. 'You had to have the bright hot spotlight,' Joel rants, as Cannata's buoyant sax solo threads in and out. Newly hired lead guitarist David Brown – who came to fame as a member of Santana in the late-1960s and throughout 1976 – starts off and reacts brilliantly to Joel's repetitive 'big shot' ranting. Brown stakes out the outro, with envelope-pushing results. DeVitto's on the money, switching gears on a dime, either with violent rolls or a truculent four-to-the-floor.

'Honesty' (Billy Joel)
B/w 'The Mexican Connection,' 'Root Beer Rag' and released as the third single in May 1979. Peak: U.S. *Billboard* Adult Contemporary: 9, France (IFOP): 1
Joel expands his vocal range here in this complex ballad about the vagaries of romantic mistrust. David Spinozza strums stunning acoustic guitar, and Robert Freedman fills out spaces with soulful horn and string arrangements.

'Honesty' represents one of Joel's most transparent studio performances, and when done live, he has historically held nothing back.

While 'Honesty' does come across as heartfelt and genuine on the surface, that simple description belies the subtext: an undercurrent of discomfort. The lyric reveals a deep hurt and a hunger to be with a person on whom the singer can ultimately rely. But there's a lot of emotional unpacking to do here. In the first verse, Joel creates a thin wall between himself and the listener. He's still in a somewhat abstract state of mind. He theorizes about what love is like; he's guarded. Then in the chorus, he spills his guts out: 'Honesty is hardly ever heard and mostly what I need from you.' That's the payoff. That's what we came for. In the second verse, Joel complains about those who spit out 'pretty lies.' The incendiary narrative belies his subdued vocal performance.

DeVitto made off-color jokes about the lyrics, at times, to keep things light. These barbs often kept Joel on track with lyric writing.

'My Life' (Billy Joel)

B/w '52nd Street' and released as a single, 28 October 1978. Peak: UK Singles (OCC): 12, US *Billboard* Hot 100: 3, US Adult Contemporary (*Billboard*): 2, Zimbabwe (ZIMA): 1

This rip-roaring song, released as a single on 28 October 1979, features a relaxed introduction with a roiling keyboard riff; fingers snapping against a strolling bass line and shades of horn that sound similar to 'Stiletto': another *52nd Street* arrangement. Chicago's Peter Cetera is one of the prominent backing singers. Javors and Brown go for the jugular.

The band drops out on one of the final verses, leaving Joel's voice soaring above DeVitto's sparkling rhythm. At this point, Joel weighs in on his newly-discovered independence; you can hear the liberation in his inflection.

The repeated tonic note in the bass acts as a pedal point, which increases the sense of thematic tension that threads through the song. In the interlude, Joel replaces triads with more complex 9th chords. The rhythm comes stacked with syncopation.

During production, Phil Ramone insisted on a disco beat to reflect the popular style of the time: a request that initially made DeVitto bristle. In his memoir, he recollected: 'It was a straight disco beat, which I thought sucked.' But the drummer ultimately complied, and later agreed that Ramone's instinct had been right: the record went gold. Along those same percussion lines, there's a sunny but short marimba solo.

Joel envisioned an intergenerational battle when he wrote the rebellious lyric – an irate, unforgiving teen slamming a bedroom door; a father accusing the kid of disrespect. There's no attempt at resolution, just the counterargument, 'Live your own life and leave me alone.'

'My Life' could be considered a close cousin to 'You Don't Own Me' by Lesley Gore, 'It's My Life' by The Animals and 'I'm Eighteen' by Alice Cooper – collective clarion calls that inspire youth to break free from controlling authority figures.

'Zanzibar' (Billy Joel)

No, it's not the tropical island that Joel gets antsy about here, despite the title. Ramone recommended that the narrative take place in an actual sports bar. The themes vary but include nods to American sports figures: baseball champ Pete Rose, heavyweight boxer Muhammad Ali ('Ali, don't you do downtown') and even the New York Yankees. The baseball theme also leads to some double entendre, particularly in the use of older-generation North American seduction slang, as in 'second base.'

Style-wise, some fans and critics have pointed to Steely Dan's Donald Fagen, due to the contrasting minor and major chords and erratic but breathtaking stops and starts.

This rapid-fire tune features a flurry of harmonic changes and Freddie Hubbard's evocative trumpet solos. Later, trumpet-master Carl Fischer would enliven key live performances. DeVitto tastefully paints with brushes near the end as an extra perk.

The landscape starts slowly but picks up momentum quickly with Stegmeyer's unyielding bass line and a host of inviting Latin persuasions. Mainieri's marimba adds one more touch of class.

'Zanzibar' reached the younger generation in early-2021, when the jazz tune went viral on TikTok. According to Frank Lovece on newsday.com on 31 January 2021: 'On his Instagram Stories account over the weekend, Billy Joel gladdened many TikTok users by reposting several of their videos in which they perform in dance inspired by his 1978 song 'Zanzibar.'

@maxmith ignited the dance craze challenge after filming the original version in her kitchen. The simple choreography included miming the driving of a vehicle and playing air guitar along to the related 'Zanzibar' excerpt: 'She's waiting out in Shantytown/She's gonna pull the curtains down for me, for me/I've got the old man's car/I've got a jazz guitar...'

Remarkably, the hashtag #zanzibar has over 122.2 million views according to *intheknow.com*, and the video has received 264,000 views. But even though this social media phenomenon drew countless youthful music lovers to the Billy Joel camp, some felt that matching the excerpt up with a silly dance put Joel's work in a demeaning light.

'Zanzibar' brought into focus boxer Muhammad Ali. In *Ali, A Life* by Jonathan Eig, the author discussed the late champion's tendency to shift focus away from his career when trying to accommodate the public. Eig used Joel's lyrics to support his findings: 'Even the singer and songwriter Billy Joel expressed concern that the distractions in Ali's life were hurting his performance in the boxing ring, opening the song 'Zanzibar' with the warning for Ali not to go downtown lest he give away 'another round for free.''

Perhaps 'Zanzibar' would've become a classic without the added exposure. After all, by the ultimate take, 'Zanzibar' contained multiple elements that led to its star quality: distinctive brass, an insidious tempo and curious lyrics and confident vocals. Similar to much of Joel's studio output, the song required brainstorming. In an interview with the author in 2021, DeVitto said:

Billy brought it in and we just did a demo. As a matter of fact, and Billy does the verse about, 'Ali, don't you go downtown,' and then the second part comes and I kind of bluffed the part, and Billy's lyric is 'da da da...you screwed up but then again, so did I!' Then, on the guitar part, 'I got a jazz guitar,' was not there yet. When Billy came to the studio the next day – because he'd always play the songs first to see if they could fly with the band – things went really well, so he went home and finished the lyric. The next day, when he came to record 'Zanzibar,' he had the part 'I got a jazz guitar.' I said, instead of doing just a normal solo over the chords, why don't we do it like we're in a jazz club, you know? So, that was a lot of fun, but it was a challenge. We're not really jazz players. We put the full-length version on the box set version that came out later on *52nd Street*, and at the end, we kind of fall apart, because that was all the jazz we could possibly play.

Producer Phil Ramone enjoyed the colloquialisms – especially the line, 'Ali, don't you go downtown': a phrase drawn from boxing jargon that alludes to deliberately losing a fight; something 'a street kid with intellect' might weave into everyday speech.

'Stiletto' (Billy Joel)
Although the band drew inspiration from the British group Traffic, finger snaps codify the 1950s American beatnik era. Joel lightly comps during the intro, alongside the lounge-style sax, but then switches to a bluesy call-and-response, starring his own vocal. 'She cuts you hard, she cuts you deep,' Joel sings and later shrugs, 'You don't really mind the pain.' This is an exciting mix of raw vocals amid energizing keyboard runs and DeVitto's synergy; even the fade's got juju.

'She's so good with her stiletto/You don't even see the blade,' Joel exclaims, yet there's no mention of an exit plan. Instead, the strings and organ cut in and out, and Joel chisels in some barrelhouse chops right before that linear sax solo.

Rumor has it Joel wrote the song about the challenges he faced during his marriage to Weber, who doubled as his manager; their union ended in 1982. Afterwards, Joel hired her brother Frank Weber, and a more harrowing story unfolded.

'Rosalinda's Eyes' (Billy Joel)
The guitar and vibraphone parts form an immutable symbiosis, but overall, 'Rosalinda's Eyes' is a percussionist's dream. Mike Mainieri's marimba sits in the driver's seat, while acoustic guitar and joyful flute vie for attention in the sidecar. With this homage to traditional Afro-Cuban standards, the band was not remiss – listen for gemstones: shaker, cowbell, maraca and snare.

The acutely balanced Latin feel comes across in a simpatico manner, an instant success when played at the Karl Marx Theater in Havana, Cuba, in 1978. The swanky percussive ideas formed a prototype 'as an American version of a Cuban beat,' as described in DeVitto's astute memoir.

'Half A Mile Away' (Billy Joel)
Joel's voice remains low but is lifted up by the strings. In a notable and forward-thinking move, Dave Grusin outdid himself by constructing a vibrant horn arrangement.

Lyrically, this is a buddy song. 'Little Geo is a friend of mine,' goes the breezy setup. Two pals sit on the curb, hiding alcohol from beat cops, dreaming about being anywhere else. It's not clear whether the subjects are newcomers who yearn for the comfort of their native country or locals who've never left the city but long for an adventure. But in the third verse, we hear, 'Angelina save a place for me' and 'I try to keep the family satisfied.' Here, we take a wild guess that the narrator has a family back home that he's struggling to provide for; his financial intentions are good and clear, yet judging by his current circumstances – where he's aimlessly drinking – we don't know if he'll achieve his goals.

Musically, Dave Grusin's stealthy horn arrangement matches DeVitto's dynamic drumming beat-for-beat. In the meantime, Joel pulls out the expected soulful stops.

'Until The Night' (Billy Joel)
B/w 'Root Beer Rag' and released as a single in the UK, March 1979. Peak: UK Singles Chart: 50

A singular bass note on the piano sets the barometer. Joel's baritone and harmonies, star. There's a sad richness in the lyric: 'So many broken hearts/So many lonely faces.' At 6:35, this is a lengthy song, which is a positive attribute because the listener has time to embrace the romantic tenor.

Joel's vocal quality changes distinctively on the second part and as the dynamic intensifies. Strings and sax meld wistfully before the final chorus convenes. Rhythm guitarist Javors doubles as a vocalist and produces superb harmonies. Lead guitarist Brown pays strict attention to the dynamic parameters. The ballad is finely structured, with a clear buildup and breakdown.

Joel channeled The Righteous Brothers when he wrote the intense lyrics. That 1960s/1970s act was synonymous with the genre descriptor 'blue-eyed soul.' Joel must have had a field day imitating the low tones of original member and baritone Bill Medley.

'52nd Street' (Billy Joel)
Although the title song is incredibly short, it does the vital job of recapitulating the album experience. I think that's the Broadway part of Joel's songwriter brain kicking in. Plus, as the core players collaborate, we get to celebrate their singular talent.

Glass Houses (1980)

Personnel:
Billy Joel: acoustic piano, synthesizer, harmonica, electric piano, accordion, vocals
Richie Cannata: organ, saxophone, flute
David Brown: acoustic and electric guitars (lead)
Russell Javors: acoustic and electric guitars (rhythm)
Doug Stegmeyer: bass
Liberty DeVitto: drums
Jim Boyer: engineer
Bradshaw Leigh: assistant engineer
Ted Jensen: mastering at Sterling Sound (New York, NY)
Brian Ruggles: technician
Steve Cohen: lighting
Jim Houghton: photography
Michele Slagter: production assistant
Jeff Schock: product management
Recorded: 1979, A&R Recording, New York City
Producer: Phil Ramone
Label: Family Productions/Columbia
Release date: 12 March 1980
Chart positions: UK: Albums (OCC): 9, US: *Billboard* 200: 1, Canadian Albums (RPM): 1, Australian Albums (Kent Music Report): 2
Running time: 35:06

Joel purportedly had fun in the studio, despite a Sisyphean songwriting experience. Ultimately though, he and his team's solid decision-making resulted in successful final cuts. It had been a landmark year for riveting radio hits, so competition was keen. The *Billboard* Hot 100 for 8 March 1980 verified that tunes by Queen, Andy Gibb and Donna Summer dominated the charts.

This seventh studio album received a ranking of 4 on *Billboard*'s 1980 year-end chart, and won the Pop/Rock Favorite Album Award. Moreover, Joel received a Grammy for Best Male Rock Vocal Performance the following year, which perhaps softened the blow when the album was nominated for Album of the Year but lost out to the lesser-known Christopher Cross and his self-titled album. Joel was up against a trio of tough contenders: Frank Sinatra's *Trilogy*, Barbra Streisand's *Guilty* and Pink Floyd's *The Wall*.

Stephen Thomas Erlewine at AllMusic.com proclaimed, 'It may not be punk – then again, it may be his concept of punk – but *Glass Houses* is the closest Joel ever got to a pure rock album.' Erlewine also praised the album's 'bold, direct melodies and clean arrangements.'

Blender.com added: 'Plenty of panicked mainstream rock stars were trying to go new wave at the time. Thanks to his brattiness and gift for stylistic wanderings, Joel was able to pull it off better than just about anyone; the snarl of the motorcycle-riding 'You May Be Right' and Cars-imitating 'It's Still Rock And Roll To Me', came naturally to him.'

But on 1 May 1980, Paul Nelson of *Rolling Stone* slammed the celebrators by insisting that Joel 'always comes off like a particularly obnoxious frat boy who hoisted a few too many while trying to put the make on an airline stewardess. His profundity is single-bars deep.' Ouch. However, with the majority of sceptics sated, Joel had reason to crow. In this love-fest of blazing guitars and counterculture riffs (and his third Ramone collaboration), the team fed off each other's seemingly endless energies.

The sonics were enriched by Brown's truculent lead guitar work, Cannata's seamless sax solos, Javors no-holds-barred strumming, and bassist Stegmeyer and drummer DeVitto's scaffolding.

Between January and July 1980, the album was aggressively promoted, with the release of singles, 'All For Leyna,' 'You May Be Right,' 'It's Still Rock And Roll To Me,' 'Don't Ask Me Why' and 'Sometimes A Fantasy.'

Album Art

When an album begins with the sound of shattering glass, it makes sense to echo that aggression visually, and that's exactly what you see. Joel stands, poised to throw a rock through the second-storey window of his very own glass house in Cove Neck. And on specific covers, Joel gazes back through a hole in the cracked glass. Repeat photographer Jim Houghton created equal amounts of angst and mystery in this high-stakes, eye-catching image.

'You May Be Right' (Billy Joel)

B/w 'Close to the Borderline' and released as a single in March 1980. Peak: U.S. *Billboard* Hot 100: 7, Canadian Singles Chart: 6

'It took nearly 30 sheets of glass, and the best-sounding take came on the last piece, with one crack of the hammer,' Phil Ramone recollected in his memoir, about creating the breaking glass effect that introduced this track.

In an interview with classicrockrevisited.com, Liberty DeVitto recalled a Columbia executive's response to hearing the opening track: 'You guys have a better Rolling Stones song on your album than they do on their album.' Indeed, the song derives much of its zeitgeist from Brown's sizzling riff: the kind Keith Richards might well have concocted in the midst of a deep slumber.

The six-bar intro begins with the bold tonic note, which repeats and serves as a drone throughout. Joel's voice starts out and stays husky. The story paints a lot of scenery within the first few lines: The subject crashes the party one night, and apologizes the next. Right away, we know this guy's fairly unhinged.

Another clue? He waltzes through 'Bedford Stuy alone.' Bedford-Stuyvesant is a gentrified neighborhood now, but in the 1980s, it was considered sketchy. Joel describes this clueless behavior as 'crazy.'

Although non-New Yorkers wouldn't necessarily catch the hint, other references remind us that the subject is a guy who lives on the edge. True to form, Joel's vocals ride out on a rebellious stallion.

So, the tone and urban narrative is perfect for this raucous rock 'n' roll anthem. Against David Brown's tense, nerve-shattering riffs, Joel has room to vocally maneuver. The tempo stays pretty much the same throughout, and there are relatively few punchy chord changes, as opposed to much of Joel's other material. The melody dips down at the end of the measure, for the most part, giving Joel multiple opportunities to vent using his mellow lower register.

'Sometimes A Fantasy' (Billy Joel)

B/w 'All for Leyna' and released as the final single in 1980, Peak: US *Billboard* Hot 100: 36, Canadian Singles Chart: 21
The story centers around a man who calls his wife long-distance and tries to talk her into having phone sex. We don't get a sense of the wife's reaction from the lyric (You'll get a better sense from the video), but he's basically telling her that he's lonely and that the act is harmless; a 'fantasy.'

This is a rapidly-moving song that starts with related effects. The single cover shows Joel dialing the number. In the video, he presses down the keys on an old-school touch-tone phone. When he sings the chorus, he gets backed up with 'woah oh oh oh's.'

There's a short synth solo, but the scratchy electric guitar and DeVitto's aggressive drumming form an incombustible bond. After the extended synth solo, Joel grabs back the spotlight. His evanescent vocals recall Buddy Holly's, sans the Lubbock native's wholesome demeanor.

'Don't Ask Me Why' (Billy Joel)

B/w 'C'etait Toi (You Were the One)' and released as a single 24 July 1980, Peak: US *Billboard* Adult Contemporary: 1, Canada RPM Adult Contemporary: 1
This hybrid was released as a single in July 1980. Joel kicks out a four-bar, rhythmic, bluesy piano riff. The Latin-tinged solo later makes a deep imprint, especially when that section ends with a shrill glissando. The ensemble establishes a powerful sound with a 12-string guitar, along with brash bass and percussion. No less than 15 pianos were used as overdubs.

Joel's voice is moderately soft and buttery smooth and, at certain moments, can be easily mistaken for Paul McCartney's upper range.

The story is about a woman who apparently forgot where she came from. The French-language reference leads us to believe she moved to France, without a forwarding address. The narrator is either miffed or surprised, but either way, he's washed his hands of the situation, hence the title.

DeVitto said in his memoir: 'I only played with one stick, which was in my left hand playing the floor tom, while I held two maracas in my right hand.'

If that's not enough, add to that image, Richie Cannata on claves and Billy Joel on castanets. But there's more – according to A&R engineer Larry Franke,

Joel used the heels of the receptionist's shoes to 'tap out a flamenco style rhythm.' This song is, certifiably, one live wire.

'It's Still Rock And Roll To Me' (Billy Joel)

B/w 'Through the Long Night' and released as a single 12 May 1980, Peak: U.S. *Billboard* Hot 100: 1, Canadian Singles Chart: 1

The band pulls out all pistons. Cannata's sax excursions are emphatic, but Joel also defends his musical turf with gang war gusto. DeVitto levies some Lennon-esque 'Instant Karma' into the mix by quoting a famed Alan White (of Lennon and Yes) fill when one would least expect it.

'What's the matter with the clothes I'm wearing?' Joel sneers. Of course, it's a rhetorical question; he's just seeking intergenerational respect. His rant is about how the founders of genres like punk and new wave simply borrowed or pilfered from the past but were not the groundbreakers they claimed to be: 'Everybody's talkin' 'bout the new sound, funny, but it's…' This is the quintessential baby-boomer banshee cry. Joel directs a verbal torpedo to critics, when he accuses no one in particular of writing articles that are 'aimed at your favorite teen.'

Fans are still sorting whether 'pink sidewinders' are sneakers, suspenders or casual socks;DeVitto suggested that they are shoes. *The Dictionary of American Slang and Colloquial Expressions* by R.A. Spears (National Textbook Co., Chicago, Il., 1975) defines the term as, 'a sneaky and despicable man.'

'All For Leyna' (Billy Joel)

B/w 'Close to the Borderline' and released as a single in January 1980. Peak: UK Singles Chart: 40, Spain (AFYVE): 16

'All For Leyna' – the lead single on *Glass Houses* – focuses on a young man's obsession which develops after a one-night stand. Despite the setup in the first two verses, where we see his downfall – 'I'm failing in school, losing my friends' – the lyrics come off as mildly ironic in the third, where we find Leyna luring this vulnerable man 'to that third rail shock' and then to a beach, where she neglects to warn the pure slug that 'there were rocks under the waves.' The lovesick masochist barely avoids the threatening undertow!

Finally, in the last two lines of the final chorus, we discover that he's not simply torturing himself, he's destroying another potential partner's self-esteem: 'There's nothing in it for you 'cause I'm giving it all to Leyna.'

The terrific rhythm is enlivened with streams of steady synth. Joel's overall presentation simmers with passion. He uses falsetto as a melodic leitmotif. I have to admit, I'm as obsessed with this rapidly-moving story as the feckless subject is with the drama queen.

In his memoir, DeVitto claims, 'The hole after he says, 'Stop,' is an edit. We played through, and when we came in to hear the mix, there was an edit: stop. It was actually difficult to learn the stop when we played the song live, because now we had to stop on that part; it was in an odd spot.'

'I Don't Want to Be Alone' (Billy Joel)

'When this magic night is through/Could it have been just anyone or did it have to be you?' Now, that's the telling line in a nutshell. Did he actually click with this woman, or is she just a place-filler for some lonely guy with a ransacked heart?

At the bridge, Joel sings, 'But don't you know that it's wrong,' and on the chorus, he reveals that she's hurt him before. As the two meet in 'the bar at the Plaza Hotel,' we can take a wild guess that he's rekindling an affair with an old flame. He's no longer looking for anything permanent: just a fling. Yet despite his bravado, he's as afraid of getting hurt as the next guy.

'Sleeping With The Television On' (Billy Joel)

After warming up with the American national anthem, the band kicks into high gear. There are a lot of warm harmonies and acid guitar, prior to the warning: 'Tomorrow morning, you'll wake up with the white noise.' The juxtaposition of lead vocal and backing harmonies is magical. The brief organ solo is classic 1960s, harkening back to the schizoid anthem '96 Tears' by Michigan's preeminent Mexican-American band Question Mark and the Mysterians.

'Nobody's found a way behind your defenses,' the lover gripes to the protagonist. It seems like her expectations will never be met. Her attitude is, 'Don't waste my time,' yet her twinkling eyes say, 'Talk to me.' Ultimately, he's urging her to wake up and take a chance, or she'll be forever haunted by a snowy screen emitting white noise: a cultural death knell.

'C'etait Toi (You Were the One)' (Billy Joel)

Joel put himself in the line of fire by reciting a French lyric. He received a lot of flak from some in the French-speaking community, but despite his perceived second-language limitations, this ballad adds an air of calm and tenderness to an otherwise fast-paced album. I'm left wondering why Paul McCartney didn't get sabotaged when he murmured sweet nothings in French on 'Michelle.'

DeVitto fills up vocal holes with respectable restraint, and the accordion riffs add a sense of romantic realism. As for the use of French? How did it go over? DeVitto recalled: 'The French in France hated it because when a translator was brought into the studio for Billy, he was French-Canadian, so it was a different dialect. It's a shame because I love that song.'

'Close To The Borderline' (Billy Joel)

DeVitto's on the money from the first beat. Joel's voice slides in and out, up and everywhere. He even emits a trill into the blistering mix. 'I didn't think I needed anything,' he proclaims in the brief bridge, but he's bluffing; he's losing it, and fast. This guitar-driven tune is comprised of simple triads. Brown's guitar solo is thrilling but frustratingly short.

'Blackout, heatwave, .44 caliber homicide'. Joel's choppy street phrases which foreshadow the rant-fueled 'We Didn't Start The Fire,' build and build until he unearths the main character's molten core: 'I'd start a revolution but I don't have time.'

Joel's got a Lou Reed thing going on; his voice is loose, completely devoid of tension. He does a stylized call-and-response with himself, a sonic selfie. Best of all, the band created a cool garage-band groove, with DeVitto upping the ante with feisty fills. Brown inserts some loopy David Bowie 'Fame' referencing at the exit ramp.

'Through The Long Night' (Billy Joel)

Here, Joel's upper register and stylistic approach, mirror Paul McCartney's romantic 'Junk' from *McCartney* (1970). 'Warm tears, bad dreams, soft, trembling shoulders,' are vivid indicators of a roller-coaster love affair. This song has a gorgeous flow. 'What has it cost you?/I could have lost you,' Joel adds in the bridge. Now, we know even more about why this relationship has to work, and the lengths this sensitive person will go to, to make this love endure.

The harmonies are bittersweet but quickly moving. Although frustratingly short at 2:43, 'Through The Long Night' is a sincere and expressive ballad.

The Nylon Curtain (1982)

Personnel:

Billy Joel: vocals, acoustic and electric pianos, synthesizer, Hammond organ, melodica, Prophet-5 synthesizer, Synclavier II (3)

David Brown: electric and acoustic guitars (lead)

Russell Javors: electric and acoustic guitars (rhythm)

Doug Stegmeyer: bass

Liberty DeVitto: drums, percussion

Additional musicians:

Bill Zampino: field snare (4)

Rob Mounsey: synthesizer

Dominic Cortese: accordion (9)

Eddie Daniels: saxophone and clarinet (9)

Charles McCracken: cello (9)

Dave Grusin: string and horn arrangements

David Nadien: concertmaster (1, 3-7, 9)

String Fever: strings (2, 8)

Phil Ramone: producer

Laura Loncteaux: assistant producer

Jim Boyer: engineer, remix

Bradshaw Leigh: associate engineer

Michael Christopher, Larry Franke, Andy Hoffman: assistant engineers

Ted Jensen at Sterling Sound, NYC: mastering engineer

Kenneth Topolsky: production manager

Paula Scher: artwork

John Berg: inner sleeve design

Chris Austopchuk: front cover design

Benno Friedman: back cover photo

Record Label: Family Productions/Columbia

Recorded: A&R Recording, Inc. and Media Sound Studios, New York City, Winter 1981-Spring 1982.

Producer: Phil Ramone

Release date: 23 September 1982

Chart positions: UK: Albums (OCC): 27, U.S: *Billboard* 200: 7, Netherlands: Albums (MegaCharts): 1, Japan: Albums (Oricon): 2

Running Time: 41:57

According to Ramone's memoir, he furnished Joel with a 'control box with Echoplexes, MXR phasers and flangers', and labeled the buttons, 'Elvis,' 'Doo Wop' and 'R&B.' Finally, the savvy producer 'put it on the piano so he could switch the effects around until he hit on one he liked.' We should all have such diligent minders!

Ramone was clearly aware of Joel's vibrant vocal capacity and that as a concert singer, he conveyed maximum emotion. Yet he sensed early on that

Joel was self-conscious about his recorded vocals. As such, the team struck a balance, using modern technology as a guidepost.

So, one might say Ramone went to extremes on *The Nylon Curtain* to incorporate specific effects. In fact, because Ramone intentionally set out to create a unique vocal quality in every track, when you survey the material, you'll likely recognize the impact of those effects. Ramone, the consummate engineer – who once upon a time had been entrusted to record John F. Kennedy's speeches – brought that same level of consideration and commitment to the studio. The musicians were in expert hands. In addition, he handpicked stellar guests – saxophone and clarinet player Eddie Daniels; cellist Charles McCracken, and arranger Dave Grusin – and forged uncharted territory by exploring the brave new world of electronica and digital technology, with newcomer Rob Mounsey hired to play synthesizer. Attention to detail paid off; another Grammy nomination got under way.

The Nylon Curtain was an album on which Joel revealed a new side to his persona. This sharp, sociopolitical edge had been less evident in prior works, or perhaps this was his time to simply air his views without apology. To that end, there's a lyrical depth and beauty in *The Nylon Curtain* that touched fans worldwide and at times even stirred controversy. By taking on tough subjects such as war, industrial and commercial changes within established communities, and disenfranchised workers in a capitalistic society, Joel had become an activist of sorts. He then had to contend with the residual flak. He'd been under fire, of course, for creating controversy with 'Only The Good Die Young,' but that reckoning had been unexpected; Joel's intentions had been misunderstood. But these themes came about deliberately.

From behind the glass, germinal ideas came to fruition. Due to Ramone's technical advice, the newly-formed arrangements could more than hold a candle to industry gold standards like The Beach Boys' *Pet Sounds* or The Beatles' *Sgt. Pepper's...* or *The White Album*.

The band was wholly committed to the album's bold ideologies. DeVitto for instance, was moved to tears by 'Goodnight Saigon,' which was fully evident in his playing, but the entire band stood by the sentiments.

Classicrockreview.com noted: 'After much commercial success with his previous albums, Billy Joel really branched out to new musical territory on his eighth studio album *The Nylon Curtain*.'

On 14 October 1982, Stephen Holden of *Rolling Stone* observed, 'While 'Goodnight Saigon' is *The Nylon Curtain*'s stunner, there are other songs in which Joel's blue-collar smarts, Broadway theatricality and rock attitude, blend perfectly.'

Album Art

A row of identical small black houses stands against an orange glow, over which Billy Joel's name is boldly printed in a pedestrian font. The light-blue stacked words of the title take up the lower half and are set against a black background.

The stark visual is ambiguous. Does it represent the homes of Joel's industrial heroes, the suburban sprawl of his youth, or boxy complexes in the former Soviet Union? It's notable too that Joel preferred to use this illustration rather than a casual portrait shot; but then again, the contents revealed that *The Nylon Curtain* contrasted greatly from his previous works.

The title is based on the term 'Iron Curtain,' which came into use as part of Western jargon after British prime minister Winston Churchill used the phrase to describe the closing off of freedoms in Eastern Europe under the Soviet Union.

'Allentown' (Billy Joel)

B/w 'Elvis Presley Blvd.' and released as a single in September 1982, Peak: U.S. Cash Box Top 100: 14, U.S. Adult Contemporary (*Billboard*): 19

Beginning with the shrill blow of a factory whistle, the thump of a clanking pile driver plops the listener into a mind-numbing, utilitarian factory setting. Lyrically, thematically and sonically, Joel paints a fiery portrait of an American tragedy: the 1970s downsizing of Bethlehem, Pennsylvania steel workers.

Joel used the name of the neighboring industrial town Allentown, however, because it had better rhyming capabilities than Bethlehem, where the actual downsizing took place, and he also felt that Bethlehem might stir up religious connotations and create thematic confusion.

The sprightly and beautiful harmonic progression is dotted with colorful suspensions, but it's Joel's rhythmic melismas that truly stand out. Those warm nonstop undulations over constantly shifting major and minor chords are as much of a draw as the electronic effects. At the chorus, while recapitulating the catchy string of chords, Joel's utterances evolve into onomatopoeia: he mimics factory noises. (Live, it's always been fun to watch Joel and band members follow suit.) Brown's brief but explosive electric guitar solo is another standout.

'Allentown' is considered one of Joel's most socially conscious songs, yet reactions from actual factory workers have been mixed. Some appreciated Joel's attention to their plight, while others thought he resorted to stereotypes. Despite the ambiguity, 'Allentown' enjoyed a successful run: the song remained for six weeks on the *Billboard* Hot 100.

Sheila Davis – author of *The Craft of Lyric Writing* – compared Joel's song to Yip Harburg's 'Brother, Can You Spare A Dime?' In 1932, during the grueling American depression, Harburg witnessed former businessmen begging for change in the streets and was genuinely moved: 'Joel, like Harburg, portrayed his miner as strong ('It's hard to keep a good man down') and similarly bewildered: ' ...and still waiting... for the promises our teacher gave if we worked hard,' Davis surmised. In essence, both writers based their content on firsthand accounts of human suffering, and treated their subjects with dignity.

To achieve the tumultuous rhythmic effect on the record, DeVitto found himself 'jumping up and down on hard shell instrument cases.' But DeVitto didn't equate the exhausting workout with any negative thoughts. He insists that 'Allentown' remains one of his favorites.

Bethlehem Steel contributed greatly to the World War II effort by providing material for airplanes, warships and naval fleets. Postwar, the company supplied steel frames for U.S. bridges and New York skyscrapers. Hence Joel's narrative: 'Well our fathers fought the Second World War/Spent their weekends on the Jersey Shore.' At that juncture, the company was doing well and the workers had reason to feel secure. But then, all bets were off. The song is sung from the perspective of the sons. Due to an influx of foreign steel, aluminum and pressed concrete, factory futures could no longer be guaranteed for these workers. Joel's lyric sums up the challenging transition: 'But the restlessness was handed down/And it's getting very hard to stay.'

Through 'Allentown,' Joel underscores the painful effects of an economic downturn that families could neither predict nor prepare for. Website comments verify that while 'Allentown' was written about American cities, the song has had universal appeal.

'Laura' (Billy Joel)
The subject is a needy woman, which Joel later revealed was his mother. With that in mind, it's an uncomfortable listen, but aside from that, Joel makes delightful use of alliteration. His voice and piano were intentionally muted – a decision that Joel and Ramone mutually made – and may have been inspired by Martin's forward-thinking Beatles sessions. Brown's electric guitar solo, more than makes the grade and recalls guitarist George Harrison's buoyancy.

In *Billy Joel: The Definitive Biography*, 2014, author F. Schruers noted how John Lennon's Phil Spector produced 'Mother' served as Joel's thematic inspiration. Of course, Lennon's Primal Scream therapy helped him release his demons with throaty, anguished shouts, which, while Joel didn't approximate, he substituted with his own brand of boiled-over rage.

'Laura' garnered many Beatles-related comments. Mark Bego compared the track to Lennon's dreamy 'Dear Prudence' and McCartney's clanky 'Maxwell's Silver Hammer.' The swooning harmonies certainly ring true, here.

On the chorus, Joel churns: 'Living alone isn't all that it's cracked up to be.' He seeks our validation: 'I'm on her side.' Throughout, he shifts from third to first person which keeps us engaged. As the story continues, he loses his sense of empathy. 'I'm her machine,' he complains; he's rapidly reaching his breaking point.

The dramatic strings definitely bring to mind the rich imagination of George Martin, especially during the Beatles' *White Album* days. Ken Bielen's remark in *The Words and Music of Billy Joel*, 2011, that DeVitto's drums mimic Starr, apply, too. And similarly to many Beatles' songs, there's that ironic matchmaking of a shiny melody with a troubling topic–Maxwell was, in fact, a killer!

At the outro, Joel wearily asks: 'How do you hang up on someone who needs you that bad?' 'Laura' is a moving example of a strained, symbiotic relationship.

Although it never became an arena staple, it's an essential piece of this emotional album and a clear window into Joel's past.

Pressure' (Billy Joel)

B/w 'Laura' and released as a single in September 1982, Peak: U.S. *Billboard* Top Rock Tracks: 8, U.S. *Billboard* Hot 100, Canadian Singles Chart: 9
In DeVitto's memoir, the main piano riff of 'Pressure' was referred to as a 'Cossack dance.' The killer riff that Joel performs on a synth, really does capture the essence of an explosive Eastern-European folk dance. Needless to say, 'Pressure' was the album's smash hit. DeVitto remembers well how that reference came to fruition:

> Billy was driving. I was in the car. Doug Stegmeyer was in the car and Russell. We were driving into the city, and he put on the demo tape that he had made at home. He was the one who would go, 'Da da da duh' and yell 'Hey,' so he was the one who was giving the song the Cossack reference.

As was typical with Joel's work, the music preceded the lyrics, but the actual theme took a hot minute to percolate. In fact, when Joel confided to his secretary that he was struggling to find an original theme to complete the studio album, she simply noted Joel's stressed-out demeanor, and advised him to write about his own dark state of mind.

The verses are built around a major chord progression, with acute, unrelenting accents, but the pre-chorus contrasts with a minor tonality. Joel's voice often approximates the late David Bowie's own jittery vocal instrument. However, Bowie and Queen's 1981 recording 'Under Pressure' bears little likeness harmonically or melodically, and is similar only in title.

Joel's right hand keeps up a staccato feel, which contrasts with the steadfast octaves in the left. The dynamics shift dramatically in the bridge: anger subsides, phrasing is subtler, and Joel lets a little steam out of the bag. Brown's electric guitar work fills in any vacancies that Joel hasn't already compounded with block chords etc.

The overall production is stellar – Joel's double-tracked anger, advances from verse to verse, not only because of the layered effect but because the lower end of his range is so clear and compelling. At certain cadence points, he emotes with the force of a fire-breathing dragon.

The balalaikas give the arrangement a distinctive shimmer too. Phil Ramone acknowledged that during the time of the recording, the crew discovered a group of Russians near the studio, carrying these unique instruments. Ramone described the instrument as 'a three-string Russian guitar with a triangular body and elongated neck.' It was all very serendipitous. But balalaikas aside, the violin stabs too, buoy up the pressure.

Joel name-checks 'Peter Pan' – James Matthew Barrie's fictional character who was known for dreading adulthood: a time when one is expected to face and solve conflicts head-on. A particularly pertinent line addresses the lack of 'scars' on the subject's face; another mocking of the subject, who is too childlike and frail to withstand pressure. A further reference is to *Sesame Street:* a once-popular American TV show directed towards children that started in 1969. It appears that Joel is juxtaposing the psyche of a still-developing child and a self-actualized adult, by inserting this cultural reference.

I asked DeVitto about his choices as a drummer. The piano part was already so rhythmic. How did he perceive his role as a drummer? 'That's what I'm saying – there's so much movement in the piano. The safest thing to do is a straight boom boom boom bah.'

'Goodnight Saigon' (Billy Joel)
B/w 'A Room of Our Own' and released as a single in 1983, Peak: UK Singles Chart: 29, U.S. *Billboard* Hot 100: 56
In *Rock of Ages, The History of Rock and Roll*, the authors pointed out that early-1980s rock musicians 'were coming up with vivid tough-minded work about the debacle of Vietnam and its aftermath.' As such, they listed The Charlie Daniels Band's 'Still In Saigon,' The Dead Kennedys' 'Holiday In Cambodia,' Stevie Wonder's 'Front Line' and Joel's own sincere effort.

Joel – who didn't go to Vietnam but whose dear friends did – wanted to honor the soldiers who returned and those who didn't, in this searing study of a group of young marines during wartime. For realism, the crew used sound effects of a chopper at the beginning and repeated the sound at the end. Percussionist and childhood friend Bill Zampino pounded out a somber rhythm on a field snare.

At 7:04 in length, Joel and the band had enough latitude to create a vast emotional canvas. Similar to what the songwriter had done with earlier material, he fleshed out specific characters by addressing them by first names and attaching meaningful chunks of information.

The slow-moving melody is stunning. Joel's voice carries out the emotion from the time the soldiers meet on Parris Island in South Carolina to the dire moment in which they commit to the possibility that they will 'all go down together.' That rousing chorus underscores the strong attachments the men create with one another.

According to an interview Joel did with onefinalserenade.com, he was inspired by the structure and arrangement of The Beatles' 'A Day In The Life' from *Sgt. Pepper's Lonely Hearts Club Band*. That song also contained war references such as 'Four thousand holes in Blackburn, Lancashire,' and bewildering sound effects. Perhaps John Lennon's world-weary vocal on the beginning verses was also an inspiration. The instrumentation on the verses was spare, mostly upheld by acoustic guitar, 'But the choruses are grander and lusher like a large symphony is playing,' Joel observed.

In a 1982 interview with DJ Sciaky, Joel was asked why he waited so long to write a song about the Vietnam vets. Joel explained: 'The actual writing began during the recording of *52nd Street*. I didn't think people were ready. I didn't think I was ready either.' Yet he knew it was going to 'be a war song.' He continues: 'And lately, things have opened up, and we're able to look at it in a different way. There's been a *Newsweek* (article), and a dearth of novels have come out.'

As a voracious reader, Joel had read fictional accounts of war, and felt he could be put to task. Yet, he had been criticized by certain critics for not taking political sides. Here is how Joel responded: 'I didn't want to write an anti-war song or pro-war song. I just wanted to write it from a soldier's point of view.'

But Joel did something unique with his subject's point of view. Author Sheila Davis illustrates how the songwriter effectively used 'a shifting viewpoint' – from first-person-plural to third-person – to further draw the listener into the soldier's harrowing world. Davis notes: 'A ghost crew member of a downed helicopter seems to be thinking aloud – almost as if he were addressing the American conscience – as he recalls the camaraderie of a crew that promised they would all go down together.' The term 'downed helicopter' implies the crew members did not survive, or were shot down, survived and were facing the jungle and the enemy together. I'm not sure what Joel's intention was, but Davis has an interesting perspective. She also emphasizes his strong craftsmanship by singling out the line 'Remember Charlie?' as if the subject was suddenly talking to his buddies. This shifted perspective works, she says, 'because it came at the top of a verse, not somewhere in the middle.' I'll explore more about that phrase and its military meaning in a moment.

Musically, there are a number of palpable effects designed to transport the listener to the war zone, starting with an airbrush of wind chimes, an orchestra of crickets, and finally, the aforementioned rattle of the oncoming chopper. Joel's lyrics go dark and deep. He wastes no time unpacking his emotions. Within the first few phrases, we're hooked. Like a beat reporter, Joel fills the listener's head with headlining information, and ironically, even though he tips us off about the sad result, the music and writing is so solid that we don't mind the spoiler alert, 'We met as soulmates on Parris Island/We left as inmates from an asylum.'

The U.S. Marines first meet up in Parris Island, South Carolina, at the Recruit Depot. Their futures hang in the balance, but their morale is mostly high. On the lines 'We were sharp/As sharp as knives,' Joel's voice is cast with an eerie reverb effect. Soon the story incorporates cultural references, such as *Playboy*, the Hugh Hefner-produced magazine – 'soft soap' and 'Bob Hope': an American comedian who was known for entertaining troops during wartime. Soldiers stayed sane by listening to The Doors and smoking hash; these references were based on statistics and stories by vets. Further down the line is the first of two military radio references: 'Remember Charlie,' followed by 'Remember Baker.' The moniker 'Charlie' harkens back to the American Military's use of the NATO phonetic alphabet which was commonly used in radio communication. Thus the Viet Cong were designated 'Victor Charlie' and shortened to 'Charlie.' As far as the next line, 'They counted the rotors and waited for us to arrive' – according to U.S. Army personnel: The number of blades a helicopter uses affects the sound they make. By counting the rotors, they would know if they were facing Army, Marines or ARVN. The 'they' may imply a specific or faceless enemy. Regardless, the tension is made clear.

Joel told American radio personality Howard Stern, that although he didn't serve in Vietnam, he was encouraged to write the song by a group of close friends who were Vietnam vets: 'I wanted to do that for my friends who did go to 'Nam. Whether you agreed with the war or not, they took it on the chin. They came back here and they got screwed. When you're getting shot at, you don't think about ideology.'

Joel also reiterated to journalist Bryant Gumbel his experience of socializing with veteran buddies as they drank beer and bared their souls: 'They asked me to write a song about it. I listened to these guys in tears.'

'Goodnight Saigon' has a unique history in that the song led to an emotional partnership between Joel and many veteran groups. As such, an excited group of Vietnam veterans 'came on stage to sing. It was the Kennedy Center, there wasn't a dry eye, and everyone applauded,' wrote Lois O'Connor and Mike McMahon of the VVMF (Vietnam Veterans Memorial Fund), about an event that took place at Nationals Park on 26 July. O'Connor also explained: 'Our current generation of service members and veterans, feel the gratitude and warmth of a grateful nation. However, this wasn't the case for our Vietnam veterans.'

The planning for the event began when Joel's camp reached out to the organization, looking for about 14 veterans to participate in singing the chorus together onstage. After the performance: 'Billy's band members dropped their instruments and hugged and thanked each and every one of them. Ultimately, the veterans on the stage were stunned. Tears filled everyone's eyes.'

Other artists followed up with cover versions. Folk singer Joan Baez – who took an anti-war stance against the Vietnam War in the 1960s – interpreted the words in her chilling soprano. Country singer Garth Brooks also championed the ballad. Joel eventually ended up writing another war-related song – 'Christmas In Fallujah' – but chose not to perform it due to his age, so Long Island singer-songwriter Cass Dillon did the honors. DeVitto was deeply affected by the song's influence:

Veterans feel it's right on. It really touched a lot of people. When we first recorded the song and we played it back for people in the studio before the record came out, people would cry because we're at that age where we all knew somebody who went to Vietnam or went to Vietnam and didn't come back. It's funny because when Billy did that musical *Movin' Out* with Twyla Tharp, he asked if I wanted to see the show. I said no, because I know those songs and how they were written and I don't need to see somebody dancing to 'Goodnight Saigon.' It's a very sensitive song. It's the one song where we're really serious when we play it onstage. Even when The Lords of 52nd Street (one of DeVitto's current bands) do that song, it's very serious. It was originally written leaning towards a World War II thing because we were demoing it during the *52nd Street* sessions, and it didn't make an album until *Nylon Curtain.*

DeVitto is cognizant that his role in the song was essential: 'I'm the powerhouse. I'm driving the reaction for the people, accenting phrases like 'it was dark,' really orchestrating it. The buzz roll came after the line 'And we all go down together.' That was played by our friend Billy Zampino.'

Ramone strategically used 'an echo chamber with a noise gate' to make Joel's voice sound 'breathless, frightened and agitated.'

'She's Right On Time' (Billy Joel)
Joel was inspired by the keyboard and vocal performance of Steve Winwood: a member of Blind Faith and Traffic, before forming a solo career. The acoustic guitar accompaniment is unapologetically gentle.

'I've had to wait forever,' Joel sings at the first verse, and later: 'She never missed a cue or lost a beat.' This well-constructed song is both sunny and melancholic. On one hand, the singer can't wait for his loved one to re-enter his life; on the other, he's aware that he's taken her for granted one-too-many times, and that their fragile relationship is slipping away.

The setting is Christmas, and the subject is busy setting up the tree, so there's already a built-in feeling of anticipation. The charming harpsichord interlude ushers in Joel's emotional pleas, revealing more clearly his vulnerability, whereas earlier, he couched his insecurities or rattled off his partner's virtues as a kind of distraction.

The video is worth checking out. It's a slapstick interpretation of the singer preparing for his lover's arrival around the holidays and destroying his home in the process. Joel has often downplayed his acting abilities, but I think he shows great comic talent here. He ranked it his second favorite video after 'Scenes From An Italian Restaurant.'

'A Room Of Our Own' (Billy Joel)
This upbeat, bass-friendly song is hard-hitting, with early Beatles-style rhythm guitar, Stegmeyer's brassy inserts and Joel's bluesy lyrics. The lovers are at odds: 'You've got diamonds and I've got spades' and 'You've got yoga, honey/ I've got beer.' This underrated tune features rough, stuttering vocals. It's 'She's a Woman' meets Joe Cocker's sandpaper version of 'The Letter.' Although Joel superbly filled out the spaces with his self-assured vocals, his lively instrumental interlude left me wanting more.

'Surprises' (Billy Joel)
This tearful ballad is laden with tender strings. Joel's vocals intrigue. When he ends a phrase with falsetto, his vocal – whether intentionally or not – sounds eerily like Lennon's.

After a leisurely entrance on the second verse, DeVitto sustains momentum. 'Surprises' is a sensitive arrangement. But because this album boasts so much pioneering material, 'Surprises' runs the risk of remaining a wallflower.

The B-section features escalating strings and intense harmonic changes. The song also includes an intricate interlude reminiscent of Paul McCartney's piano work on The Beatles' 'Martha My Dear' from the *White Album*.

'Scandinavian Skies' (Billy Joel)

In this well-orchestrated homage to psychedelia, Joel again sounds divinely Lennonesque. 'I guess this is the weirdest one off the new album,' he tells a live audience. The song begins with a flight attendant making an announcement in her native language. The narrative takes place on that flight, hence the title.

From the time Joel sings 'We pulled the shades and closed our eyes' to 'The Stockholm city lights were slowly starting to rise' – all against measured military drumming – the band creates a cinematic marvel. The repeated octave notes on the keys to create a drone effect bring back memories of The Beatles' ethereal 'Tomorrow Never Knows' and the minimalist landscape of 'Dear Prudence.' The Prophet-5 solo is a definitive nod to psychedelia.

Joel wrote this dizzying song about his one-off experience doing hard drugs. When he sings 'They exhausted our supplies,' the statement may be a thinly-disguised observation about the after-effects of a bad experience, as Joel claims he never took that drug again. DeVitto recalls:

> It was one of the most difficult ones, and there was a different way of doing that song. The basic track was myself on drums, Doug Stegmeyer on bass and Billy playing the Hammond organ. It was just us, and that was really a powerful thing because every album that we did, we used to think about how we can duplicate this live. Songs from *Glass Houses* could be played live, no problem, but when we did *Nylon Curtain*, Billy said, 'Don't even think about how you're going to duplicate these songs, just play whatever you feel we need to play on these tunes.' That's why on 'Scandinavian Skies,' on the drum part where it goes 'on the plane,' those drum fills? – I may be copying myself three or four times on that song to get that sound.

'Where's The Orchestra?' (Billy Joel)

In terms of tone and theme, this deep cut recalls, to me, Peggy Lee's bittersweet rendition of 'Is That All There Is?' (Leiber/Stoller) with its veiled skepticism, but Joel has stated in interviews that he had Harry Nilsson in mind.

I also hear Tom Waits' wear-and-tear in the legato phrasing. But yes, Nilsson's elongated phrases and dramatic modulations come to mind as well.

This heart-wrenching closing ballad reminds me of 'Is That All There Is' made famous by Peggy Lee in 1969. In, *Is That All There Is? The Strange Life of Peggy Lee* by James Gavin, the origin of this Lieber and Stoller ballad referenced in the title is clearly explained. It was inspired by Thomas Mann's 1896 short story 'Disillusionment' as well as the songs of Kurt Weill and Bertolt Brecht which both convey feelings of resignation.

'Let's break out the booze and have a ball,' Lee ultimately proclaims. Similarly, Joel throws up his hands in dismay and asks, 'Wasn't this supposed to be a musical?' Both storytellers struggle with disappointment; neither enjoys a satisfying resolution.

Musically, the *Nylon Curtain* finale is spiked by saxophone at significantly dramatic moments. The slick melding of classical orchestral instrumentation and a penetrating saxophone keeps the arrangement contemporary; relying strictly on the former model might've led to cliché.

Randy Newman orchestrated Lee's version of 'Is That All There Is?,' and also played piano in part. Perhaps that's another reason the two songs feel similar: both artists use piano as their primary means of expression and know how to bring out the heart of a song.

What I appreciate most is the unpretentiousness – Joel has written an absorbing story with utterly simple phrases: 'The role the actors played, the point the author made.' Finally, he sings, 'The curtain falls on empty chairs' before repeating the title. There's a constant juxtaposition of glamor and utter despair from beginning to end.

Joel's superb arrangement includes sought-after accordionist Dominic Cortese (known for his session work with Elvis, Spike Jones and Bob Dylan), plus a seamless clarinet part, courtesy of Eddie Daniels, set against a persuasive synthesizer. Cellist Charles McCracken – an avid appreciator of Ludwig van Beethoven, like Joel – adds a subtle and mellow exuberance.

It's clearly written from the standpoint of a star who is evaluating the after-effects of fame. The arrangement is touching, well-produced and meaningful in a predictably melancholy way. It's also an efficient composition that, surprisingly, only lasts 3:17 and yet eludes time because all elements come together in such an organic manner. And with the wit of a Broadway hitmaker, when Joel does bring the song to a close, he includes a slowed-down, heartbreaking ode to 'Allentown': a reference that many fans will definitely note (and that most fans will consider evocative). By quoting another emotional track, he coaxes us into acknowledging his deepest feelings and breaks down the fourth wall between artist and audience.

Perhaps the sadness so inherent in this dark finale had to do with Joel's breakup with his first wife and manager Elizabeth Weber.

An Innocent Man (1983)

Personnel:

Billy Joel: Baldwin SF-10 acoustic piano, Fender Rhodes electric piano, Hammond B3 organ, lead and background vocals

Liberty DeVitto: drums

Doug Stegmeyer: bass

David Brown: lead electric and acoustic guitars

Russell Javors: rhythm electric and acoustic guitars

Mark Rivera: alto saxophone on 'Keeping The Faith,' 'This Night' and 'Christie Lee'; tenor saxophone, percussion, backing vocals.

Ralph MacDonald: percussion on 'Leave A Tender Moment Alone' and 'Careless Talk'

Leon Pendarvis: Hammond B3 organ on 'Easy Money'

Richard Tee: acoustic piano 'Tell Her About It'

Eric Gale: electric guitar on 'Easy Money'

Toots Thielemans: harmonica on 'Leave A Tender Moment Alone'

String Fever: strings

Ronnie Cuber: baritone saxophone on 'Easy Money,' 'Careless Talk,' 'Tell Her About It' and 'Keeping The Faith'

Jon Faddis: trumpet on 'Easy Money'

David Sanborn: alto saxophone on 'Easy Money'

Joe Shepley: trumpet on 'Easy Money,' 'Careless Talk,' 'Tell Her About It' and 'Keeping The Faith'

Michael Brecker: tenor saxophone on 'Careless Talk,' 'Tell Her About It' and 'Keeping The Faith'

John Gatchell: trumpet on 'Careless Talk,' 'Tell Her About It' and 'Keeping The Faith'

Tom Bahler, Rory Dodd, Frank Floyd, Lani Groves, Ullanda McCullough, Ron Taylor, Terry Textor, Eric Troyer, Mike Alexander: background vocals

Producer: Phil Ramone

Recorded: Chelsea Sound and A&R Recording, Inc., New York, NY

Mixed at A&R Recording, Inc., New York, NY

Mastered at Sterling Sound, New York, NY

Engineers: Jim Boyer and Bradshaw Leigh

Assistant Engineers: Mike Allaire and Scott James

Production Coordinator: Laura Loncteaux

Mastered by Ted Jensen

Horn and String Arrangements: David Matthews

Background vocal arrangements: Tom Bahler

Musical Advisor: Billy Zampino

Photography: Gilles Larrain

Cover Design: Christopher Austopchuk and Mark Larson

Release date: 8 August 1983

Chart positions: UK: 2, US: 4, New Zealand: 1, Australia (Kent Music Report): 3, Iceland (Tonlist): 3, Japan (Oricon): 3

Running time: 40:25

When Joel returned to the studio after a Mexican divorce from Elizabeth Weber, it was as a newly single man. To his surprise and elation, he found himself sought after by supermodels, including Elle McPherson and Christie Brinkley: the latter who starred in the 'Uptown Girl' video and would become Joel's second wife. That being the case, Joel supposedly felt inclined to write a series of youthful ballads that reflected his recently-acquired social status. Because he was feeling rejuvenated, the song ideas came to him easily, and the entire songwriting process merely took about six weeks.

Joel's ninth studio album is a concept album that pays homage to the doo-wop and soul heroes of his transistor-radio youth. The doo-wop vocal style originated primarily in black and Italian neighborhoods in Detroit, Chicago, Philadelphia and New York. Young singers would often practice on a street corner or under a bridge: the right physical environment often helped the groups capture a specific acoustic effect.

In hindsight, those times weren't always so innocent. Sometimes the singers were restricted to certain urban areas, or had nowhere else to rehearse. In any event, it was a matter of groups independently creating a unique set of harmonies. Young singers developed their ears and strengthened their vocal-range capacity, usually without the benefit of trained teachers. Traditionally, singers would be assigned parts based on their vocal range. And in lieu of actual words, nonsense words could be used, hence the name doo-wop. In some cases, singers would imitate a trumpet or stand-up bass, and often harmonies were sung *a cappella*.

Joel paid homage to a number of *streetlight singing* acts on *An Innocent Man*, including Little Anthony and the Imperials – a charismatic act from Fort Greene, Brooklyn – and Frankie Lymon and the Teenagers, who hailed from Harlem.

In an author interview with singer Anthony Gourdine at the end of this album section, the frontman shares anecdotes about his auspicious interactions with Joel.

Joel also paid tribute to a bevy of American soul singers, including the aforementioned Ray Charles and Wilson Pickett. With his exceptional ear, Joel identified the qualities that these vocalists used in their signature tunes, and synthesized them into his originals.

An Innocent Man was nominated for the 26th Grammy award for Album of the Year, as were Joel's three prior studio albums, but he lost to Michael Jackson's *Thriller*. In addition, Joel received a Grammy nomination for Best Male Pop Vocal Performance for the Frankie Valli tribute 'Uptown Girl': but again, Jackson walked away with the honors.

In-demand saxophonist Michael Brecker's CV included sessions with his brother Randy Brecker, James Taylor, Chaka Khan, Art Garfunkel and Chick Corea. Brecker returned to the Joel camp for the recording of *The Bridge*.

Saxophonist and multi-instrumentalist Mark Rivera did not play on *The Nylon Curtain*, but joined the Joel contingent in 1982 for the Nylon Curtain tour, replacing Cannata. In describing *The Nylon Curtain,* Rivera told Rolling Stone writer Andy Greene: 'I was very involved in that record from playing in the horn section with Michael Brecker, David Sanborn and Ronnie Cuber on 'Tell Her About It' and 'Easy Money', and singing the backgrounds on 'Uptown Girl' and 'Tell Her About It', and playing the triangle on 'An Innocent Man.''

Album Art

Joel sits on the steps of a Soho establishment at 142 Mercer Street in Manhattan, gazing into the distance. He's wearing a black leather jacket, dark jeans and black boots, with fingers crossed over his right knee. It's ironic that Joel's remaining studio albums don't feature similarly-posed portrait shots, as the photography here provides so much detail about the attitude and personality of the inside material. Joel's name is on the upper-left-hand corner, and the album title rests on the bottom. The pale yellow lettering modestly offsets the stark and stunning black outfit and stairway.

The objective of Gilles Larrain (the French photographer responsible for the cover shot) has been to 'capture the landscape of the soul of a person.' He nailed it.

'Easy Money' (Billy Joel) (Homage to James Brown and Wilson Pickett)
The track 'Easy Money' was heard during the opening credits of the 1983 film by the same name and starring American comedian Rodney Dangerfield.
DeVitto kicks off the tune with great enthusiasm, followed by a maelstrom of horns. Joel's voice is sandpapery and soulful. The phrasing is uncomplicated and direct: 'Roll me like the numbers/Roll me like the dice.' The subtext is, 'I want the good times I never had.' Pendarvis handled the Hammond B-3 like a Stax-label insider. As a 1983 movie theme song, 'Easy Money' captured the imagination of a new, youthful audience.

'An Innocent Man' (Billy Joel) (Homage to Ben E. King and The Drifters)
B/w 'I'll Cry Instead' and released as the third single in 1983, Peak: UK Singles Chart: 8, US *Billboard* Hot 100: 10, US *Billboard* Hot Adult Contemporary Tracks: 1
The first few bars are subtle instrumentally, save for light taps from DeVitto and a faint line from Stegmeyer. Then, with extraordinary articulation, Joel takes off, accompanied by finger-snapping. The melody is strident with a well-crafted rise as Joel explores his vocal range. His low notes are so extraordinarily low, that when his falsetto erupts, it's a delightful surprise.

More importantly, he does a fine job giving the listener a taste of an important musical era in which singers relied on their natural talents rather than electronic effects like autotune.

The first verses refer to general attitudes that 'some people' possess. Joel ticks off the disparities, and these third-person references continue for several verses. But then the story grows more heated and personal when we discover that the subject's friend/lover is treading a cautious path. The subject responds to this guarded behavior by acknowledging it: 'I know you don't want to hear what I say/I know you're gonna keep turning away.' We now understand that they've had a history together; that they're both on tenterhooks at the moment. But the subject then conveys that he's been in a vulnerable place before; he's gotten through it and he'll try to stand by his partner and see things through.

After Joel deviates from the lyric, with acrobatic riffs over the title phrase, he reasserts his philosophies – 'Some people hope for a miracle cure/Some people just accept the world as it is' – but he's unwilling to play somebody else's game; he's an 'innocent man.' At the heart of the song is a kind of savior aura that the subject conveys: 'I'm not above making up for the love you've been denying you could ever feel.'

Joel exploits the outer edges of his range for a soulful effect. DeVitto's light cymbal work puts the song in the scene. The strings work their way into the arrangement in a predictable manner, but it's the core rhythm section that keeps things fluid.

Intrigued fans wonder if this is about a therapist and client?; a partner consoling another vulnerable partner?; a friend advising a friend?

'The Longest Time' (Billy Joel) (Homage to doo-wop groups like Frankie Lymon and the Teenagers)

B/w 'Christie Lee' and released as the fourth single in March 1984m Peak: UK Singles Chart: 25, US *Billboard* Hot 100: 14, US *Billboard* Hot Adult Contemporary Tracks: 1

Although this option didn't coincide with Ramone and Joel's original plan, Joel furnished all of the lead and backing vocal parts, and the blend is fantastic. With multiple listens, you can appreciate the skill that goes into creating these separate parts that sparkle with personality.

As for the handclaps and finger snaps? Joel orchestrated those too. Finally, this wasn't the first – nor would it be the last – song conceptualized as an instrumental that would blossom into a full-blown arrangement. But ultimately, the music and words fit together – as Joel might say – like a marriage.

'This Night' (Billy Joel) (Homage to Little Anthony and the Imperials; chorus is based on Beethoven's 'Piano Sonata No. 8' (Pathetique)

B/w A-side 'Leave a Tender Moment Alone' (U.S.), B-side 'I'll Cry Instead' and released as the fifth single in 1984, Peak: UK Singles Chart: 78, Belgian Singles Chart (Flanders): 21

Leave it to Joel to co-write a song with the great Ludwig van Beethoven. Who owns the intellectual property rights to that? For this arrangement, Joel chose an especially melodic piece, yet the theme was contemporary. Joel allegedly wrote it about his brief relationship with supermodel Elle Macpherson.

The *shoo-wop* harmonies that sandwich Joel's earnest voice, are period-perfect. The Beethoven chorus is so playful, that one can easily disregard its 18th-century origins. Many Beethoven biographers paint the European composer as a sourpuss rather than an emotionally available man, to which specific letters attest. Regardless, Beethoven's emotions consistently came through in his compositions, which Joel here brought to light.

Joel's team shores up hard edges: Mark Rivera's riveting alto sax solo ushers in an unanticipated but exciting modulation.

Keep in mind that Little Anthony and the Imperials inspired the groove, although it must be said that lead singer Anthony Gourdine went on to explore many other styles in his career. But during the act's golden years, he commanded compassion when fronting 'Tears On My Pillow' and 'Goin' Out Of My Head.' Their rendition of 'Hurt So Bad' by Teddy Randazzo, Bobby Weinstein and Bobby Hart was a top-10 hit in 1965. These songs conveyed a youthful purity that Joel – even at this relatively later stage of life – could respectfully imitate.

'This Night' was only available as a single in the UK and Japan, but didn't chart especially high in either country. In the US, it was the B-side of 'Leave A Tender Moment Alone.'

'Tell Her About It' (Billy Joel) (Homage to Motown groups like The Supremes and The Temptations)

B/w 'Easy Money' and released as a single spring 1983, Peak: UK Singles Chart: 4, U.S. *Billboard* Hot 100: 1, U.S. Cashbox Top 100: 3, U.S. *Billboard* Hot Adult Contemporary Tracks: 1

There's team effort here. The lead vocal, backing harmonies and vibrant cacophony of horns, come together with incredible vigor. At the bridge, Joel confirms he's the leader of the pack.

The narrator gently reminds his friend to open up emotionally to his current girlfriend. He states with a quiet urgency: 'You got to tell her about it before it gets too late.' Further on, he warns the friend to hold nothing back: 'Tell her all your crazy dreams.'

The song reached number 1 on the *Billboard* Hot 100 for a solitary week on 24 September 1983.

'Uptown Girl' (Billy Joel) (Homage to Frankie Valli and the Four Seasons)

B/w 'Careless Talk' and released as a single 29 September, 1983, Peak; UK Singles (OCC): 1, U.S. *Billboard* Hot 100: 3, U.S. Adult Contemporary (*Billboard* : 2

Being a natural mimic, maybe it was easy for Joel to channel the silky-voiced Frankie Valli. Whatever the case, there are times when you close your eyes, you swear that the former Four Seasons frontman has seized the microphone. Joel's backing vocal arrangement is precise and heartwarming. Kudos to him for doing all the parts. It's one of his jewels.

The opening drum fill on 'Uptown Girl' has as many syllables as the name Liberty DeVitto. The drummer elaborates on his unique learning style here: 'I don't read music, so I have to think of something that has the same number of syllables of that fill that I have to do, so 'Liberty DeVitto' just happened to come out that way, just like, 'butter beans': bada ba bada ba.' According to the award-winning drummer, construction sounds and bird tweets also morph into rhythms that go 'right into the brain.'

'Careless Talk' (Billy Joel) (Homage to Sam Cooke)

'Everybody's telling lies. I don't know why.' Deception is the theme here. Joel portrays a suspicious guy. 'They've been talking ever since you've been around.' But as it's a homage to the great Sam Cooke, I longed for a more developed storyline.

'Christie Lee' (Billy Joel) (Homage to Little Richard or Jerry Lee Lewis)

Joel's raw vocal sets the band on fire. Rivera's sax spins in and out of the verses. While the piano-playing echoes the rock-and-roll ethic of Jerry Lee Lewis, Joel's vocal derives its spirit from the Little Richard oeuvre.

'Leave A Tender Moment Alone' (Billy Joel) (Homage to Smokey Robinson)

B/w 'This Night' and released as a single 1984, Peak: UK Singles Chart: 29, U.S. *Billboard* Hot 100: 27, U.S. *Billboard* Hot Adult Contemporary Tracks: 1

Musically, the crisp stepwise movement makes the melody emotionally accessible. The lyric zeroes in on insecurity within a monogamous relationship: 'Just when I ought to relax, I put my foot in my mouth.' The poor guy is drowning in an abyss of romantic confusion: 'Just when I'm in a serious mood, she's so quiet and shy.' Are they compatible? Is he living inside his head?

Joel makes every phrase meaningful, not just with his voice but through his rest stops. He slows our frantic world down with this film noir type ballad. Another reason for the song's success is Belgian Toots Thieleman's dynamic blues-harp solo. He and Joel created a perfectly balanced duet.

'Keeping The Faith' (Billy Joel) (Homage to pre-British Invasion rock 'n' roll)

B/w 'She's Right on Time' and released as a single in 1984, Peak: U.S. *Billboard* Hot 100: 18, U.S. *Billboard* Hot Adult Contemporary Tracks: 3

Although the song soared to number 3 on the US *Billboard* Adult Contemporary Chart, it neglected to curry favour with the UK Singles Chart. In fact, it was the only single from the album that did not chart in the UK, while the album, overall, was well-received there.

That said, the commercial 1950s references to Lucky Strike cigarettes, matador boots, 'a tight pair of chinos' and Old Spice shaving lotion may have left U.K. fans out in the cold or simply uninspired. While the references are fun, they lend themselves to a particular demographic.

This straight-ahead, nostalgic rocker tells a solid and inspirational story, but pales in comparison to the impact of the surrounding tracks. I like it, but I don't find it as catchy or memorable as the others.

However, the combination of two trumpets and three saxophones truly flesh out the production. Joel's voice stays deep throughout, and although there's not a full choir in the background, it almost feels like there is, as his lead vocals are full-bodied and demonstrative.

The best parts include Joel's delightful phrasing. 'Comb my hair in a pompadour like the rest of the Romeos wore.' And the invaluable lessons learned, as in the bridge: 'You can linger too long in your dreams.'

Interview with Anthony Gourdine (from Little Anthony and the Imperials)

Over the years, I admired the work of Billy, but I'd never met him. He was a Long Island guy and a New Yorker, and that was it – everybody knows everybody – I'd never met him, but I loved his work. In fact, I sang a couple of his songs in my show. Back in the 1980s and '90s, I was really into his music, and thrilled at how he was looking at everything: it was different from how everybody else was, especially his interpretation. 'New York State Of Mind' blew me out of the water.

In 2006, we were told we'd been nominated into the Long Island Music Hall of Fame, and I told my publicist George Dassinger, 'I ain't from Long Island, I'm from Brooklyn.' But he reassured me: 'They nominated you because you lived there for a few years. That made you official.' That was a big to-do, and they had everybody's who's-who – either those who were there posthumously or those that were there physically – but it was a great night. Tony Bennett was there, Richie Havens, just a ton of people. It was huge, the red carpet, the whole bit.

We were backstage and I heard this piano playing. I went around the curtains, and there was Billy, sitting on the bench. So as I walked in, he said, 'There he is. If it wasn't for him, none of us would be in this business.' That was quite thrilling. Really? And something happened during that moment, in which we connected. And after time, little things would happen. So around 2006-2008, I'd get messages: 'Hey man, did you read that article? He's talking about you.' Billy was focused on me more than I was focused on him. Well, I realized he was a fan of my work.

One day, I was in New York. George told me that Billy was going to be at Madison Square Garden, and that he'd like me to come backstage. 'He wants you to come before the show,' George confirmed. He told me that Billy likes to meet people before the show rather than after. When I got there, there were all sorts of dignitaries in the suite; all these famous people, and I'm going,

'Gee.' Billy comes out and goes, 'Hey, man,' and goes past all of these people, sits with me and starts talking like nobody else was in the room: like old friends. He said, 'I hate when I have to go on stage when my throat is like…,' that kind of talk.

Bill O'Reilly (from ABC and CBS News) was there, and asked me afterwards: 'Do you know Billy?' I replied, 'Not really really well. Just over the years, I really like his music and I found out that he really likes mine.' Even Bill noticed that we were real admirers of each other.

I also saw Billy at the 25th-Anniversary Rock and Roll Hall of Fame televised show, where, with the Imperials, I sang 'Two People In The World.' Everyone was there, from Stevie Wonder to Stevie Nicks. But it seemed like, when I was in the room, Billy would stop anything that he was doing. I told George that if I moved back to New York, we'd probably be good friends. We'd probably hang out. It's like I knew him for a long time.

I've been a great admirer of Billy's work and his genius. There aren't too many cats that come along like that, it's rare. Something about his work fascinated me; it was different. He did this one song at The Troubadour in Los Angeles on Santa Monica Blvd., that's where he recorded it live. We'd show up and he'd say something to somebody else. People would say to me, 'Billy said to say hello.'

I'm like the old man in the sea. I'm the senior senior of that era, and to me, Billy's a young man. I was out there a gazillion years before he started, but still, I have many people in the business today that still stand out to me. There are just as many singers out there today, but the format is different. I think they were better in my day. They might not have had all the advantages to learn about their craft, but now they throw them into the lion's den and say 'Be a star', and they don't learn how to fail. We came from the bottom, and Billy was that kind of cat; he came from that kind of background. He struggled. He went after failure after failure after failure, until he made it because nobody would accept his style. He says it better right there in 'Piano Man.' He's a saloon guy. He's the kind of guy, he's plinking around on the piano, like Hoagy Carmichael. He was homespun; earthy. He plays his piano because he likes to. He wasn't writing to save his life, he does it because he likes it and all that stuff that came with it. That's probably the thing that gave him the strength and the fortitude to overcome all of that failure from the beginning, and I admire that as well.

There were about 22,000 people in the audience at Madison Square Garden, and I'm in the audience. I was sitting down right in the front row. All the people I admire were sitting in this one row; movie stars were on my left. I'm sitting there with George. Billy looks up at the screen and says, 'God, I look like my dad.' Then he says, 'Ladies and gentlemen, there's a guy out in the audience …' He didn't introduce anybody else. It was very flattering. And I'm sitting there slouching in my chair, feeling like I don't deserve this honor, but with all these other great stars around me, Billy singled me out. George remembered that I had tears in my eyes. Billy intended to surprise me, and he really did.

Whenever I do interviews, I always talk about Billy Joel: how he's doing, what he's doing. We all have a tendency to do that; we're very conscious of each other. Like I said, cats like that don't come along, except for every 50 or 60 years. They're like a comet – they leave with such a mark on everybody musically in such a way that you go, 'Did that really happen?' That name is Billy Joel.

We sang under the lights and in the subway. We were the stone age of rock and roll. We were the pioneers. We settled the land for people to come in, but I didn't know the street-corner singing had that kind of influence over what Billy Joel was doing.

Above: Native New Yorker Billy Joel onstage in February 1979. (*Alamy*)

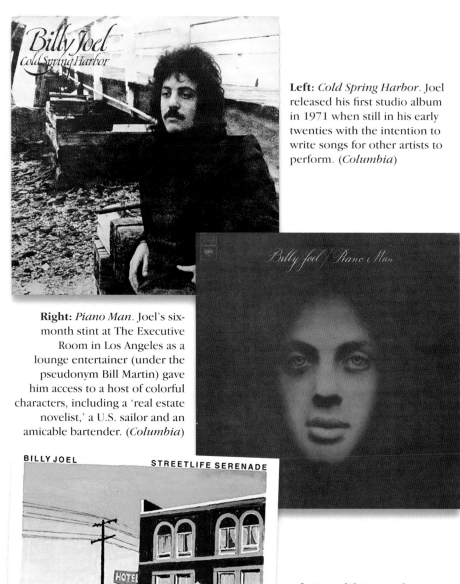

Left: *Cold Spring Harbor*. Joel released his first studio album in 1971 when still in his early twenties with the intention to write songs for other artists to perform. (*Columbia*)

Right: *Piano Man*. Joel's six-month stint at The Executive Room in Los Angeles as a lounge entertainer (under the pseudonym Bill Martin) gave him access to a host of colorful characters, including a 'real estate novelist,' a U.S. sailor and an amicable bartender. (*Columbia*)

Left: *Streetlife Serenade* Released in 1974, Joel's third studio album included multi-instrumentalist Tom Whitehorse and guitarist Don Evans. (*Columbia*)

Right: Released in May of 1976 and recorded in Colorado and New York, Joel's fourth studio album, *Turnstiles*, marked a literal turning point in his career. (*Columbia*)

Left: With producer Phil Ramone at the helm, *The Stranger*, released in September 1977, ushered in a period of creative ingenuity, technological advances and a spectrum of hits including 'Movin' Out (Anthony's Song,)' and 'Just the Way You Are.' (*Columbia*)

Right: *52nd Street.* This 1978 release cast a bright light on American jazz, especially with 'Zanzibar,' featuring guest trumpeter Freddie Hubbard. (*Columbia*)

Left: New Orleans native Dr. John and Long Islanders Billy Joel and Elliott Murphy talk shop backstage at the now defunct The Bottom Line, Greenwich Village. NY, circa 1977. (*Photo courtesy of Elliott Murphy*)

0402 Then known as The Billy Joel Orchestra Doug Stegmeyer, Billy Joel, John Almond, Rhys Clark and Don Evans gear up at the SIR Studio for the Great American Music Hall gig, San Francisco, 1975. (*The Rhys Clark Collection*)

Left: Known for his palpable New York style approach to drumming, Liberty DeVitto became the piston that drove the engine of the Billy Joel Band for over thirty years. (*Liberty DeVitto*).

Right: Liberty DeVitto, Doug Stegmeyer, Billy Joel, Richie Cannata, Russell Javors and David Brown, the quintessential lineup, take five before 'Movin' Out' for a promotional tour. Photo courtesy of Liberty DeVitto.

Associate producer David Thoener added wisdom and color to 'Shades of Grey' on the *River of Dreams* album, 1993. (*Derrick Berryl*)

Right: Co-producers Peter Asher and Joe 'The Butcher' Nicolo with Billy Joel behind the glass during the 'To Make You Feel My Love' (w. Bob Dylan) sessions for *Billy Joel – Greatest Hits Volume III*, 1997. (*Joe Nicolo*)

Left: Joel's crisp white shirt and necktie reflect his high regard for onstage convention, reproduced in this video for 'My Life'.

Right: While Joel's vision has included sophisticated orchestrations, he looks quite at home in herringbone at the acoustic piano in the 'My Life' video.

Left: Rehearsal time often translated to takeout, twilight hours and kidding around but the band's work ethic ultimately prevailed, hence Joel's enormous catalogue.

Right: On the Jay Dubin directed video of 'Uptown Girl,' Joel, surrounded by dancing garage mechanics, portrays a 'downtown guy'. His second wife, model Christie Brinkley, co-starred.

Left: After a pal of Sean Lennon's insinuated that people in Joel's generation had it easy, Joel penned the list song, 'We Didn't Start the Fire' from *Storm Front*, 1989.

Right: 1985: 'You're Only Human (Second Wind') addressed teen suicide. Proceeds were donated to charity. To offset the sobering theme, Joel composed a light-hearted melody.

Left: *Glass Houses*, Joel's seventh studio album released in March 1980 featured hard-edged deliveries and gratuitous electric guitar. (*Columbia*)

Right: *The Nylon Curtain*, Joel's eighth album from June, 1982, embraced digital technology ahead of its time and was greatly inspired by material written by The Beatles and produced by George Martin. (*Columbia*)

Left: Joel's ninth studio album, *An Innocent Man*, released on 8 August 1983 yielded seven singles and honored the doo-wop and soul genres popularized in the late 1950s to early 1960s. (*Columbia*)

Right: Joel's tenth studio album, *The Bridge*, released on 9 July 1986 was recorded on two North American coasts and was the last studio album vetted by Phil Ramone. (*Columbia*)

Left: With rapt attention to detail by musical director David Rosenthal, 1989's *Storm Front* broke political and socio-economic barriers. (*Columbia*)

Right: Released on 10 August 1993, *River of Dreams* involved co-producers Danny Kortchmar, David Thoener and Joe Nicolo and was promoted with four singles, including the bittersweet, 'All About Soul.' (*Columbia*)

Above: Philadelphia producer Joe Nicolo takes a break from the mixing board to bond with beloved studio icon Marty. (*Joe Nicolo*)

Right: Fans 'leave a tender moment alone' as Joel serves up a solo at Madison Square Garden, New York, under brilliant blue lights. (*Dawn Richter*)

Above: Joel holds court under the 'white hot spot light' at Madison Square Garden, New York, November 2021 after several concerts were cancelled due to the coronavirus pandemic. (*Madeline Torem*)

Below: Baseball fan, Billy Joel, at the historical Wrigley Field Ball Park, Chicago, in August 2017. (*Madeline Torem*)

Left: Like Joel, singer-songwriter Elliott Murphy started his career in Long Island. Joel inducted his long-time friend into the Long Island Music Hall of Fame in 2018. (*Michel Jolyot*)

Right: Singer and front man Anthony Gourdine of Little Anthony and The Imperials inspired 'This Night' from *An Innocent Man*. (*Tony Gourdine*)

Left: Billy Joel and early drummer Rhys Clark reunite at Joel's 20th Century Cycles, Oyster Bay, New York. (*Marilyn Clark, Rhys Clark Collection*)

Above: Howard Emerson (middle) with Ivan Elias (left) and Liberty DeVitto (right) at The Action House, Island Park, New York, circa 1971, in support of 'Supa's Jamboree.'

Right: Fingerstyle guitarist Howard Emerson poses in front of his guitar cabinet. (*Nancy Schoen*)

Left: The Phil Ramone-produced *Songs In The Attic*, Joel's first live album, was released on 14 September, 1981 during the *Glass Houses* Tour. (*Columbia*)

Right: *KOHUEPT (Concert)*, Joel's sophomore live album released on 26 October 1987 was recorded during The Bridge tour and required the expertise of long-term sound engineer Brian Ruggles and mixer Jim Boyer. (*Columbia*)

Left: *Billy Joel: 2000 Years, The Millenium Concert* released 1 May 2000, contained two discs and a whopping 25 songs. (*Columbia*)

Right: Released on 2 September 1985, the double-disc *Billy Joel Greatest Hits Volume I & Volume II* bypassed *River of Dreams* and *Cold Spring Harbor* but included both upbeat favorites and romantic balladry from his collection. (*Columbia*)

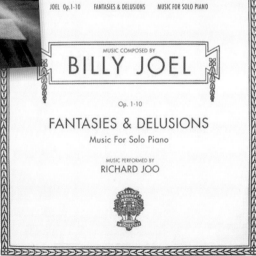

Left: Billy Joel, Live at Shea Stadium: The Concert, with accompanying CD and DVD, was Joel's fifth live project, which was released on 8 March 2011. (*Sony*)

Right: *Fantasies and Delusions*, Joel's thirteenth and final studio album, was released on 27 September 2001 and comprised of a series of original, classical compositions performed by pianist Richard Hyung-ki Joo. (*Columbia*)

Left: Joel's monthly gigs at his 'second home' have attracted international audiences, as well as New York natives. (*Dawn Richter*)

Below: Picture of author with Emily Torem and Madeline Torem celebrating Billy Joel's reappearance at Madison Square Garden. (*Madeline Torem*)

The Bridge (1986)

Personnel:
Billy Joel: lead and backing vocals, acoustic piano (1-3, 5-9), synthesizer (1-4, 6-8), electric guitar (3), Fender Rhodes (9)
David Brown: guitar (1-4, 6, 8, 9), 12-string acoustic guitar (8)
Russell Javors: guitar (1-4, 6, 8, 9)
Liberty DeVitto: drums (1-4, 6-9), percussion (9)
Doug Stegmeyer: bass (1-4, 6, 7, 8)
Mark Rivera: tenor saxophone (4), alto saxophone (7)
Additional personnel:
Rob Mounsey: synthesizer (1), orchestration (2, 4, 6)
Jeff Bova: synthesizer (3,8), orchestration (7)
Ray Charles: acoustic piano (5), lead vocals (5)
Steve Winwood: Hammond B3 organ (9)
Dean Parks: guitar (5)
John McCurry: guitar (9)
Neil Stubenhaus: bass (5)
Ron Carter: acoustic bass (6)
Neil Jason: bass (9)
Vinnie Colaiuta: drums (5)
Jimmy Bralower: percussion (4)
Eddie Daniels: alto saxophone (6)
Michael Brecker: tenor saxophone (6)
Ronnie Cuber: baritone saxophone (6)
Dave Bargeron: trombone (6)
Marvin Stamm: trumpet (6)
Alan Rubin: trumpet (6)
Don Brooks: harmonica (8)
Patrick Williams: arrangements (5)
Philippe Saisse: orchestration (7)
Peter Hewlett: backing vocals (1)
Cyndi Lauper: harmony vocals (8)
Production:
Producer: Phil Ramone
Production coordinator: Joseph D'Ambrosio
Engineer: Jim Boyer
Associate engineers: Steve Boyer, David Dickson, Bradshaw Leigh and Fred Tenny
Technical support: Ricki Begin, Peter Bergren, Mark Betts, Steve Butler, Cary Butler, Gary Ciuzio, Ed Evans, Bruce Howell, Joe Lopes, Frank Rodriguez, Billy Rothschild, Joe Salvatto, Audrey Tanaka and Phil Vachon.
Support system: Barry Bongiovi, Jim Flynn and The Power Station staff.
Digitally recorded at The Power Station, Chelsea sound and RCA Recording Studios (New York, NY); Evergreen Studios (Burbank, CA)
Mixed at The Power Station (New York, NY)

Mastering by Ted Jensen at Sterling Sound (New York, NY)
Acoustic piano supplied by Yamaha
Design: Mark Larson
Cover painting: Brad Holland
Photography: Patrick Demarchelier
Sleeve photos: Larry Busacca, Phil Ramone and Charles Reilly
Chart positions: UK Albums (OCC): 38, US *Billboard* 200: 7, Australia (Kent Music
Report): 2, Japan (Oricon): 2

In September of 1986, Anthony DeCurtis, of *Rolling Stone* stated, 'The album's
formal simplicity allows its meanings to emerge in a natural, unpretentious
way.' The result is a smart, sophisticated collection of songs that seemingly
bring us closer to Billy Joel than we've ever been before.

A major change took place after these recording sessions that greatly
influenced the future of the band and affected specific members – though
they all had enjoyed tremendous commercial and creative success with
producer Ramone, Joel decided to end his long-term partnership with the
producer after the recording of *The Bridge*. Ramone and the band had spent
a professional decade together, so the dissolution – whether perceived as
temporary or not – left certain people in the team, untethered, and fans
somewhat mystified.

When Joel responded to a question about that dissolution during a master
class in 1996 at the CW Post on Long Island, he hinted that he'd consider
collaborating again with Ramone in the future, however: 'It was becoming a
treadmill. After ten years, it's difficult. You've got to keep the passion going.
You have to keep doing different things.'

Original Topper members – guitarist Russell Javors and bassist Doug
Stegmeyer – also said their goodbyes, and as in the case of Ramone, the exit
was not of their own choosing. Plus, Joel surprised his fans by collaborating
on a ballad. This intrepid move involved distinguished keyboardist/singers Ray
Charles and former Traffic member Steve Winwood.

The era was ripe for dramatic artistic change. Conservative politics abound.
UK Prime Minister Margaret Thatcher created an atmosphere that would usher
in rebellious music. Ronald Reagan – President of the United States – also
triggered intergenerational division.

Advanced technology during this time led to increased mobility for fans.
VCR equipment allowed them to record and play music whenever convenient.
Videos quickly became a new revenue source, yet this phenomenon was a two-
edged sword for the camera-shy Billy Joel, who insisted that he only wanted to
play in a band and never wanted to be a 'rock star.'

'Running On Ice' (Billy Joel)
Not since 'Pressure' had Joel pitched such a frenetic nerve ball. 'There's a lot
of tension in this town,' he begins. His voice sounds strained as if it had been

squeezed through a wind tunnel. In the first verse alone, as Joel pops out the words 'symptoms' and 'anxiety,' you feel like you're hearing an ad for a migraine remedy.

DeVitto lays down his soul. Thrashing fills and beastly attacks comprise 50 percent of this maddening overture. Needless to say, Joel and DeVitto were enthralled by the quickly-paced tunes of The Police for a couple of reasons – first of all, Joel and Police frontman Sting had similarly-permeable voices. Secondly, Police drummer Stewart Copeland's hypnotic sound whet DeVitto's percussive appetite. Finally, both acts thrived on creating musical upheaval.

Joel had written 'Every Step I Take (Every Move I Make)' with The Hassles, which later appeared on the 2005 compilation *My Lives*. Lyrics there predated similar ones in The Police hit 'Every Breath You Take,' which the new wave band released in May 1983.

But in Joel's tightly-wound narrative, he gives concrete examples of a hamster-wheel existence, lyrically and vocally. It's tunnel-vision mania.

DeVitto described 'Running On Ice' as 'a colossal opener', which 'really energized me for the remaining tracks.' Moreover, his performance here runs parallel to an early rock influence: 'Sometimes – like on this song – I become the lead instrument. On a lot of those songs – like Ringo with The Beatles – we become the lead instruments because we do fills after the singer stops.'

'This Is The Time' (Billy Joel)

B/w 'Code of Silence' and released as the third single in December 1986, Peak: U.S. *Billboard* Hot 100: 18, U.S. *Billboard* Adult Contemporary: 1

The evocative introduction features Brown's melodic guitar lines; Brown and Joel create a cool call-and-response. When Joel reflects back on a more-vulnerable state of mind – 'I know we've got to move somehow/But I don't want to lose you now' – Brown's shredding is a healing force. When DeVitto changes up the rhythm in the second half, this arrangement especially sizzles. Best of all, Brown cycles back for a beautiful wrap.

'A Matter Of Trust' (Billy Joel)

B/w 'Getting Closer' and released as the second single in 1986, Peak: UK Singles Chart: 52, U.S. *Billboard* Hot 100: 10, U.S. *Billboard* Hot Adult Contemporary Tracks: 17, U.S. *Billboard* Mainstream Rock Tracks: 14

'A-one, two, three, four,' Joel counts off and catapults us behind the glass with the rest of the band. His voice throbs with conviction all the way through this finely-structured song.

'A Matter Of Trust,' to me, is about a lover still reeling from a painful past that bravely holds out hope for a shared future.

Instrumentally, it's a guitar lover's dream realized. The kinetic riffs are exhilarating. The related video shows Joel with an electric guitar slung over his shoulder – he doesn't actually play, but he convinces us that he's the consummate shredder.

The eloquently-articulated verses grow even more arresting when the major tonality ushers in minor-7th chords. 'You can't go the distance with too much resistance/But for God's sake, don't shut me out,' Joel sings in the short but powerful and delicately-worded bridge.

'Modern Woman' (Billy Joel)

B/w 'Sleeping with the Television On' and released as the first single in 1986, Peak: U.S. *Billboard* Hot 100: 10, U.S. *Billboard* Hot Adult Contemporary Tracks: 7

'Modern Woman' was strongly influenced by the driving rhythms and disquieting horns of Huey Lewis and the News: known for – among other tracks – the 1980s' award-winning 'The Power Of Love.' Bassist Stegmeyer and tenor saxophonist Mark Rivera, star here, but riveting stabs of synth fall not far behind.

Vocally, Joel's rhythmic images fly and soar in this song about 'an old-fashioned man' who is essentially walking on eggshells: 'She's an intellectual/ What if she figures out you're not very smart?'

In the 'Uptown Girl' tradition, Joel places his love interest on a pedestal while apologizing for his blue-collar past. The subject perceives the 'modern woman' as being out of his league. We could sympathize, or get out of the middle and just get up and dance, which is what the song really seems to be about.

More ambiguity awaits: 'She says she loves you, but she doesn't know why,' Joel puzzles. What's more exciting is the outro, where Joel whips through a series of vocal iterations.

'Modern Woman' made a splash when used for the American film *Ruthless People*; it rocketed to number 10 on the *Billboard* charts. The song deviates from the 'Uptown Girl' world when Joel looks past the purely romantic arena and twins 'rock and roll' with 'politics.'

'Baby Grand' (Duet with Ray Charles) (Billy Joel)

B/w 'Mulberry Street' and released as the fourth and final single off the album, Peak: U.S. *Billboard* Hot 100: 75, U.S. *Billboard* Adult Contemporary: 3

Playing piano and singing with an early hero must have been exhilarating, to say the least, and fans might have been happy with the simplest of arrangements, but Joel did not rest on his laurels. Most importantly, the men respected one another's vocal and instrumental boundaries; neither superstar overshadows the other.

This is an immaculately produced recording. Joel wrote a piece that holds a space for the past but enlists the present. The song rose to number 3 on the Adult Contemporary Chart.

The men first bonded when Charles heard through the grapevine that Joel gave his daughter Alexa the middle-name Ray. Charles contacted Joel, and the creative negotiations began.

With both men having extraordinary ears, they could've fallen into a mimic fest once in the room together. After all, Joel enjoyed mimicking Ray Charles' easygoing style in the early years of his career. Would he choose to go that route with his hero in the studio or stick with his own signature sound? Frankly, when listening to the track, I can't always determine which man is singing, but that's part of the fun.

Charles was agreeable from the beginning as long as the song was right, and Joel apparently came up with the goods. It only took Joel one night to complete the song once he conceptualized the idea, although he spent much of the time pacing frantically inside a warehouse. The theme is essentially a love song to the piano but can be construed as a metaphor for an all-consuming romantic relationship.

One of the hallmarks here is the use of the stride jazz piano technique. Originally referred to as ragtime on the American East Coast, this style harkens back to 1920 and was best explored in the popular song 'Harlem Stride Piano.' Pianists Willie 'The Lion' Smith and James P. Johnson were early proponents; Fats Waller ushered this catchy phenomenon into the swing era.

Merriam-Webster describes this jazzy style as follows: 'the right hand plays the melody while the left-hand alternates between a single note and a chord played an octave or more higher.'

Despite having had little time to come up with a blueprint, Joel nailed the architecture. His elevating stride-based arrangement of 'Baby Grand' doubles as a fitting tribute to an essential musical era. His admiration for all things Ray Charles shines through.

Furthermore, the composition is glowingly reminiscent of Ray Charles' own classic arrangements, such as the bluesy and tender 'You Don't Know Me.' And last but not least, the narrative gently places the baby grand on as high a pedestal as a love interest. Joel masks the true identity of the subject until the end of the second verse. But until that point, we're led to believe he's referring to a romantic partner and not an 88-keyed ivory and ebony instrument: 'Late at night when it's dark and cold/I reach out for someone to hold.' These verses highlight the narrator's vulnerability. I get swept away by the dreamy, earnest phrasing. But at the bridge, music in and of itself becomes just as sacrosanct as the longing for love: 'But only songs like these played in minor keys, keep those melodies holding on.'

Chicago Sun-Times critic Dave Hoekstra said that Joel 'demands and deserves respect as a songwriter in this genre.' The Philadelphia Inquirer added that the song was 'the obvious high point' of the album.

Musically, Joel strove to approach the quality of 'Georgia On My Mind' – a bluesy ballad written by the Indiana-born Hoagy Carmichael – which Charles recorded for *Genius Hits the Road* in 1960.

'Big Man On Mulberry Street' (Billy Joel)

The musicians authentically captured the American big band sound of the 1940s. Joel's phrasing is suitably relaxed, but as he edges towards the outer limits of his upper range, that strain detracts from his scat approach to singing. Joel's early piano fills are spare, but exciting. Hold on; there's more to come.

Rob Mounsey's walking bass line in the bridge keeps the song on solid ground. The seasoned instrumentalist had worked with Paul Simon on 'You Can Call Me Al.' Whether improvised or not, he had Joel's back.

'Why can't I lay low?/Why can't I say what I mean?,' Joel posits. The ambling lack of resolution contributes to the laid-back vibe.

This horn arrangement was performed by highly talented guests Marvin Stamm and Alan Rubin on trumpet; Dave Bargeron on trombone; Ronnie Cubor on baritone sax; Michael Brecker on tenor sax; Eddie Daniels on alto sax, and Ron Carter on acoustic double bass – who has been cited as the most recorded jazz bassist in American history, and whose CV includes performing with The Miles Davis Quintet from 1963 to 1968. Needless to say, Carter was on fire.

The only issue, perhaps, was negotiating status. Bassist Doug Stegmeyer – according to DeVitto – may have felt he'd been taken out of the loop.

In his memoir, DeVitto mentions trying to approximate the Purdie Shuffle, which was named after New York drummer Bernard 'Pretty' Purdie – legendary for this specific technique, and for providing drum tracks for hundreds of legends over the course of his career. In Purdie's 2014 memoir *Let the Drums Speak!*, the Purdie Shuffle is described as 'a bread-and-butter pattern figure that is common to the blues, jazz, and some pop music, with a half-time feel driven by hi-hat chirps and delicate triplets woven around a very sturdy backbeat.' DeVitto explained: 'I can't do the Purdie shuffle, but that's my interpretation of it, and I just let that swing on the hi-hat. The song, the lyric, is so cool: this guy walking down Mulberry Street. He's thinking about what a big shot he is, but then he worries, 'What if somebody really knows who I am?' Still, the man walks the walk, and talks the talk.'

'Temptation' (Billy Joel)

Joel wrote 'Temptation' about his relationship with his first daughter Alexa. Joel was committed to being an all-aboard father; after all, he knew what it was like to feel abandoned at an early age, and as such, he struggled with the push-me-pull-you dilemma he faced. As a touring musician, he had the challenge of juggling financial responsibility with the amount of quality time he could spend with his daughter.

The lyrics are deeply emotional, with some lines being more suggestive than others. So it made sense that some fans confused the content with a straight-ahead romantic ballad. Still, some lines get right to the point – 'I've got business to conduct and I've got places to go' – and it's easy to relate to a theme about missing moments that one will never get back, whether that involves a child or a partner.

Mark Rivera's evocative lines soar in and out of Joel's narrative. This pleasing ballad with an edge, highlights a human and universal phenomenon. DeVitto points out the give and take process that went into this recording: 'I loved when I played on this track; it's weird and it's different. It's a strange track to play; it's kind of a ballad, but it's not. There are a lot of holes. If you listen to Billy Joel songs, you hear me at the vocal. We go back and forth all the time.'

'Code Of Silence' (Backing vocals by Cyndi Lauper) (Billy Joel, Cyndi Lauper)
This was a case of serendipity which remarkably led to a co-write. When Joel was stuck with writer's block, vocalist Cyndi Lauper happened to walk through the studio door. She partnered up on the songwriting process and also contributed vocals. Sometimes the two voices blend well; Lauper adds a decidedly forceful texture. However, her vocals sometimes overwhelm Joel's. Don Brooks guests on the intro and exit with blazing hot blues harp licks. DeVitto, meanwhile, stays steady and strong.

'Getting Closer' (Billy Joel)
The thematic digs possibly reflect the bitterness Joel felt after signing an allegedly one-sided contract with producer Ripp early on in his career. Despite the aftermath, Joel's look-back includes a resolution: 'Though I've lost quite a bit, I'm still in control.'

On the purely musical front, this closer features Steve Winwood on the infectious Hammond organ. His solo is fantastic. Bassist Neil Jason – who worked with the likes of Mick Jagger, Janis Ian and Luciano Pavarotti – contributes a solo that goes down smoothly as well, so with these guests close at hand, the final track boasts a distinctively-tailored sound.

DeVitto – who considers Winwood a hero – sounds like he's having the time of his life. Incidentally, 'Coloured Rain' – co-written by Winwood – was a Traffic song that Joel played in Long Island bars. DeVitto acknowledged in interviews that he and Joel shared similar tastes.

Album Art
Artist Brad Holland created the contemporary painting on the cover. It's an immense geometric construct comprised of gleaming steel against a Picasso-blue background. Joel's name and the title appear in small white letters across the top. During that same decade, Holland's paintings adorned the album covers of musicians Jelly Roll Morton and Stevie Ray Vaughan.

Storm Front (1989)

Personnel:

Billy Joel: vocals, acoustic piano (1, 4, 6, 7, 8, 10), clavinet (2, 3, 6), accordion (3), percussion (3), Hammond organ (4,6,9), harpsichord (5), organ (8), synthesizers (10)

Jeff Jacobs: synthesizers (1-9), backing vocals (1), horn arrangements (6)

David Brown: lead guitar (1-9), MIDI guitar solo (6)

Joey Hunting: rhythm guitar

Schuyler Deale: bass (1-9)

Liberty DeVitto: drums (1-9), percussion (2)

Crystal Taliefero: backing vocals (1, 2, 5, 6, 9), percussion (2)

Additional musicians:

Don Brooks: harmonica (1)

Kevin Jones: keyboard programming (2)

John Mahoney: keyboards (2), keyboard programming (7)

Doug Kleeger: sound effects (2), arrangements (2)

Sammy Merendino: electronic percussion (2)

Dominic Cortese: accordion (3, 7)

Itzhak Perlman: violin (3)

Lenny Pickett: saxophone (6, 9)

The Memphis Horns: (6)

Andrew Love: saxophone

Wayne Jackson: trombone, trumpet

Arif Mardin: orchestral arrangement (7)

Frank Floyd: backing vocals (1, 5, 6)

Mick Jones: backing vocals (1, 4, 8), guitar (6), guitar solo (8)

Patricia Darcy Jones: backing vocals (1, 5, 6, 9)

Richard Marx: backing vocals (1, 6)

Brian Ruggles: backing vocals (1)

Ian Lloyd: backing vocals (4, 8)

Joe Lynn Turner: backing vocals (4, 8)

Chuck Arnold: backing vocals (7), choral leader (7)

Hicksville High School Chorus: backing vocals (7)

Bill Zampino: choral accompaniment (7)

Brenda White King: backing vocals: (9)

Curtis King: backing vocals: (9)

Production:

Release date: 17 October 1989

Recorded: May 1988-July 1989

Label: Columbia

Studios: The Hit Factory Times Square Studio, New York City; Right Track Recording, New York City; The Warehouse Studio, Vancouver, British Columbia, Canada; The Power Station, New York City

Producers: Billy Joel, Mick Jones

Mixing: Tom Lord-Alge (1-3); Jay Healy (3-10)
Engineer: Jay Healy
Assistant engineers: Dana Becker, Tim Crich, David Dorn, Suzanne Hollander, Joe Pirrera and Gary Solomon
Mastered by Ted Jensen at Sterling Sound (New York, NY)
Art direction: Chris Austopchuk
Back photo: Timothy White
Front photo: Frank Ockenfels
Chart positions: UK (OCC): 5, US *Billboard:* 1, Australia (ARIA): 1
Running time: 44:34

What a year! On the international scene, big news included the tumbling down of the Berlin Wall. And in the studio, major changes (okay, not as major as two parts of the same country unifying) were also on the horizon. One might say that Joel went 'to extremes' in the personnel department when firing two-thirds of his backing band (Stegmeyer and Javors), leaving only longtime drummer DeVitto. Moreover, after letting go of Ramone, Joel gave the green light to British producer Mick Jones of Foreigner and Spooky Tooth fame. Jones played guitar for Peter Frampton and George Harrison in the 1970s, as well as on every Foreigner album. Three years prior to producing *Storm Front*, he produced *5150* for Van Halen, and *Fame and Fortune* for Bad Company.

It had been three years since Joel had recorded new tracks. *Storm Front* would be his 11th album, but would this moment in time be considered his 11th hour due to these monumental changes?

The album was recorded with new-recruit guitarist Joey Hunting, who was hired for studio work. Hunting also contributed to *Souvenir: The Ultimate Collection,* and provided additional in-house instrumentation until 2000. Guitarist Tommy Byrnes was assigned to tour, and has remained as touring lead guitarist and musical director. Bassist Schuyler Deale would from here on furnish bass for *Storm Front* and *River of Dreams*, an assortment of Billy Joel collections, and *My Lives*. DeVitto, Brown and Rivera were kept on. Massachusetts-born multi-instrumentalist (percussion, saxophone, harmonica, guitar, drums) and vocalist Crystal Taliefero – who had toured with John Mellencamp and Bruce Springsteen – was added. She became a permanent band member after her initial tour, and was a background-vocal arranger for *River of Dreams*. The American organization NAMM (National Association of Music Merchants) conducted a video interview with Taliefero on 21 October 2019. When asked, 'What makes for a great gig for you?,' she responded: 'When you go to a level, and the guys go there at the same time. You can't explain it; you don't want to – when you look at the other person in the face and they're feeling the same way. We've hit that a couple of times with 'You May Be Right.'

Rolling Stone wrote: 'Billy Joel throws off pop complacency for an angry, committed – and often moving – exploration of life in modern America.'

Some say the popular press maligned Joel's music throughout his career to the point of getting personal. This reviewer was refreshingly straight-forward about the work itself: '*Storm Front's* aggressive tone is immediately established by the surging slide guitar and growling blues harp that kick off 'That's Not Her Style,' the record's opening track.'

And as for the song in which Joel constructed the lyrics first, rather than the melody, rollingstone.com remarked that the album 'gets down to business with its second cut, 'We Didn't Start The Fire.'

Joel has often said in interviews that he would've been a history teacher had he not been bitten by the rock bug. Perhaps the slew of historical events strung together in 'We Didn't Start The Fire' served as his long-awaited credentials.

Needless to say, this Grammy-nominated album yielded two extremely different smash hits: 'We Didn't Start The Fire' and 'I Go To Extremes.'

'That's Not Her Style' (Billy Joel)

B/w 'And So It Goes' and released as the fifth single in 1990, Peak: UK Singles (OCC: 97, US *Billboard* Hot 100: 77, US Mainstream Rock (*Billboard*): 18
The opener's compelling atmosphere is courtesy of Don Brooks on blues harp, but the theme of the high-stylin' woman had sort of run its course by this point in Joel's career. Musically though, the guitar riffs are riveting, and get us in the mood for this album of varied tones.

'We Didn't Start The Fire' (Billy Joel)

B/w 'House Of Blue Light' and released on 27 September 1989, Peak: UK Singles (OCC): 7, *U.S. Billboard* Hot 100: 1, U.S. Adult Contemporary (*Billboard*): 5
According to *thelistenersclub.com*, 'List songs are built around extensive inventories of people, places, and things.' This prototype has been popular with Broadway songwriters and their audiences for decades. In 1928, Cole Porter employed this technique in 'Let's Do It, Let's Fall in Love.' Oscar Hammerstein hopped aboard in 1959 with 'My Favorite Things.' 'Tchaikovsky (And Other Russians)' – written for Danny Kaye in 1941 – featured an ambitious list of acclaimed composers.

Maybe baby boomers 'didn't start the fire,' but kindling crackled after Sean Lennon and a 21-year-old pal cornered Joel (comfortably in his 40s) and questioned the legitimacy of the baby-boomer generation. After all, the friend mused, people growing up in the '50s had it easy, but the current generation, the young man reasoned, faced insurmountable challenges. Joel quickly realized that the young man had no idea how many tragedies had taken place during the songwriter's childhood and beyond. Using the book *Chronicles* as a guide, Joel documented 118 icons, tragedies and discoveries that had an impact on his life from his birth year 1949 up to 1989, and set them to a dance beat.

On a YouTube video of an Oxford master class Joel led, he described the melody as being similar to the sound of 'a dentist's drill.' During the video, he rolled his eyes and stabbed a finger repetitively against a couple of piano notes to illustrate his point.

Joel finds the melody jarring; I just find it innocuous. It's really the narrative that matters, and what led up to constructing the tongue-twisting theme. But being a one-man orchestra, it's understandable that Joel had a bee in his bonnet about this issue: he *is* accustomed to fine-tuning all parts of a song.

What's interesting, too, is how the song can be viewed through the pop culture lens. Stipe, Mills, Buck and Berry's 'It's The End Of The World As We Know It (And I Feel Fine)' by R.E.M. was released two years earlier, and has often drawn comparisons to Joel's rant due to its own swift apocalyptic message. The rhythm of the verses is similar, although R.E.M. concentrates more on alliteration, e.g., Leonard Bernstein, Leonid Brezhnev, Lenny Bruce, Lester Bangs. But R.E.M. certainly 'didn't start the fire' either. Guitarist Peter Buck told *Guitar World* magazine in 1996 that their creation was inspired by Dylan's 'Subterranean Homesick Blues' from his 1965 album *Bringing It All Back Home*. And neither did Dylan! His work was preceded by a series of 'talkin' blues' songs, such as Woody Guthrie's 'Talking Dust Bowl Blues' (1940) and 'Talking Blues' by Christopher Allen Bouchillon (1926).

Joel used rhyming couplets to get his points across but varied from that description by increasing the intensity of his vocal throughout. True, he settled on a sing-song melody, but he did adjust his dynamics and pace accordingly.

In addition, he opted to use an ABCB approach to create excitement: 'Harry Truman, Doris Day, Red China, Johnnie Ray', and used each stanza to convey a specific time period. The chronology included sports icons, movie stars, literary figures, politicians and landmark events.

The single – released on 27 September – was 20 seconds shorter than the album version, which begs the question: what major event was left out?

A comparison between the album and single versions reveals that the latter sacrificed a few lines. In the first chorus after, 'I can't take it anymore,' there's an omission, and the actual line, 'No, we didn't light it, but we tried to fight it' is also omitted. The single version faded at an earlier point, but the same events were included on both versions!

Despite Joel's misgivings about the melody, his thematic formula went on to be a winning success for academicians. Legions of history teachers use the song to supplement generic curricula; the US *Billboard* Hot 100 designated the song number 1. And in what other sphere do Khrushchev, Kerouac and Ho Chi Minh occupy the same sonic space; or dreamy James Dean and brainy Einstein form a couplet?

Joel explained to the *L.A. Times* that the content sometimes goes over peoples' heads: 'I sing 'U-2', and a lot of people say, 'I didn't know that band was out in 1960.' I have to tell them it was the spy plane that wrecked the peace conference between Khrushchev and Eisenhower.'

Joel's team also added flares. The sound effects were implemented by Doug Kleeger: an AV professional who added sparkle to multiple Joel recordings.

'The Downeaster 'Alexa'' (Billy Joel)

B/w 'And So It Goes' and released as a single in April 1990, Peak: UK Singles Chart: 76, U.S. *Billboard* Hot 100: 57, U.S. *Billboard* Hot Adult Contemporary Tracks: 18, U.S. *Billboard* Mainstream Rock Tracks: 33

Poignantly conveyed through heartfelt lyrics about a laudable cause, Joel's story is about a generation of fishermen – the Long Island baymen – who, because of the passage of strict government regulations, can barely make a living or keep their boats (downeasters) afloat.

Joel has explained their significance in multiple interviews: 'It struck a chord. The bay men have been here since colonial times. They were the original pioneers of the island.' He became aware of the situation after reading Peter Matthiessen's book *Men's Lives*. When younger, Joel spent time on an oyster boat, 'swabbing the deck' and doing pedestrian tasks, so he came to the cause with a strong degree of compassion for the hard work involved.

Joel performed two benefits on behalf of the bay men cause, for which he did more than give lip service. In fact, he got arrested during a protest against the regulatory bodies, and donated the proceeds of the single to the fishermen as well.

Musically, 'The Downeaster 'Alexa'' is one of Joel's finest and most mature compositions. His voice is rugged and persuasive; the lyric structure recounts classic poetic works. The accordion playing is especially fierce, and even the inclusion of this almost-forgotten instrument is significant: the protagonist in this sea shanty feels isolated from community-at-large too. That's not to say that the instrument hasn't found its way back to pop culture; it's just that it's still a rarity. Talking Heads embellished 'Road To Nowhere' with accordion in 1985. The following year, Paul Simon enhanced *Graceland* with full-out bellows on 'The Boy In The Bubble.' But in general, the wearable, transportable instrument seesaws in and out of vogue.

Joel puts himself in the center of forgotten voices, and his empathy and ear for dialect cannot be understated: especially, 'Since they told me I can't sell no striper/And there's no luck in swordfishing here.'

Joel went for the top by hiring violinist Itzhak Perlman as an uncredited guest (due to label issues). Perlman's sweeping strokes added the perfect combination of class and pathos. Then, to bring us down to earth again, Joel ends with the plaintive fisherman cry 'ya-ya-ya-yoh,' which in the real-world, would-be part of a social call-and-response, but here the subject faces the world devastatingly alone.

Although DeVitto empathized when Joel got arrested for protesting with the fishermen out on Long Island, he had his own technical issues to contemplate:

The sports fishermen are just fishing out the waters. It used to be a different situation, but now, because of the laws that have been passed, that song is about protesting the laws and saying what it was like before, so I had to come up with the sound of a boat. Billy's boat is called the Alexa Ray. The body of the boat – the hull shape – is a downeaster. It's got a big transom that you can fish off of, but the front is very short. Billy spoke to a lot of fishermen, and based the song on their stories like he was one of them, and wrote about the suffering that he was going through. So, I came up with the sound of a boat, like we're on a boat. I've gone out on the Alexa, and I threw up. It was a challenge to come up with that groove, but I think we nailed it.

'I Go To Extremes' (Billy Joel)
B/w 'When in Rome' and released as the second single in 1990, Peak: UK Singles (OCC): 70, US *Billboard* Hot 100: 6, US Adult Contemporary (*Billboard*): 4, US Mainstream Rock (*Billboard*): 10, Canada Top Singles (RPM0: 3, Canada Adult Contemporary (RPM): 2

Joel's lifelong struggle with mood swings inspired the confessional lyrics: 'Sometimes I'm tired, sometimes I'm shot/Sometimes I don't know how much more I've got.' 'I Go to Extremes' includes some of the songwriter's most emphatic phrasing to date.

The sad progression of the bridge and chorus and Joel's teetering-on-the edge vocal, combine to make this ballad an all-consuming experience, but Joel couldn't have done this job alone.

In a commanding performance, DeVitto drives emotions sky high, only relenting when Joel inserts an exceptionally bluesy keyboard solo. DeVitto explains the process of keeping up the momentum: 'Right from the get-go, you're playing, and you play that way all the way to the end. It's like running a race. It's more physical when you swing and start to keep that going all the way to the end without seeming like you're tired.'

DeVitto related to the sizable ups and downs:

That was easy to relate to; we're all kind of like that. Musicians have these highs and these very lows. Like I explain in the book, what it's like, not playing for a while; you feel like somebody else is molesting your girlfriend when they're playing, and you set into this depression; you don't want to go out anymore. When you're onstage, you get so high; if you have any aches and pains, they go away.

'Shameless' (Billy Joel)
Released as a single in January 1991, Peak: US Adult Contemporary (*Billboard*): 40

Joel's objective was to channel the Jimi Hendrix sound when composing 'Shameless.' He approximated the guitarist's distinguished drawl, and in this homage, he ends each cadence with a shimmering chord: an effect the Seattle shredder would whip up with his whammy bar.

'Shameless' tells the story of a usually-in-control person who suddenly finds himself going to great lengths to please his lover. Yet, at the same time, feels depleted when ending up in such a vulnerable state: 'I never lost anything I ever missed/But I've never been in love like this.'

Joel's version merely reached 40 on the US Adult Chart (*Billboard*) in 1989, but the ballad sprang to life when covered by country artist Garth Brooks on his album *Ropin' the Wind:* earning the country singer a number-1 placement on the *Billboard* country chart in 1991.

But how did this Hendrix-inspired ballad originally make its way into Brooks' country catalogue? As a member of a CD club, the award-winning star returned from tour to find *Storm Front* in his mailbox: 'One of his songs really captured me, a song called 'Shameless',' he explained in the article 'Story Behind the Song: Garth Brooks' Chart-Topping Billy Joel cover, 'Shameless.'' In the aftermath, Brooks' team kept a close watch on the ballad. When it failed to be released as a single, Brooks leapt at the opportunity to cut it, and did so with Joel's blessing. As a matter of fact, Joel was overjoyed to discover that the Hendrix-inspired song could enlist a crossover audience. As such, he boasted to fans at the Boston Garden a few years later: 'My kid grew up to be a country-western star.'

The record's success led to several live appearances together. When Brooks performed in Central Park in 1997, Joel showed up to sing 'New York State Of Mind'. They performed the song at Last Play at Shea in 2008, and in 2011 when Brooks was inducted into the Songwriter's Hall of Fame, Joel made the speech, and on that performance, Brooks' wife – country singer Trisha Yearwood – added harmonies.

Brook's decision was prophetic. The lyrics lent themselves to the Americana genre. The chord progression is straight-ahead, the lyrics are heartfelt, and it's driven by twangy guitar and a steady beat.

'Storm Front' (Billy Joel)

Painted with strident bass and brass courtesy of The Memphis Horns, the title song addresses the red-flag-a-flying on the cover. The arrangement feels like Steely Dan due to a splash of intermittent chords, but there's also a soulful undercurrent. Mid-song, we discover a love interest, but 'he drove her away,' which heightens the suspense. But the plot is just one positive element; the alliteration and basic word feel are infectious. 'We got the cumulonimbus and a possible gale,' Joel cautions, steering the listener across raging seas.

'Leningrad' (Billy Joel)

B/w 'Goodnight Saigon,' 'Vienna,' 'Scandinavian Skies' and released as a single in 1989, Peak: UK Singles (Official Charts Company): 53, West Germany (GfK Entertainment Charts): 14

The stately piano introduction, suggested by DeVitto, is a classy prelude. The storyline revolves around a Russian man named Viktor whom Joel met on tour in the USSR. Working as a professional clown, Viktor cheered up Joel's daughter Alexa, and the two men became good friends over the course of the following years.

Against a few simple chords, Joel documents Viktor's life through a brief biography, and then juxtaposes that information with his own childhood in Levittown, Long Island. Through these touchstones, Joel brings Viktor's personality and trials to life. In his youth, Viktor was 'sent to some red army town,' and ultimately, 'The greatest happiness he ever found/Was making Russian children glad,' while back in Joel's hometown, 'Children lived in Levittown/Hid in the shelters underground.'

'State Of Grace' (Billy Joel)
In this pop confection, Joel relies on an escalating and descending melody line. He laments that his lover is 'slipping away,' as he tries to sort out what's left of a relationship that's quickly going south. Brown's too-brief, but brilliant guitar solo runs counter to the storyline.

'When In Rome' (Billy Joel)
Joel gives his voice a decent workout by adding a lot of variation to the clever words in this catchy tune. The horn solos are quick and dirty. He ad-libs over the backing singers for a total R&B explosion. Think Otis Redding or Wilson Pickett, and you get the drift.

'And So It Goes' (Billy Joel)
Released as a single in 1990, Peak: U.S. *Billboard* Hot 100: 37, U.S. Adult Contemporary (*Billboard*): 5, Japanese Singles Chart: 12
The simple church-style chords which shadow the voice are breathtakingly beautiful. In the first verse, the subject keeps a cool distance. But in the next verse, he examines what went wrong with more skin in the game. On the bridge, he throws up his guard once more, when musing about romantic misfortunes, but it's not clear if he's singing directly to his love interest or not; he could be speaking to anyone: 'And every time I've held a rose/It seems I only felt the thorns.' Finally, he re-establishes a bond by telling his lover, 'You're the only one who knows.'

Related Track
'House Of Blue Light' (Billy Joel)
Somehow relegated to the B-side of 'We Didn't Start The Fire,' this extravaganza is riddled with bellowing blues harp, and sharp accents courtesy of wild brass players. Joel sings confidently against inflammatory orchestra hits.
   This search for lust entails taking on the open road and overcoming grief. 'They had a man playing blues,' Joel wails, adding a description of an old roadhouse. With gutsy lyrics and an unapologetic flow, this is a fitting soundtrack theme for a hard-boiled, cinematic production.

Album Art
The blood-red flag on the cover is the maritime storm-warning flag, which shows wind forces 10-12: numbers that correspond to the highest intensity on the Beaufort scale. That image offers a glimpse into the turbulence of the contents.

River Of Dreams (1993)

Personnel:

Billy Joel: lead vocals, clavinet (1, 4), Hammond organ (1, 4, 6, 8, 10), acoustic piano (2, 6-10), organ (1, 4, 6, 8, 9, 10), backing vocals (2), synthesizers (3, 8), keyboards (5)

Jeff Jacobs: synthesizers (2), additional programming (8)

Tommy Byrnes: guitar (1, 3, 5, 6)

Danny Kortchmar: guitar (1-4, 6, 8-10)

Leslie West: guitar (1, 2, 4)

Mike Tyler: guitar (8)

T. M. Stevens: bass (1, 2, 4, 6, 9, 10)

Lonnie Hillyer: bass (3, 8)

Schuyler Deale: bass (5)

Jeff Lee Johnson: bass (8)

Chuck Treece: bass (8)

Zachary Alford: drums (1, 2, 3, 4, 6, 8)

Liberty DeVitto: drums (5)

Steve Jordan: drums (9, 10)

Jim Saporito: percussion (2)

Andy Kravitz: percussion (8)

Arno Hecht: baritone saxophone (4)

Richie Cannata: tenor saxophone (4)

Osvaldo Melindez: trombone (4)

Laurence Etkin: trumpet (4)

Ira Newborn: orchestration (2, 6-8)

Lewis Del Gato: orchestra manager (2, 6-8)

Frank Simms, George Simms: backing vocals (1, 2, 8)

Color Me Badd: guest vocals (5)

Wrecia Ford, Marlon Saunders, Crystal Taliefero, B. David Witworth: backing vocals (6, 8)

Curtis Rance King, Jr.: choir conductor and contractor (6)

Choir on 'All About Soul': Phillip Ballou, Katreese Barnes, Dennis Collins, Will Downing, Frank Floyd, Diane Garisto, Stephanie James, Devora Johnson, Marlon Saunders and Corliss Stafford.

Production:

Producers: Danny Kortchmar (1-4, 6-10); Billy Joel (5)

Associate producer on Track 5: David Thoener

Co-Producer on Track 8: Joe Nicolo

A&R: Don DeVito

Production Coordinator: Bill Zampino

Engineers: Carl Glanville (1-7, 9 and 10); Joe Nicolo, Phil Nicolo (8)

Recorded by: Jay Healy, Bradshaw Leigh, Bob Thrasher and Dave Wilkerson

Mixing: Niko Bolas (1-4, 6, 7, 9, 10); David Thoener (5); Joe Nicolo, Phil Nicolo (8)

Time: 49:10

Label: Columbia
Producers: Billy Joel, Danny Kortchmar, Joe Nicolo, David Thoener
Release date: 10 August 1993
Recorded: September 1992-May 1993
Studios: The Boathouse at the Island Boatyard, Shelter Island; Cove City Sound
Studios, Glen Cove, New York; The Hit Factory, New York City
Assistant Mixing on Track 8: Dick Grobelny
Mastering: Ted Jensen at Sterling Sound (New York, NY)
Technical Support: Andrew Baker, Lester Baylinson, Steve Bramberg, Laura Delia, Jon
'J.D.' Dworkow, Greg Garland, Peter Goodrich, David Hewitt, Dave Hofbauer, Doug
Kleeger, Howie Mendelson, Larry DeMarco, Artie Smith and Courtney Spencer
Art and Commerce: Jeff Schock
Art Direction: Christopher Austopchuk
Cover Artwork: Christie Brinkley
Design: Sara Rotman
Photography: Glen Erler
Chart positions: UK(OCC): 3, US *Billboard* 200: 1, Australia (ARIA): 1, New
Zealand (RIANZ): 1

Related Album
A Voyage on the River of Dreams (Australian 1994 box set)

Album Art
Dressed in a formal suit jacket and tie, Joel stands up to his waist in sky-blue
water.

Christie Brinkley was awarded 'Top Picks' by Rolling Stone magazine in 1993
for the colorful illustration she created for Joel's 12th studio album. Joel's
forward-facing head with closed eyes is the central focus, but other images
include a verdant tree forest, a shimmering lake, a crater exploding lava, a
boat floating in the distance, roaming wild cats, and a human male and female
engaged in a heated embrace.

'The River Of Dreams' (Billy Joel) (1993)
B/w 'The Great Wall of China' and released as a single in the UK: 19 July 1993, U.S:
1 September 1993, Peak: UK Singles (OCC): 3, US *Billboard* Hot 100: 3, U.S. Adult
Contemporary (*Billboard*): 1, Canada Top Singles (RPM): 2, Australia (ARIA): 1,
Canada Adult Contemporary (RPM): 1
DeVitto played a strong role in Joel's most recent studio album of lyrics and
music: 'When Billy played me the song, I said, 'What's that line?: 'We traveled
along on the river of dreams?' What are you saying?' Billy said, 'Do you think
that should be the name of the song?' I said, 'That should be the name of the
album. That's a great title.''

The recording began at Shelter Island, New York, as Joel wanted to remain
close to home. Seven tracks were completed, but the final cuts did not meet

his standards. For further production assistance, he sought out the expertise of Danny Kortchmar: a guitarist, producer and songwriter who achieved acclaim working with Linda Ronstadt, James Taylor, Carole King and Carly Simon in the 1970s. Like Stewart and Martin, 'Kootch' insisted on using session musicians. Thus, the original tracks were redone, and only 'Shades Of Grey' from the initial sessions was included on the final album.

There were major lineup changes here: bassist T. M. Stevens played on the majority of the tracks, replacing the long-term Stegmeyer; Byrnes was now in charge of major guitar responsibilities. Original sax player Richie Cannata returned to play tenor saxophone on 'A Minor Variation'; 30-year drummer DeVitto only played on 'Shades Of Grey'; Steve Jordan played on 'Two Thousand Years' and 'Famous Last Words,' and drummer Zachary Alford played on the remaining tracks.

'It's difficult, because it's probably the most biographical album I've ever done; it was very self-directed,' Joel explained to *Dateline NBC* about his last studio album with lyrics. In interviews after that time, he said he wanted to concentrate on writing more instrumental music for the studio rather than to write new ballads, so *River of Dreams* represented a significant turning point in his career. In fact, disappointed fans even went as far as to set up a petition to get Joel to produce one more pop/rock album. Yet others felt that Joel had already created a plethora of material that resonated with multiple generations and had paid his dues; they were happy listening to his existing hits. Moreover, they understood his reluctance to produce new music on a highly-pressured continual basis.

Paris-based American singer-songwriter Murphy shared a similar opinion with *rockhistorymusic.com* after recalling a Billy Joel performance in Germany: 'He played in a huge stadium: it was over 50,000. He played all those songs. It was like they were out yesterday with the audience reaction. You did not get the sense this was an oldies show in any way, so maybe in that sense he doesn't feel the need. He's doing so well with the catalogue he's got.'

Joel told the press that he might record an occasional single, but that his heart lies for the moment with composing classical music in whatever form that may take.

Joel's then-wife Christie Brinkley designed the colorful award-winning album cover. *Sputnikmusic.com* has noted that, 'Joel allows his music to mature and progress, resulting in his best album since *The Stranger,*' and 'Arguably the two best songs on the album – 'All About Soul' and 'Two Thousand Years' – are both serious expressions that sound and feel like humble-though-still-very-impassioned retrospectives.'

'No Man's Land' (Billy Joel)
B/w 'No Man's Land (Live)' and released in August 1993, Peak: UK Singles (OCC): 50, U.S. Mainstream Rock (*Billboard*): 18
This truculent dystopia was a fascinating choice for an opener. The first line steers the listener into a sobering graveyard of fear. 'I've seen those big

machines come rolling through the quiet pines.' Is Joel depicting a massive political takeover? Tanks catapulting through the streets of a potentially powerless nation?

As the theme progresses, Joel's allusions take on a more commercial aggression – the likes of 'discount outlet merchandise' and 'raise up a multiplex' – and come the chorus, he drives home the point that we've been pawns much longer than we ever considered: 'Who remembers when it all began?'

Joel's voice holds a heedless flatness, that not only keeps the song eerie in a Bowie way, but we believe in him because he never breaks character; the robotic tone is sustained from beginning to end. At a time when acts like R.E.M., Nirvana and Sting were experimenting with theme and emotion, 'No Man's Land' came across as culturally relevant in terms of fitting into an increasingly dark musical landscape.

'The Great Wall Of China' (Billy Joel)

Had we not known the tragic backstory, this ballad could've been construed as a metaphor for an embittered, widening distance between ill-fated lovers. But most Joel fans were well aware of the songwriter's anger towards his former brother-in-law and manager Frank Weber – whom he'd been battling in court over alleged misappropriation of funds – and in this song, Joel pulls no punches when expressing his disappointment.

It made sense too that Joel chose China as a landing point – for all intents and purposes, China remained a somewhat-unexplored terrain to many Americans, and Joel had already demystified Russia. 'This was not your calling/ Just look how hard you've fallen,' he laments. Lyrically, he juxtaposes Weber's fall from grace with the age-old Humpty Dumpty rhyme. In Fred Schruer's biography *Billy Joel*, he reveals Joel's original title: 'Frankie My Dear I Don't Give A Damn.'

But in this final version, Joel replaces some of the harshness with a quiet sense of loss; the two could've built a successful empire together. They could've traveled to that 'Great Wall,' 'if you'd only had a little more faith.'

It's a return to classic rock. The instrumental hooks in the chorus suggest the wild exuberance of T-Rex; some recording techniques parallel Martin's ideas for *Sgt. Pepper*. There's solid guitar work, courtesy of Leslie West (founding member of Mountain: famous for 'Mississippi Queen'). The loopy electronic effects and full-on backing vocals may find you wailing for a chorus more.

'Blonde Over Blue' (Billy Joel)

Heavy percussion and a tense keyboard riff start off this story about a disheartened soul overwhelmed by the stresses of everyday life: 'The TV works, but the clicker is broken.' As the story unfolds, the role of Joel's muse, his then-wife, Christie Brinkley, becomes clearer, although Joel has stated in interviews that 'Blonde Over Blue' has a wider application.

The palpable lyrics have a stream of consciousness feel that remind me of Jack Kerouac's *On The Road*. The phrases in the verse move along in a carefree way, like shoppers on an escalator: 'In hell there's a big hotel where the bar just closed and the windows never opened.'

But Joel shifts confidently from observer to first person here: 'but in the darkness, I see your light turned on.' In the chorus, the phrasing is shorter, and the love interest is described, using a meaningful metaphor: 'Your hands are cold. Your eyes are fire.'

There's a great deal of nuance on this song. When Joel sings, 'Sometimes when I'm wound so tight,' the electric guitar riffs configure neatly around his words. His warm, impressive vocal leaps, inspired by Roy Orbison, go beyond mere imitation.

A related *vrbo* video from that same year shows Joel struggling to find the right drum part. He and producer, Danny Kortchmar, are at odds about how to make the song swing. Christie Brinkley added that Joel's disquieting repetitive riff reminded her of the film, *Psycho*.

'A Minor Variation' (Billy Joel)

On one hand, Joel compares his ever-mounting troubles to a 'hungry pack of wolves when it's feeding time.' His resilient vocal against the vibrant horn section throbs with a sultry R&B vibe at the verses. At the chorus, he's Wilson Pickett personified. There's a good helping of common-sense philosophy thrown in for good measure: 'I've gotten tough, it doesn't faze me.'

'And so it goes,' Joel commiserates about his plight against humanity, against guitar riffs aggressive as 16-wheelers merging into rush-hour traffic.

Arno Hecht on baritone sax, Richie Cannata on tenor, Osvaldo Melindez on trombone, and Laurence Etkin on trumpet, meld together silky tones; T. M. Stevens serves up a rad bass; drummer Zachary Afford kicks it all off but remains vigilant, and Joel pumps up the heat with layers of shimmering clavinet, Hammond organ and acoustic piano.

'Shades Of Grey' (Billy Joel)

Joel declared production rights for this song and smartly swung guitarist Tommy Byrnes, bassist Schuyler Deale and Liberty DeVitto into the fold. Oklahoma quartet Color Me Badd polished up the backing vocals with soaring harmonies. Joel exclaimed on YouTube: 'I think it's easier to write when you're younger, because you have a certain arrogance, a certain confidence. You don't question your beliefs when you're young, you look at things as black and white.' He concluded though, that 'maybe' when people get older, they open up more and develop a different point of view: hence 'Shades Of Grey.'

'All About Soul' (Billy Joel)

B/w 'You Picked a Real Bad Time' and released as the second single in October 1993, Peak: UK Singles (OCC): 32, U.S. *Billboard* Hot 100: 29, U.S. Adult

Contemporary (*Billboard*): 6, U.S. Mainstream Top 40 (*Billboard*): 17
The B-side 'You Picked A Real Bad Time' ultimately appeared on the compilation box set *My Lives* in 2005 but did not make it onto this album. The CD single released in the UK featured a radio edit, an extended 6:05 remix, and an LP version of comparably equal length.

This slow, steady, but immensely evocative song is well-supported by multi-instrumentalist Crystal Taliefero, the quartet Color Me Badd, and a small but story-sensitive string section.

Refreshingly, Joel celebrates enduring love here, or what he referred to in a 1993 *Washington Post* article as 'married love: people who've been together for a long time,' rather than obsessive or unrequited love, which he had been known for posturing about in the past. That said, he comes off as more philosophical and reflective than ever before. 'All About Soul' is a life-affirming song in which the virtues of trust and faith stand alongside each other and where those content with mere infatuation need not apply.

Tommy Byrnes on guitar, T. M. Stevens on bass and Zachary Alford on drums contribute heavily to this airtight ship, as do the three backing singers and convincing ten-person choir conducted by Curtis Rance King: best known for work with David Bowie, Meat Loaf, Celine Dion and Madonna.

Producer Joe Nicolo – an award-winning Philadelphia-based studio owner – worked with Joel on 'All About Soul' and 'River Of Dreams.' He has worked on material by John Lennon, James Taylor, The Police, Kriss Kross and Cypress Hill, among others. In September 2021, I interviewed Nicolo regarding his work on specific cuts on *River of Dreams*. I included those comments under their respective track titles, but I also asked him to answer general questions that I felt would bring the Billy Joel studio persona to life. These answers appear at the end of this section.

Nicolo describes how he got started working with Joel on the album and on 'All About Soul.'

LT: Had you worked with Billy Joel prior to these sessions?
JN: Actually, no. I had become staff producer for Columbia Records. I had the label Ruffhouse through Columbia. Cypress Hill: 2020's *Insane in the Brain* was big. Kriss Kross was huge, so I became staff producer and the go-to guy if singles didn't come up to what Donnie Ienner – President of Columbia Records 1989-2003 – thought was radio-friendly; Ienner would call me, and I was the ringer who would make the singles. That's what happened with Billy. I remember the first time I talked to Billy about it: he was like, 'Dude, I wrote that song. You can take it to hell in a handbasket. I don't care because I wrote the song. I trust your judgment.' He seemed to know what was happening in radio, so I did 'River Of Dreams' and 'All About Soul.' Up until then, Danny Kortchmar – who I had enormous respect for – you know, James Taylor, Carole King; but for whatever reason, they weren't happy with where the singles were going, and that's how I started working with Billy.

LT: Were you a fan? Does it matter if you're a fan or not?

JN: It definitely does. I think you're always a little bit intimidated by, I mean, at this point, that record came out a hundred and three years ago (laughs), but at the same time, I was in my middle-30s. Of course, I was a huge fan of Billy Joel because he was an icon at that point, but at the same time, that was the thing: 'Do you want to work with Aerosmith?' Sure. 'Cyndi Lauper?' Sure. 'Bob Dylan?' Uh. Okay. It was definitely intimidating because we all have self-doubts about how good we are, but I was definitely a fan.

It started with what Danny (Kortchmar) had come up with, and I loved Billy's vocal and his piano-playing on that song. I asked Billy, 'Are you happy with this vocal?' and he said, 'Yeah. I thought the vocal was done.' So, on that song, I started with the vocal and piano and brought my own band in, almost like a live performance; Joel was playing piano and vocal, and they all played around him. There are these crunch guitar parts, up parts. There were some overdubs, but for the most part, that was just the band performing behind Billy. Liberty DeVitto said, 'Whomever you used, it sounded just like me.' This was backstage when I first saw him after the record came out. It wound up being a great experience.

When I cut the band around 'All About Soul,' Billy wasn't there. He was like, 'Dude, just do what you want.' The band would have felt really self-conscious if he was sitting there, so I preferred to just have them cut without Billy there, so they wouldn't feel any pressure, you know?

I never tire of it, it pushes all my buttons. It's one of my favorite songs of all times that I happened to have the privilege of producing. Two things – one: there's a long version of 'All About Soul' that has an additional verse in it, that is on one of the *Greatest Hits* collections – *She's Got a Way: Love Songs* – that was released on 22 January 2013, and that probably wasn't the single. It says 'All About Soul' remix. It's really the actual version of the song; we just called it a remix. But here's something that's really interesting. In the center of 'River Of Dreams,' Billy put a reprise of 'Lullaby,' and he wanted it to have a calliope, which we accommodated him with. But after we were done, he said 'No, man. I was going for The Beatles reprise on *Abbey Road*, like, the 'You Never Give Me Your Money' reprise, but I'm not The Beatles. Take it out.'

'Lullabye (Goodnight, My Angel)' (Billy Joel)

B/w 'Two Thousand Years' and released as the fourth and final single in February 1994, Peak: U.S. *Billboard* Hot 100: 77, U.S. Adult Contemporary (*Billboard*): 18
When Joel's first child Alexa asked her father what happens after we die, he gently wove healing thoughts into this stately ballad, which he originally constructed and conceptualized as an instrumental reminiscent of Frederic Chopin's ballades.

On the first verse, Joel gently pulses out a mixture of major and minor triads against mellifluous vocals. On the second verse, the piano commands the spotlight, but the string section liberally joins in.

Joel comes across as a devoted and doting father with his vocal, without clever conversation or turn-of-phrase; no dramatic Broadway ending. Instead, the dramatic piano fills act as an extension of his protective parental thoughts.

'The River Of Dreams' (Billy Joel)

B/w 'The Great Wall of China' and released on 19 July, 1993 (UK), 1 September, 1993 (US), Peak: UK Singles (OCC): 3, US *Billboard* Hot 100: 3, US Adult Contemporary (*Billboard*): 2, New Zealand (Recorded Music NZ): 1

The first single off the album was released on 19 July 1993 in the UK and 1 September 1992 in the US. This award-winning song which is structured around a highly-infectious beat, included the talents of three bassists. Meanwhile, Zachary Alford was back on drums, and Mike Tyler manned the electric guitar.

In the U.S. and across the pond, the song peaked at number 3. It also aced in Australia, New Zealand and the Canadian and US Adult Contemporary charts.

The lyrics are pure poetry, or what one might describe as a flow-of-consciousness, in contrast to earlier Joel songs that relied on punchy phrasing. A clever touch is the brief addition of the song 'Gloria' during the fade-out.

The following is a continuation of the interview with Joe Nicolo, focusing on the song 'The River Of Dreams.'

LT: How did you balance out the various musical influences on *River of Dreams*: doo-wop, gospel and R&B?

JN: I think, at the time, what the radio people – when you're dealing with a record, whether it sells two million or seven million, is a big deal. At the time, the number-one person – aside from Billy: he's the number one artist – the number-one person that I would have had to please at that point was a gentleman by the name of Jerry Blair. He had headed radio promotions (at Columbia Records from 1988 to 2000) because back then there was no social media, so if the record didn't get played on the radio, the record didn't happen, so it was my job to make sure that the record got played on the radio.

It was my style at the time that was getting played. I wanted to have an urban-rap influence, but not make it sound like a miniskirt on gramma, and it just evolved into this very percussive African sound, but the elements I used were rap elements. That's why it worked across so many different styles of music. You have to cater the sessions to the artists. At that point, it's funny, because I was a 35-year-old white guy from the suburbs, who had been working with rap for almost ten years. But since I started in the early days of rap, my concept was, whether it was The Fugees or Cypress Hill or Kriss Kross or Lauryn Hill, I wanted to cater to the person who said, 'I'm really not a big fan of rap, but I like *that*.'

So, I wanted to work in the opposite with Billy's record, especially with 'River Of Dreams,' to add what sounded like stuff on the radio – just like today, country music is 808 and 909 drum machines with very boomy 808 bass sounds with country guitar and vocals. So, I was trying to incorporate the modern style to Billy. When I worked with James Taylor, he said, 'Dude, don't put a miniskirt on gramma,' so I didn't want to put a miniskirt on Billy Joel. So, what happened was 'River Of Dreams' became very percussive: African tribal as opposed to rap. But if you were to tear that track apart, it's Schoolly D loops; there's the big tom-tom; thunderous drums in the back of that song. D-loops is like a four or eight-beat drum performance that you put in the back of the record to add a percussive element. And the same thing with that rolling bass sound. Good producers borrow, great producers steal. I was thinking, Paul Simon's 'Graceland.' I didn't want the song to sound like Billy Joel featuring DMX. It had to sound like organic Billy Joel, and I thought it came out great. He loved it, and that's what we went with.

The live drummer on there is Andy 'Funky Drummer' Kravitz. He was my drum guy. He's the one who put that thunderous 'cha choo' which really set the song into that African percussion oeuvre, and the rest of it is just all of these different drum performance loops that just place under it. It makes this cacophony of drums. You can't single out what it's doing, but you like it.

This is my analogy of the University of Wisconsin Marching Band. Andy had a marching band bass drum, the kind you strap on and you play on both sides. We turned that on its side, he got two mallets and he did that 'cha choo' which we recorded about four or five times to make it sound like this big thing. Then the rest of the drum sound, when we got that, that's the silver bullet. So, all of the other percussion and percussive sounds revolved around that big, marching drum sound.

LT: 'River Of Dreams,' to me, is a spiritual, philosophical song. From a technical standpoint, how much did the actual backstory matter?

JN: It definitely matters, because you're trying to create an emotion, and especially in the way the background singers approach it. If you look at the video, it's very gospel. The lyrics? It depends on the artist. Sometimes it's not as important, and songs just evolve. You go with your head and you go with your heart. It's like, 'Uh, no, no. We're off the road a bit, let's get back on the road.' You listen to a song when you're recording it, thousands of times, and the cool thing about that is, it's going to get played thousands of times. So, you're into the process, and all of a sudden you wake up in a cold sweat, you go back in the studio: 'I don't know, man, something ain't right.' But most of the time with great artists, the song and the artists know where it should go, and it goes there.

Vocally, Billy has such control: that's what makes people superstars. He was able to sing it, and I didn't really have a lot of trouble from a technical standpoint. One of the magic boxes in the studio from way back to the beginning of my career until now is a thing called a limiter. What the limiter does is it makes sure the low parts, volume-wise, aren't too low, and the high parts aren't too high. So, from that standpoint, a good limiter will be an engineer's best friend, because if you do have somebody who, dynamic-wise, is all over the place, that's really going to save you. It's been done since the beginning of the recording process. It's still one of the key elements, especially when you're recording vocals. It's the butcher knife in your toolbox. It's the number one: equalization to change the tone, and limiting to make sure it doesn't go too loud or too low are in every engineer's toolbox. You can't live without them.

LT: Were there any issues regarding the combination of session players and long-term players?

JN: Liberty DeVitto was definitely not happy with the direction that Columbia Records wanted to take the record. They've got this rap producer, Joe the Butcher, with a Kriss Kross, Schoolly D, and they're forcing that on a Billy Joel record. This is going to be a nightmare, you know, a dumpster fire, but I have to say, Liberty was like, 'Dude, you knocked it out of the park on 'River Of Dreams'; it was great.'

LT: I had gotten the impression that all producers were in the studio together.

JN: You don't want the album to seem like it's a splintered process. I don't want to paint Danny in any kind of light aside from… The rest of that record, really, is Danny. It's absolutely stunning.

LT: With Billy Joel playing multiple keyboard instruments throughout, and Danny providing stealth guitar parts, how did you go about delineating these textures?

JN: Basically, when you want to put textures on a record, you want to find the specific frequency in terms of basement-range treble, where each instrument can sit and have its own space. And the two ways you're trying to do that, of course, is with equalization, where you make sure that the EQ on each instrument is separated, and the other way you do it is with stereo separation; so you would put, let's say, Billy's organ on the left and Danny's guitars on the right.

LT: Can you comment on the use of reverb?

JN: When you go into an unfinished basement and there's just cinder block walls, you go 'Hey,' and you hear this echo in the space: that's reverb. So, it all depends now. Back in the day, they actually threw the sound into a big concrete room. That's what the Capitol Chambers at the Capitol Studios was: eight reverb chambers used for generating natural reverb. Now, of course, it's all done digitally, electronically, but that actual sound is what reverb is. Big ballads usually have quite a bit of reverb on them. Up-tempo songs, usually not so much, as it's not appropriate for that song, but that's what reverb is. It depends on the song and your common sense as to how much reverb you would think a song would need.

LT: How about microphone placement?

JN: He'd say, 'That's your job. My job is to write and sing amazing songs. That's enough.' If he doesn't like it, of course, he'll tell you. He was like, 'I'm the shortstop. You're the center fielder.'

'Two Thousand Years' (Billy Joel)

Joel starts this epic off simply, sans sturm and drang, and builds the story up with care. He ushers in the phrase 'In the beginning,' before welcoming in the piano and a contagious Celtic-sounding riff. This section continues, essentially, with more crystal-clear vocals and block chords. Danny Kortchmar's soothing strum is an ambient tour de force, but the hum of the accordion also adds a wistful air.

While it was magical to hear Joel pour out such uncompromised emotion in that spare lo-fi manner, the story needed to move forward, and within a few measures, the rhythm section kicks in, lending a sense of raw immediacy to the text. There exist no wasted words here, especially in the first verse. From the insightful 'Too many kingdoms/Too many flags on the field' to 'Time is relentless/Only true love perseveres,' Joel continually overturns fresh lyrical ground. But embedded in these phrases is the holy grail: his eternal devotion to a special person, as well as to posterity.

In verse two, Joel wonders how our children will fare in this new world, and the lyrics grow temporarily dark: 'Is this a curse or a blessing that we give?' His lyrics shimmer with intelligence, intensity and an enduring hope overall, but in the third verse, he's more direct: 'There will be miracles after the last war is won,' he posits. And in terms of prospects for the future, he injects a sense of spirituality and even clairvoyance, by adding, 'Prophets and angels gave us the power to see.'

Unlike 'We Didn't Start The Fire' with its blunt specificity, Joel's journey focuses on his perception of overall human achievement in anticipation of the millennium. He makes allusions to fire and the *Book of Genesis* and raises questions about how we choose to live. Finally, the penultimate line points to brighter days ahead: 'We're on the verge of all things new.'

The invigorating outro features Steve Jordan's excellent drumming and a recapitulation of the contagious Celtic riff.

Joel stopped performing the song live after the desecration of New York's twin towers on 9/11, as the optimism he strove to obtain at the time the song was written no longer felt achievable.

'Famous Last Words' (Billy Joel)

Joel's imagery cites the summer-season-end and 'the last of the souvenirs.' He makes it clear that whatever we came for, is over. 'They're pulling all the moorings up,' and 'They swept up all the streamers' after a parade. He softens the blow by using 'they' – there's really no one specific to blame, yet the thoughts are sad ones.

'But now it's time to put this book away.' Paradoxically, the major tonality belies the thematic despair.

Joel was undoubtedly preparing his fans for his exodus from rock music writing and recording. For many, this was dismal news. But Joel had been consistently open with fans; melody had always come first, and he often struggled with lyrics. Finally, the pressure valve to do both on a consistent basis would be shut down. There'd been that Samuel Barber moment when he'd heard 'Adagio for Strings' and yearned to write similarly haunting compositions.

But at the same time, it was important to recognize that fans still had Billy Joel at their disposal. He was still committed to touring, and with his pick of hundreds of songs from the vaults, he'd keep the buzz going.

Years later, after the afore-mentioned Columbia executive Clive Davis moved to Sony Records, he had a heart-to-heart with Joel, in which he tried to encourage his former client to create original arrangements and resume his studio career. Since the two had enjoyed a strong professional relationship over time, Davis felt comfortable broaching the delicate subject. In his memoir, Davis recalled: 'He didn't yell. He didn't flee,' but added that he received a call from Joel's attorney Lee Eastman, Jr. five months later, and the bottom line was that Joel 'loved the meeting, but just couldn't muster the desire to go back into the studio again.'

More insights from Philadelphia producer Joseph Nicolo:

LT: The album achieved great acclaim.
JN: The record was nominated for Album, Song and Record of the Year, and the two producers of the year were Danny Kortchmar and Joe Nicolo. I had never met Danny. They just took the project away from him and gave it to me, so I never even called Danny. I thought, this is going to be weird, because at the time, I thought, this guy's a legend and I'm the new kid on the block, so to speak, so I never talked to Danny, never. So, we were seated in the front row of the Grammy awards that year. I was sitting down and Danny sits down next to me. He couldn't have been more gracious. He was thrilled. Dude, we're sitting here for Album, Song and Record of the Year. I'm not complaining, okay? Danny was just awesome about it, so everything was fine.

This is a Billy organ story. I forget what studio we were at. It might have been Sony or the Record Plant. It doesn't matter. Billy's sitting at the Hammond organ with the Leslie spinning speaker. He looks at me and goes, 'Do you know how to make a Hammond organ really howl?' I say, 'I'm sure you're going to show me.' He says, 'Get me a butter knife.' So, I say to my assistant, 'Get Billy a butter knife.' So he runs out, goes into the kitchen and brings Billy back a butter knife. Billy gets up and proceeds to unscrew the screws on the back of the Hammond organ with a butter knife. He wanted a screwdriver, but I guess, when he's home, you know, a butter knife works, so he unscrewed the back of the Hammond with a butter knife.
LT: Does Billy prefer to record vocal tracks separately from keyboard tracks?
JN: It depends on the song and it depends on what Billy's feeling. Sometimes he will cut piano and vocals together at the same time. So, it depends. On other songs, he would take the time to go back and spend a lot of time. He's performance-oriented, so, if he felt like it, he nailed a vocal.'

David Thoener interview, September 2021

Triple Grammy-winner David Thoener began his career as an assistant engineer at the Record Plant in New York City in 1974. He subsequently worked as a mixer, engineer and producer/co-producer with Aerosmith, Winona Ryder, John Waite, Roseanne Cash, Sammy Hagar, Meat Loaf, John Lennon, David Bowie, Jason Mraz, The J. Geils Band, Cher and Bob Dylan, among others. Having worked with Billy Joel on *River of Dreams* in 1993, Thoener agreed to share his valuable insights.

LT: As part of a production team, how did you choose which producer handled which arrangement?

DT: Most of the album was complete before I was hired. Billy decided to add 'Shades Of Grey' as the last recording. With an artist as gifted as Billy, he decided the arrangement of his songs. He was open to ideas or comments, but he knew what he wanted as far as arrangement.

LT: 'Shades Of Grey,' according to the liner notes, included guitarist Tommy Byrnes, bassist Schuyler Deale, drummer Liberty DeVitto, and Billy Joel on keys. Did Billy Joel come to the studio with the vocal and piano arrangement already figured out, or did he request assistance with structuring and/or completing the song? Some critics say that the lyrics show a reflective Billy Joel, as compared to his earlier recordings. Did such comments influence the instrumentation?

DT: Billy chose the players. Some decisions in that respect are made on availability or the artists' desire to try someone new he has admired or heard positive remarks about. He had the arrangement in his head. He presented it to the band, and they fine-tuned it in the studio in an hour or so. I had always wanted to work with Billy, and let his A&R guy Don DeVito know several times. An artist can sometimes formulate a team. Phil Ramone was Billy's producer for many years because success can follow success and they don't want to jinx the formula. I felt very honored to be able to work with Billy even if it was only for a few days.

LT: You came to the project having already worked with, among others, singer-songwriters Bruce Springsteen, John Lennon, David Bowie, John Waite and Meat Loaf. Did what you learned from working with those artists, influence your process for working with Billy Joel?

DT: Working with major artists is a matter of knowing what *not* to say, as much as what to say and when. If I feel strongly about an idea, I wait for the right time to express it. Major recording artists don't want to be told anything, but want a person to bounce their ideas off of and look for acceptance or an alternative idea. The egos are tremendous. Some leave them outside the studio door. Some walk in the studio with them. It was my job to sort out for myself the best way to make the session as constructive as possible and how to gain respect from them. I was very young when I started. Only 19 or 20 when

I was working with John Lennon and David Bowie. So, I had to learn these lessons very early on. I had some excellent engineers I assisted, and watched how they confronted situations. That helped me learn the boundaries.

LT: You used the term 'spontaneous creativity' in a previous interview. Did you see this phenomenon occur during the Billy Joel sessions? Liberty DeVitto had had a long history with Billy Joel, but the other musicians hadn't. Did any of those dynamics affect the performance?

DT: Billy surrounded himself with talent. The musicians he would hire were some of the best on their instrument. Musicians like that are full of ideas that flow the more they rehearse together. So, the key is to rehearse, watch and listen. As the musicians are rehearsing a song, it starts to come together and *gel*. As the producer and engineer, the key is to start recording the takes before the magic is gone. Over-rehearsal can be detrimental because brilliant ideas can disappear. I always felt I had a sense of the right time to roll tape. Sometimes it was roll on the first rehearsal. Sometimes, I'd wait a bit for ideas to gel. Part of the job.

LT: What technical choices did you make in terms of capturing Billy Joel's vocals?

DT: I don't remember exactly what microphone I used, but my favorites on vocals were Neumann U-67 tube, Telefunken 251 tube, and sometimes a Neumann U-87 or 47. I usually would put up a few of those and ask the artist to sing a bit on each, then make a decision which one brought out the best of their vocal with no equalization or compression. Then if needed, add a touch of equalization and compression to maximize the vocal sound.

LT: Were you surprised to see that Billy Joel did not record other studio albums after this point in time (other than the all-instrumental *Fantasies and Delusions*)?

DT: I wasn't surprised. I saw it coming. He was going through a lot in his personal life, and it was a strain. Would have been fantastic if he would have continued, but he did what was right for his life. It's a cherished memory for me, as are the 47 years my career lasted.

Related Album
A Voyage on the River of Dreams

Release date: 1994, Label: Columbia, Formats: CD, Chart positions: AUS: 1
This Australian three-CD rarity is comprised of the original *River of Dreams* CD, six live tracks from the related tour, and 'An Evening Of Questions And Answers' recorded at Princeton University.

Fantasies & Delusions (Music for Solo Piano)

Released: 27 September 2001
Running time: 76:17
Label: Sony Classical, Columbia
Producer: Steve Epstein
Recorded at Cove City Sound Studios, Glen Cove, New York, with Bill Zampino and
Richie Cannata; re-recorded in Vienna, Austria for final release.

Joel's 13th studio album features British-Korean pianist Richard Hyung-ki Joo
playing Joel's original compositions. It is the sole album in Joel's collection thus
far that contains classical compositions and no rock songs. Joel mentioned to
American talk show host Charlie Rose that he didn't have specific expectations
of how the album would impact his career; he primarily wrote the album to be a
bridge for non-classical audiences so that they could get a taste of the genre and
become more serious fans of classical music in general: 'I have this theory that
people will discover classical music and say, 'This stuff's great,' and they find it
on their own rather than having it forced on them, and when you find it on your
own, that's the best way,' he explained to fans on the Billy Joel and Hyung-ki
Joo *Fantasies and Delusions: The Making Of* video from 2007.

While many fans applauded Joel's classical studio effort, some wondered why
he didn't simply perform the pieces himself (The query had no bearing on Joo's
abilities). According to the video, Joel considers himself a decent rock pianist
but feels he lacks the skills needed to survive in the classical world. As such, he
needed a classical pianist who could 'find all the nuance and get all the dynamics.'

Joo was introduced to Joel by Joel's half-brother Alexander Joel, who resides
in Vienna and is a world-class orchestra conductor. Joo called Joel's music 'very
intricate and sophisticated,' and acknowledged that Joel 'is in love with people
like Chopin and Liszt and Schumann.' The men recorded the album in Vienna,
the site where many of Joel's favorite classical composers performed. He won
the Stravinsky piano competition. Said Joel, 'He has great ears.'

Joel started his musical trajectory at four, studying the classics, but then at 14,
dove into rock. He uses this metaphor to explain his full-circle journey: 'I left
the girl next door and I ran away with the rock and roll woman,' but then, he
came home to 'the girl next door.'

'I never left the world of instrumental classical music; I always loved it,' Joel
confided to American talk show host Charlie Rose. But perhaps his prophesy
was first revealed on the song 'Famous Last Words,' specifically with the line
'These are the last words I have to say,' on the 1993 *River of Dreams* album.
Joel was quick to add, 'A lot of classical performers dabbled in art forms
which were very popular at the time.' He started this new phase of his life by
revisiting Beethoven but traveled far beyond the master's scope.

Stephen Thomas Erlewine of allmusic.com wrote, 'It's a nice collection
of pleasingly modest, melodic, solo piano pieces, mostly sonatas ... As pop/
classical crossovers go, this is among the best in recent memory.'

Sputnikmusic.com was less generous: 'Joel's last effort is a classical throwback that sounds nice but lacks personality.' The main gripe *sputnikmusic.com* had was that the album was 'a sharp divergence from everything he's done,' suggesting that Joel, after a lengthy studio hiatus, was asking too much from his tried-and-true fans. That said, the reviewer summarized by saying, 'Technically speaking, the music is fine, but there's next to no distinguishing characteristics.'

Perhaps by charting classical waters, Joel got a break from rock/pop reviewers who insisted he was 'derivative' or ahead-of or behind a trend. But would fans stay afloat?

'Opus 3. Reverie ('Villa d'Este')' – 9:31 (Billy Joel, Hyung-ki Joo)
The lengthiest piece of this collection is light and airy, with a chord progression that recalls Chopin. The occasional low bass notes come off as more of a suggestion than an active participant. The piece feels like a constantly interrupted dream; lovely and full of spirit, yet slightly laced with jagged glass. The B-section sustains an aggressive and constant motion that often approximates hysteria. Then, there's a Spanish dance-like tempo that feels as if it was modeled after some timeless American songbook standard.

'Opus 2. Waltz #1 ('Nunley's Carousel')' – 6:58 (Billy Joel, Hyung-ki Joo)
This waltz has a very playful feel and is structured like many standards from Western culture. The booming bassline and constant interplay between treble and bass are infectious. It's bright, brassy and very maturely structured. The B-section virtually explodes with jumping chords, undulating bass lines, and a mirroring of rhythm between Joo's hands, so much so that it's difficult to determine where each line is coming from. Nevertheless, it's an optimistic melding of textures. The piece hints at Brahms.

'Opus 7. Aria ('Grand Canal')' – 11:08 (Billy Joel, Hyung-ki Joo)
This lilting and tearful melody awakens the senses. There are times when the two parts merge to become a blur; other times, it's the feather-light ornamentation that hits the spot. About four minutes in, Joo's runs are so tenderly executed that they almost overwhelm. Around six minutes in, the melodies again stubbornly separate. The constantly moving bass line is very reminiscent of Chopin.

'Opus 6. Invention In C Minor, Opus 6' – 1:04 (Billy Joel, Hyung-ki Joo)
A thrilling duel between equally ambitious parts. It was feathery and light, and I wanted to hear more, but then his delightful jaunt ended. I'm still curious: why did Joel choose to write a piece that lasts less than a minute?

'Opus 1. Soliloquy ('On A Separation')' – 11:26 (Billy Joel, Hyung-ki Joo)

After Joel's daughter came to visit, he watched her get in the car for the ride home to her mother's house. That scene – which made him melancholy – became the thematic basis. Perhaps, because the theme was conceived from such a human place, 'Soliloquy' feels the most genuine. The composition features many mellifluous fills.

'Opus 8. Suite For Piano ('Star-Crossed'): I. Innamorato' – 7:46 (Billy Joel, Hyung-ki Joo)

Very spacious and achingly slow; reminiscent of a typical Chopin ballade, yet slightly less tragic in mood. Joo's capable fingers capture the dark dissension of the bass line, and then he adds a few boastful runs.

Afterwards, one can imagine being transported to a tranquil lake, a bed of shrubs; a spiritual getaway. The serenity is not to last: the following measures spell angst. The rubato melody, again, feels Chopin-esque. Joo builds and builds; there is an uptick of richly-constructed chords.

'Opus 8. Suite For Piano ('Star Crossed'): II. Sorbetto' – 1:30 (Billy Joel, Hyung-ki Joo)

This brief exhilarating gallop, sustains its verve throughout. It echoes the synergy of Schumann.

'Opus 8. Suite For Piano ('Star-Crossed'): III. Delusion' – 3:37 (Billy Joel, Hyung-ki Joo)

The three parts of this suite leave one with a bittersweet aftertaste.

'Opus 5. Waltz #2 ('Steinway Hall')' – 7:00 (Billy Joel, Hyung-ki Joo)

Clocking in at seven minutes, the composition engages the listener with its rubato rhythm, which is fleshed out with a fragile, jewelry box-type beauty. Overall, 'Waltz #2' intrigues because of its undulating call and response.

'Opus 9. Waltz #3 ('For Lola')' – 3:28 (Billy Joel, Hyung-ki Joo)

Dynamically, the pretty, chromatic melody stays on an even keel for most of the time, the occasional dramatic rise notwithstanding. But due to its brevity, the piece feels compromised.

'Opus 4. Fantasy ('Film Noir')' – 8:56 (Billy Joel, Hyung-ki Joo)

The strong repetitive melody line is often supported by rolling arpeggios. There's a simple, sweet sadness that arises from Joo's phrasings. One can easily detect strains of Scriabin.

The B section starts out terse, and the right and left-hand parts almost melt inside each other. Then, dynamics soften and a sort of jazz dance erupts.

There's a Chopin ballade tension. But finally, all tensions subside, and a carnival atmosphere is evoked. There's a lot of heart and soul in this lengthy piece; a fine articulation of mood and dynamics. When the tension arises again, it drops more abruptly, and Joo's technique becomes ever-so apparent.

Joel has always had an old soul; this composition feels like it's come out of a post-depression time capsule. There's a cinematic quality to it.

'Opus 10. Air ('Dublinesque')' – 3:46 (Billy Joel, Hyung-ki Joo)
In the first section, the arrangement is very haunting and simple in contrast to the other pieces. In the next section, Joo's melody bursts forward with energy. It finally evolves into a traditional Irish jig of sorts. It almost feels as if Joo is preparing to play a few verses of the traditional Irish tune 'Danny Boy.'

Note: The grand performance **'Symphonic Fantasies For Piano And Orchestra'** (Billy Joel) featured several of these compositions.

2007 Singles
'All My Life' (Billy Joel)
Released: 14 February 2007
Label: Sony
Recorded: Legacy Studios, 29 December 2006
Chart positions: U.S. *Billboard* Hot Singles Sales: 1, Japan Oricon Weekly Singles Chart: 94

Produced by Phil Ramone, and written to commemorate the second anniversary of Joel's marriage to then-wife Katie Lee, it became available in the iTunes Store on 20 February 2007. The B-side 'You're My Home' was originally written for *Cold Spring Harbor*. Fans found reason to celebrate, as 'All My Life' was the first ballad made available to the public since the 1993 release of *River of Dreams*.

After a short, crisp piano solo, lithe strings drift in. The accompaniment features stand-up bass. This is a largely reflective song. 'I've been a wild restless man,' Joel confesses. 'All my life, my stars were truly crossed.' The thematic payoff is that Joel has finally found his true love: the one 'I've wanted all my life.' If Frank Sinatra came back to life, he'd *surely* make a comeback with this crooning ballad.

'Christmas In Fallujah' (Billy Joel)
Release date: 4 December 2007
Recorded: 2007
Joel followed-up 'All My Life' with this second single. This record was also released from the iTunes Store, and the song ultimately appeared on Long Island native Cass Dillon's EP *A Good Thing Never Dies*. Joel had become acquainted with the 21-year-old singer because of their mutual connection: musical director Tommy Byrnes, with whom Dillon had studied. When it came time to consider recording the song, Joel handed the baton over to Dillon, because he considered himself too old to sing a song from a young soldier's point of view – and besides, Joel banked on Dillon's animated voice, which he felt would more appropriately interpret the visceral lyrics and more accurately represent a typical soldier's age.

Although Joel and Dillon debuted the song live in Chicago, Joel had a change of heart and decided to perform the song live, solo, in Australia in 2008. 11 December 2008 marked another crucial turning point in this unique song's evolution, when Joel opted to record his own version. He announced his intentions at Acer Arena in Sydney, and also revealed that the new version – available as a download and CD single – would honor both the American and Australian servicemen stationed in the Middle East. According to Moran, J. in the article, 'Billy Joel's Tribute Song to Troops in The Middle East,' this version 'is the only official recording of Joel singing 'Christmas In Fallujah' that is available.'

Recorded with acoustic guitar and Mideastern textures, this rendition is essentially a powerful anti-war anthem. The related video depicts civilians – many of them wounded – coping to the best of their abilities with being in a war zone.

Joel was inspired to compose the song after receiving letters from soldiers engaged in combat during the Second Battle of Fallujah. Although the song may draw thematic comparison to 'Goodnight Saigon' (because, in both pieces, Joel funnels his empathy through the first-person perspective of the soldier), the similarities end there: 'Christmas in Fallujah' relies on a heated vocal delivery and the already-mentioned Mideastern instrumentation. The phrase 'We came with the crusaders to save the holy land,' aptly describes the tense setting. Joel's definitive verbal hook speaks agonizing volumes: 'And no one gives a damn.'

Cover Art
The cover shows the profile of a soldier in full uniform against a setting sun. Perhaps to dignify the serious subject at hand, the art is simple in contrast to many of Billy Joel's former projects. The title is written in English and Arabic.

Live Albums
Songs in the Attic (1981)
Personnel:
Billy Joel: vocal, piano, synthesizer, harmonica, liner notes, design concept
David Brown: electric guitar (lead), acoustic guitar (lead)
Richie Cannata: saxophones, flute, organ
Liberty DeVitto: drums, percussion
Russell Javors: electric guitar (rhythm), acoustic guitar (rhythm)
Doug Stegmeyer: bass
Producer: Phil Ramone, remixer, liner notes
Concert producer: Brian Ruggles
Digital remastering: Ted Jensen
John Naatjes: tape research
Recording Engineers: James Boyer, Bradshaw Leigh, Larry Franke, Paul Hulse
Engineer, Remixer: Elliot Scheiner:
Assistant Engineer: Chaz Clifton
Production assistant: Laura Loncteaux
Design: Paula Scher
Photography: Dan Weaks
Label: Family Productions/Columbia
Recorded: Sterling Sound, NYC, June-July 1980 during *Glass Houses* tour
Release date: 14 September 1981
Chart positions: UK: Albums (OCC): 57, US: *Billboard* 200: 8, Japan: Albums
(Oricon): 3
Length: 48:00

Joel's first live album offered fans who had not gotten aboard until *The Stranger,* a chance to savor earlier cuts. As one can imagine, recording a new album during the *Glass Houses* tour may have proved overwhelming, although, with this project, Joel was not under the gun to write new material within a relatively short period of time.

This was an opportunity for the band to test the waters and potentially get a lift from hearing audience reactions to tried-and-true material.

Album Art
Joel – in loosely fit striped pajamas – is depicted entering an attic. He shines a flashlight (the glare is visibly seen) at an almost imperceptible acoustic piano that has seen its best years. An uneven stack of music books is positioned along the top. The walls, which are a warm brown, are purely background, but give a sense of age to the dimly-lit area.

The album title is in bright yellow letters, which from left to right get increasingly smaller: it's like looking at a train track dissolve along a hazy horizon line.

Kohuept (or Kontsert) (26 October, 1987)

Label: Columbia
Recorded: Summer 1987
Producers: Jim Boyer, Brian Ruggles
Chart positions: UK: 92, US: 38
Running time: 72:52

When discussing Joel's second live album, it's imperative to acknowledge its historical significance. Although Joel was not the first American act to perform in Moscow and Leningrad during the Soviet era, his overall vision surpassed that of his predecessors. DeVitto confirmed: 'Other acts had played in the USSR, but not with a full production.'

Joel largely funded the concert, and spared little expense, because he wanted the Russian rock fans to experience the state-of-the-art sound, lighting and acoustics that American fans simply took for granted. To make this happen, he traveled with a crew of more than 100. Moreover, he envisioned a future in which the U.S. and the USSR would coexist on friendly terms, and what better way to create such inroads than through the common denominator of rock music? Yet, political tensions certainly did exist, and Joel was put in the unenviable position of arbitrating between the two superpowers when facing his fans. As such, when the band first announced to a New Jersey audience their intention to perform in this then-communist-bloc country, they were booed. To smooth things over, Joel shot back, 'Hold on: they are people too.' Joel won at least *that* crowd's approval.

Although DeVitto would genuinely warm up to the Soviet people he met on tour and they to him, he had to confront childhood fears prior to taking the trip abroad. He examined his preconceptions about the Soviet citizens in his memoir: 'I thought of them as the enemy. We used to hide under our desks at school because of them.' DeVitto was referring to a rampant fear of nuclear bomb blasts during the Cold War. To that end, American school children underwent classroom drills, so that if the U.S. was suddenly bombed, they'd be protected. Where did such classroom fear come from? In part, through propaganda and misinterpretation. In 1956, Soviet First Secretary Nikita Khrushchev gave a televised speech to Western ambassadors, in which he allegedly said, 'We will bury you.' Although future historians claimed Khrushchev really intended to state, 'We will outlast you,' suspicious American adults passed their paranoia onto their children.

At that time of the tour – when political wounds on both sides of the globe were still fresh – DeVitto claimed he was even scared to disclose his name: 'As soon as they found out my name was Liberty, I thought they'd arrest me and put me away.'

Joel hoped to recoup money allegedly confiscated by his former manager and brother-in-law Frank Weber, and so traveled with a live film crew with the hope of creating a documentary of the six concerts. But unfortunately, he hadn't anticipated the number of things that could go wrong and that were seemingly not under his control during this olive-branch tour. The international press had a field day, printing headlines about Joel's 'tantrums,' yet few writers disclosed the backstories that led to Joel's dissatisfaction. First of all, as mentioned, he had to defend his decision to perform behind the Iron Curtain to his steady stream of American fans. Secondly, having paid expenses out of his pocket, Joel had hoped to recoup said money from a documentary project and double CD, but he had no way of confirming that this would happen. In essence, he was taking a leap of faith, which many peers were unprepared to do.

Carlos Santana, Stevie Wonder and Bruce Springsteen all cried 'Nyet' (No) when asked to tour the USSR, so Joel deserved respect for entertaining in unchartered territory, and for all the right reasons – during the late-1980s, the concept of glasnost (best translated as meaning openness and transparency) was being hailed by head of state Mikhael Gorbachev. As such, this was an unprecedented opportunity to spread goodwill among the nation's youth, through live music. The Kremlin had invited Joel and the band to divide their time in equal parts between Moscow and Leningrad.

While the political timing was in sync, the personal timing was not. Joel had just come off an 11-month tour, where he'd been subject to major throat issues and was exhausted. Furthermore, on opening night, he came face-to-face with stern bureaucrats in the first row. Prior to that, he'd been persuaded to play an acoustic set in Tbilisi, with no choice but to sing through a poor sound system, requiring him to again misuse his vulnerable vocal instrument. During the second show, the film crew shone bright lights directly onto the audience. Joel and his camp had no way of knowing how harsh security would be to the fans. Prior to the extreme lighting, fans danced joyously to the music. But when the lights shone, they froze in fear of reprisal from the authorities, and when Joel attempted to reach out to the technicians in charge, he got no reaction. Thus, Joel became furious during a live show (although it may have been that the powers-that-be never got the actual message due to the sound system), but was also visibly confused and upset about performing for a suddenly unresponsive audience, as compared to the enthusiastic audiences he typically enjoyed throughout the world. He discovered (too late) that security forces were carefully monitoring the audience, which affected their spontaneity. While they were allowed to clap at the end of a song, random bursts of excitement often triggered security guards, who were fearful of Western influences negatively affecting Soviet youth. But Joel's aim was, of course, to perform to this sold-out crowd according to his typically high standards, and the pressure was on from both sides of the international community. The Olympic-sized arena seated 20,000, and tensions could've easily escalated. The glaring intrusion of bright lights could've destroyed the experience for all concerned, but what the press focused on was Joel's resulting behavior, not the factors that foreshadowed it.

According to a review by the *Los Angeles Times* on 27 July 1987, Joel 'overturned an electric piano and smashed a microphone on stage.' In a YouTube video of the event, Joel can be heard screaming, 'Stop lighting the audience. Let me do my show....' To his professional credit, he kept right on singing ('Sometimes A Fantasy') during the tantrum. Ironically, the theme of that song related so much to losing control that many members of the audience assumed his aggressive behavior was simply part of the act.

Joel and his crew anticipated cultural differences. The live show required adjustments. When he introduced songs or styles of music of which many Americans had a basic understanding, a translator repeated his explanations, which gave the Russian audience an opportunity to learn about American musical history and related genres such as doo-wop. Joel eventually seemed comfortable with the back-and-forth format, although, of course, his typically spontaneous comments got lost in the translation process. The supreme payoff was that this pioneering American rock act and the Russian fans, truly connected, despite some logistical casualties. According to Michael Sauter in the article 'Billy Joel Rocks the USSR in 1987' (*Explore Entertainment*): 'The peak of the mania hit on August 2, when 17,500 Leningrad fans jumped up and down on their seats, breaking some 200 chairs, then lifted Joel over their heads and passed him around on a sea of hands.' That decidedly rock-and-roll response incited fear in the Soviet officials, who 'threatened to cancel the remaining dates.'

Album Art
The cover is simply red with raised lettering. On the back, the photo by Neal Preston shows Joel standing in front of the colorful onion-domed St. Basil's Cathedral in Moscow, Russia. On the single version, the image is exponentially larger.

2000 Years: The Millennium Concert
Release date: 2 May 2000
Label: Sony
Recorded: 31 December1999/1 January 2000
Running time: 128:39
Chart positions: UK: 68, US: 40, Japan: 17

Joel's third live album was taped on New Year's Eve at New York City's Madison Square Garden during The Night of Two Thousand Years Tour. Multiple songs were transposed to accommodate Joel's fluctuating vocal range, and the original tracks received minor edits prior to release. As expected, the New York audience was especially geared up to celebrate this historical event, and Joel did not disappoint. He spiced up his setlist of traditional fare by adding Beethoven at the onset, 'Auld Lang Syne' to appease the elders, and Rolling Stones and funky Sly Stone covers for good measure. All songs by Billy Joel except where noted.

Previously unreleased songs
'Auld Lang Syne' (Burns/Trad.)
Joel does the traditional New Year's Eve countdown before performing the holiday song based on Scotsman Robert Burns' poem. The first time around, it's simply done, with basic triads on acoustic piano and a straight-ahead vocal. But then, Joel jazzes it up considerably to ring in the new year, complete with full band.

'Dance To The Music' (Sly Stone)
This is a full-blown production – similar in fervor to Sly Stone's (of Sly and the Family Stone) 1968 hit – fattened up with funky bass, punchy choral responses, screaming organ, and fierce guitar by longtime compadre Tommy Byrnes.

'Honky Tonk Women' (Mick Jagger, Keith Richards)
Of course, every band who dares to cover this classic is obligated to include Keith Richards' hypno-riff – which, as all good rock fans know, startled the rhythm guitarist out of a deep slumber. But there are, in addition, a smattering of instrumental add-ons, especially by way of twangy Duane Eddy-style electric guitar. Joel's chest voice gets buried amid crowd noise and virtuosic solos, but the instrumentals make up for that misstep.

12 Gardens Live
Release date: 13 June 2006
Label: Columbia
Producers: Steve Lillywhite, Billy Joel
Chart positions: UK: 95, AUS: 11
Running time: 2:32:47
Formats: CD, download

Recorded at Joel's home-away-from-home: Madison Square Garden. This album uniquely included the only live version of Joel's signature song 'Piano Man.' In addition to the expected fare, iTunes made available 'Stiletto' and 'Honesty.'

Live at Shea Stadium: The Concert
Release date: 8 March 2011
Label: Sony Legacy
Chart position: US: 35

New York's Shea Stadium was built in 1964 to house the Mets. But in 1965, the place became synonymous with rock royalty after The Beatles played there. The Who, The Police and The Rolling Stones, and many others, followed suit.

Fast forward to 2008, by which time plans for demolishing the beloved-but-dated stadium were finally set in stone. Joel jumped at the chance to perform the final concert – scheduled for 16 and 18 July in front of 110,000 excited sports lovers and music fans. The much-anticipated two-and-a-half-hour send-off included performances by vocalists Tony Bennett, Garth Brooks, Steven Tyler, Roger Daltrey, and even a surprise visit by Paul McCartney: with whom Joel belted out the Beatles standards 'Let It Be' and 'I Saw Her Standing There.' The rest of the 25-strong setlist consisted primarily of Joel chestnuts, and duets with John Mayer and Bennett, while the encore featured covers of 'Walk This Way' with Aerosmith's Steven Tyler, 'My Generation' with Roger Daltrey, and 'Pink Houses' with John Mellencamp.

A Matter of Trust – The Bridge to Russia
Release date: 19 May 2014
Co-producers: Jim Boyer, Brian Ruggles
Format: Double-disc CD, DVD/Blu-ray

This re-release of the 1987 Kontsert recorded during Joel's tour of the USSR was substantially upgraded to include eleven tracks of previously unreleased material on CD, and seven previously unreleased tracks on DVD. The fascinating documentary includes interviews with key personnel and journalists, who shared firsthand revelations.

Album Art
Against a blood-red background stands an all-black replica of the striking St. Basil's Cathedral in Moscow, Russia. Joel's name is in large yellow letters. The title *A Matter of Trust* is printed in large white letters. *The Bridge to Russia*, contrasted in bright yellow, is considerably smaller. Finally, 'The Music' is printed in white against a black background.

Previously Unreleased songs
'Odoya' (Traditional)
The song was recorded at the Djvari Monastery in Tbilisi, Georgia, USSR, and performed by the Georgian Rustavi Ensemble of the USSR with Zhournalist. The full-male choir packs warmth and rhythm into this brief anthem. At a certain point, a lead singer raises his voice above the others, who continue to chant dramatically in tandem.

'What's Your Name?' (Claude 'Juan' Johnson)
Joel and the band members fan out to sing this lighthearted 1962 American doo-wop ballad made famous by Don and Juan: a one-hit-wonder. Joel explains via a translator that he and his group of friends sometimes stayed out of school and harmonized on street corners. After Joel and the band demonstrate this unique style of singing, the crowd cheers sporadically.

'The Longest Time' (Billy Joel)
Again, the audience responds excitedly to the *a cappella* singing. But unlike their spontaneous western counterparts, they clap along rhythmically.

'Back In The USSR' (John Lennon, Paul McCartney)

Joel subs out the 'Ukraine girls' line, replacing it with 'The Leningrad girls make me sing and shout.' Joel and the band really ham it up to the excited crowd that can't get enough. The minute Joel states in English that he'll be playing a Beatles song (which is, of course, translated), the audience is in his pocket.

'The Times They Are A-Changin'' (Bob Dylan)

'This song has been going around and around in my head since I've been here,' Joel shares via the translator. As he strums his acoustic guitar, his voice mirrors Dylan's grainy quality. It's a priceless folksy arrangement: something seemingly completely different from what the audience expects from a rock artist. Did Joel deliberately omit the political lines 'Come senators, congressman/Please heed the call' for fear of reprisal?

'She Loves You' (John Lennon, Paul McCartney)

This is an extraordinary cover version of this early Beatles Lennon/McCartney-penned song. DeVitto nailed Ringo Starr's hard-hitting accents and fills; Joel's voice sounded as innocent and youthful as the fab four in the original version; the triple harmonies are absolutely joyful, especially at the infamous 'woos.' When the backing singers collectively hit that closing major sixth (which the Beatles thought was genius but Martin thought was a cliché), you can sense the crowd's excitement. There are imperceptible instrumental nuances: perhaps a homage to Harrison's country-flecked inserts. The crowd reaction is more reserved than that of the typical American audience, where hoots and shouts often interrupt the singer. For the most part, they wait courteously until songs end to respond; but when they do, it's with great gusto.

The band had a choice of doing an alternative version or honoring the original. They made the better choice of the latter.

Live at Carnegie Hall 1977

Recorded: 3 June 1977
Release date: 13 April 2019
Label: Legacy
Formats: Double LP

According to *setlist.fm*, the actual setlist included a cheerful birthday tribute to Joel's long-term sound engineer Brian Ruggles, and the brief, nostalgic 'Souvenir' as the closer. Joined by a live orchestra, Joel and his energetic cohorts premiered 'Scenes From An Italian Restaurant' and 'Just The Way You Are.' The musicians were unaware that a major sea change was about to occur: Phil Ramone – the future producer of fifth album *The Stranger* et al. – was spellbound by the act's dynamic performance. The rest, of course, is Ramone history.

Howard Emerson: 'At that point it was just me on the guitar. Russell had been let go in December of 1976 or January of 1977. Eric Weissberg was on banjo. They had to do three nights because the concerts sold out in about half an hour. 'The reality is, not months prior to that, we couldn't sell out half a room at a college in certain areas of the country. But in New York, Billy was on fire.'

Compilations and Box Sets
Piano Man: The Very Best of Billy Joel
Release date: 15 November 2004
Recorded: 1971-1993
Label: Columbia
Running Time: 79:43
Re-released 10 July 2006 with DVD; CD includes 18 hits; DVD contains ten videos.

My Lives (Box Set)
Release date: 22 November 2005
Recorded: 1965-2001
Label: Sony BMG
Running Time: 284:50 (4-CD); 85 Minutes (DVD)
Includes songs from The Lost Souls, The Hassles, Attila, B-sides, soundtracks, and a bonus CD from the River of Dreams tour.

Billy Joel: The Box Set
Release date: 1980
Label: Columbia
Formats: 12" box set
Chart position: Only charted in New Zealand: 45

Greatest Hits – Volume 1 & Volume II
Release date: 1 July 1985
Label: Columbia
Formats: CD, CS, 8T, LP
Chart positionss: Nor: 1, NZ: 1, AUS: 2, UK: 7, US: 6, Nor: 1, NZ: 1, AUS: 2

Previously Unreleased tracks
'You're Only Human (Second Wind)' (Billy Joel)
Proceeds from this pop song went to suicide prevention agencies. On the related video, Joel approaches a teen who is planning to jump off a bridge and offers advice and consolation. Joel deliberately created a lighthearted tune that would appeal to vulnerable youth.

'The Night Is Still Young' (Billy Joel)
Joel's vocals rise hauntingly above thrumming bass, brass, sultry cymbals and shimmering instrumental hooks, yielding a romantic tone.

Starbox
Release date: 26 August 1988
Label: CBS/Sony

Formats: CD
Chart position: Japan: 20

This 18-track project contained remastered tracks and was solely released in Japan.

Souvenir: The Ultimate Collection
Recorded: 1973-1990
Release date: 17 December 1990
Producers: Michael Stewart, Billy Joel, Mick Jones, Phil Ramone
Label: Columbia
Formats: CD, CS
Chart position: AUS: 1

This comprehensive, five-album box set, only released in Australia, garnered great acclaim. Disc one – *Live at Yankee Stadium* – opens with the gospel-inflected Isley Brothers' 'Shout,' followed by extended versions of Joel staples.

   Greatest Hits, Volume I includes the live version of 'Say Goodbye To Hollywood,' surrounded by studio recordings. *Greatest Hits, Volume II* also includes one live cut: 'She's Got A Way.' Disc 4 *Storm Front* included only studio tracks, while disc 5 – which includes in-depth interviews with Joel – ends with the short but touching 'Souvenir.'

Greatest Hits Volume III
(Note the 12-year gap between Volume III and Volumes I & II)
Release date: 19 August 1997
Label: Columbia
Formats: CD, CS, LP
Chart positions: UK: 23, US: 9, AUT: 7, NOR: 7

Previously Unreleased Tracks
'To Make You Feel My Love' (Bob Dylan)
'Make You Feel My Love' was written by Bob Dylan for the 1997 album *Time Out of Mind,* and has been covered by over 450 performers. The lyrics are wildly cinematic: 'When the rain is blowing in your face/And the whole world is on your case,' and so it goes. In this song about fierce romantic devotion, Joel – true to form – takes on the style of the person whose song he's covering – in this case, the Minnesota to Greenwich Village troubadour who became an ad hoc hippie prophet. There's even a compact blues harp solo to take you back to Dylan's folksy era, followed by screeching organ. The drumming, in stark contrast, is military in style.

   Producer Joe Nicolo recollects:

Billy had some great ideas. He made me bring in drummer Anton Fig, who was David Letterman's drummer, and record 24 tracks of snare drum on that song,

141

and it kind of made it sound like the University of Wisconsin Marching Band. When we were finished with it, I wasn't happy with how it came out. I just didn't like it, and 'til this day, I'm not really happy with the record. About two or three years ago, I went back to the multi-tracks and I completely rebuilt the song, starting with Billy's vocal and piano. I'm finally done.

Nicolo redid the song with producer Peter Asher (formerly of Peter and Gordon). Asher's clients include James Taylor and Linda Ronstadt. Post-production yielded Nicolo's story:

One last story about *The Greatest Hits*. It was a Sunday night and I had to finish. Peter was there, Billy was there. I was going to go to Walt Disney World the next day. So I said, 'Billy, we have to get done, this song.' He said to his assistant, 'When's the latest the helicopter can leave?' And he looks at me and says, 'That's a rock and roll question.'

We finished late. We were in New York. It was me and Peter and we walked out of the studio, turned right, and said, the very first bar we come to, we're going to go in and have a toast. We're walking down the street. We come to a bar, and outside the bar is an ambulance with the lights on and they're wheeling in a stretcher. We walk in the bar and there is a guy on the ground. Either he's passed out, or whatever, with his legs under the bar. So, we step over him and we sit down. The bartender says, 'Hey, guys, what do you have?' And Peter looks at the guy on the ground, winks at him, and says, 'I'll have what he's having.'

'Hey Girl' (Gerry Goffin, Carole King)
This soulful American ballad became a top 10 hit on the *Billboard* Hot 100 in August 1963 when recorded by Freddie Scott (and in 1971 by Donny Osmond). It was penned by the husband-and-wife songwriting team of Gerry Goffin and Carole King years before King pursued a successful solo career.

Joel committed to the tear-stained story song in 1997. 'Hey Girl' is governed by a strikingly sad progression and fearless modulations. Joel completely embodies the dramatic words. 'How will I live/How can I go on?' he posits, supported by a barrage of female singers. In the video, Mark Rivera boasts an era-appropriate saxophone solo.

In an interview I conducted with Joe Nicolo in September 2021, I asked the producer how he determined when a recording artist – in this case, Billy Joel – has successfully completed the final take. Joe Nicolo:

On that record, that's Billy's piano and vocal: one take, all the way though; one take. So it all depends on the song and whether he feels he needs to spend more time. But the vocal on that song is stunning: he killed it. Sometimes you almost have tears in your eyes. With any artist, you know when you have that ultimate take.

'Light As The Breeze' (Leonard Cohen)

'There's blood on every bracelet/You can see it, you can taste it,' Joel gasps. But that's simply one killer line that Joel configures with grit, amidst a gorgeous gospel arrangement.

Joel's earlier recording of this poetic masterpiece occurred in 1995 when he contributed to a Cohen tribute album titled *Tower of Song: A Memorial Tribute to Leonard Cohen*, which included offerings by Don Henley, Elton John, Tori Amos and Bono, among others. (The song originally appeared on *The Future*, released in 1992.)

One could grasp at straws and compare the song to Joel's 'She's Only A Woman' – particularly based on the line 'There's still a woman beneath this resplendent chemise' – since both female subjects show passive-aggressive tendencies, but otherwise, they're of a different species.

Although the album got mixed reviews, Cohen appreciated specific contributions. In fact, during an interview at radio station KCRW on 18 February 1997, he told DJ Chris Douridas that he preferred Joel's version over his own.

The Complete Hits Collection: 1973-1997

Release date: 13 October 1997
Label: Columbia
Formats: CD, CS, LP
Chart positions: UK: 33, NZ: 17

Of the four discs, the latter is unique, where Joel does spoken-word in regards to music concepts and history, and Beatles influence, and sings the minor-tinged 'You Never Give Me Your Money' and the lively 'A Hard Day's Night' in homage.

The Ultimate Collection

Release date: 20 December 2000
Label: Columbia
Formats: CD, LP
Chart positions: UK: 4, Sweden: 3, NZ: 2, Denmark: 2, Norway: 3

This collection was not issued in the United States, but *The Essential Billy Joel* served a similar purpose there. An unarguable commercial success, this collection raced up European charts.

The Essential Billy Joel

Release date: 2 October 2001
Label: Sony
Formats: CD
Chart positions: US: 15, NZ: 14

Piano Man: The Very Best of Billy Joel
Release date: 15 November 2004
Label: Columbia
Running time: 01:18:21
Formats: CD, download
Chart position: UK: 7

This cross section of romantic ballads, classic rock, psychedelia and nostalgia sets a gold standard. A few dark themes, a live version of 'Honesty' and a 'radio edit' of 'Just The Way You Are' are included for good measure. Too bad 'The Downeaster 'Alexa' didn't make the cut.

My Lives
Release date: 22 November 2005
Label: Sony BMG
Formats: CD box set
Running time: 284:50 (4-CD); 85 Minutes (DVD)
Chart position: US: 171

With liner notes by *Rolling Stone* writer Anthony DeCurtis and an assortment of outtakes, live tracks and B-sides, *My Lives* stands out among the compilations.

The Hits
Release date: 16 November 2010
Label: Sony Legacy
Formats: CD, download
Chart position: US: 34

This contains remastered versions of tracks drawn from all Joel albums. If you're gainfully unemployed or are the quintessential fanatic, this one's for you.

She's Always a Woman: Love Songs
Release date: 23 November 2010
Label: Sony
Formats: CD
Chart position: Japan: 113

Eighteen of Joel's most romantic songs on one disc! Just add a roaring fireplace and a cognac.

Billy Joel: The Complete Albums Collection
Release date: 8 November 2011
Label: Sony
Formats: CD box set

A balance of deep and lesser-publicized tracks culled from Joel's 14 albums, and the 17-track *Collected Additional Masters*.

Collected Additional Masters
Release date: 8 November 2011
Label: Sony
Formats: CD, streaming
Chart position: Did not chart

Previously Unreleased Songs
'Elvis Presley Boulevard' (Billy Joel)
Joel name-checks popular Elvis song titles and despairs over cheap plastic merch in this swinging ballad. True to form, Joel captures the magic of an earlier era with humor and style.

'House Of Blue Light' (Billy Joel)
I agree with the fans that this riveting road song should have been on *Storm Front*. It's glorified with earthy blues harp, brass and monstrous percussion.

'Nobody Knows But Me' (Billy Joel)
Joel sounds incredibly playful as he mumbles at warp speed about a secret friendship.

'Heartbreak Hotel' (Tommy Durden, Mae Boren Axton)
Vocally, Joel highlights the desperation behind this 1956 Elvis Presley hit through escalating dynamics. Joel's obvious love for this classic shines through every cadence; the band supports the underlying theme with a mixture of jazz and blues licks.

'In A Sentimental Mood' (Duke Ellington)
A stellar piano and brass arrangement which harkens back convincingly to the Duke's golden era, but Joel's voice is slightly under the radar.

'You Picked A Real Bad Time' (Billy Joel)
This track was born as an early cut from the *Shelter Island* sessions which morphed into the *River of Dreams* release, and was also the B-side to 'All About Soul.' Joel's story is woeful: he's shaking loose a lover whose timing is abominable. The arrangement is a meaty, guitar-friendly Southern blues, heaped to the sky with rhythm.

'All Shook Up' (Otis Blackwell)
A YouTuber said it well: 'Finally, a cover that doesn't butcher the original.' Joel approximates 'The King's' charm, and the backing singers lure us back to the late-1950s, but Joel makes this cover his very own.

'Where Were You On Our Wedding Day?' (Lloyd Price)
Woah. Joel, a true lover of explosive archival hits, grandly reproduces the gritty vocals of the soulful Lloyd Price, complete with compelling backing vocals and rockabilly piano. The song was featured in the American film *Runaway Bride*.

'Don't Worry Baby' (Brian Wilson, Roger Christian)
Joel performs this much-covered 1964 Beach Boys love song from *Shut Down Volume 2* with a tear in his throat, above all the expected harmonies. This cover made it onto the All-Star Tribute to Brian Wilson DVD, alongside versions by Vince Gill, Elton John and many more.

'When You Wish Upon A Star' (Leigh Harline, Ned Washington)
Cliff Edwards sang the original version of the song that eventually became the Disney Corporation's theme. Joel's laid-back Ray Charles phrasing makes for a cool, breezy ride. Catch the video, where an animated Joel shoots the breeze with sassy Snow White and Peter Pan.

Opus Collection
Release date: 20 March 2012
Label: Starbucks
Format: CD
Chart position: US: 80

With the exception of the cantankerous 'My Life,' the heaving *'Downeaster Alexa'* and the garage rock anthem 'You May Be Right,' this 16-track package features Joel's more subdued material, appropriately marketed to hot chocolate and caffeine imbibers of all ages.

She's Got a Way: Love Songs
Release date: 22 January 2013
Label: Sony Legacy
Formats: CD
Chart position: Did not chart

The 18-tracks regale a spectrum of emotions that Joel evoked in the 1970s and carried out over the course of his multi-decade career. Some – such as 'State Of Grace' and 'The Night Is Still Young' – have been couched in the shadow of hits; 'All For Leyna' and 'Shameless' teeter on the obsessive aspects of partnership, while 'Honesty,' 'Just The Way You Are' and 'She's Got A Way' point to pure romantic escapism.

Billy Joel Goes to Extremes

Joel's songs run the gamut stylistically yet intersect emotionally as he explores the capacity of the human spirit. Compare my favorite examples to yours:

'All About Soul'
'Allentown'
'All For Leyna'
'A Matter Of Trust'
'Big Shot'
'Captain Jack'
'The Downeaster 'Alexa''
'Goodnight Saigon'
'Leningrad'
'Lullabye (Goodnight, My Angel)'
'Miami 2017 (Seen The Lights Go Out On Broadway)'
'New York State Of Mind'
'Pressure'
'Scenes From An Italian Restaurant'
'Souvenir'
'Tell Her About It'
'Uptown Girl'
'Vienna'
'Where's The Orchestra?'
'You May Be Right'
'Zanzibar'

Coda: On 'The Entertainer,' Joel crooned, 'I'd love to stay but there's bills to pay and I just don't have the time.' In 'New York State Of Mind,' he cautions, 'It comes down to reality.' 'And so it goes,' I've enjoyed deconstructing Billy Joel's extensive discography with you.

Big Shot, Guest Spots

Always in high demand, Billy Joel is certainly no stranger when it comes to studio guest spots. In 1985, he sang backing vocals on Patti Austin's 'Talkin' About My Baby' from *Getting Away with Murder,* and played piano on Twisted Sister's 'Be Chrool to Your Scuel' from *Come Out and Play.*

In 1986, Joel supported singer-songwriter Julian Lennon with 'You Get What You Want' off *The Secret Value of Daydreaming,* and wrote 'Modern Woman' for *Ruthless People.* Cyndi Lauper sang and co-wrote 'Code Of Silence' from *The Bridge.* Joel backed up Lauper on 'Maybe He'll Know' from the award-winning *True Colors.*

It wasn't hard to predict that Joel would assist producer Mick Taylor on projects. The year the Berlin Wall toppled, Joel played and sang on 'Just Wanna Hold' from the reigning Foreigner member's self-titled album.

Joel added ivories to Chicago musician Richard Marx's 'I Can't Get No Sleep' from 1991's *Rush Street.* After lauding '52nd Street' and 'Easy Street,' heralding an esteemed Chicago entertainment district, kept things on an even keel.

His lively cover of Elvis Presley's 'Heartbreak Hotel' was featured on 1992's *Honeymoon in Vegas* movie soundtrack, but Joel also struck a homer with the feminist-themed movie *A League of Their Own* by recording the Ellington classic 'In A Sentimental Mood.'

Joel accumulated more movie song credits in 1999, with 'Where Were You (On Our Wedding Day)' from the Julia Roberts comedy *Runaway Bride,* and with 'Have Yourself A Merry Little Christmas' for *A Rosie Christmas* with American actress Rosie O'Donnell.

Perhaps it was a dream come true to record *Duets: An American Classic* with his idol Tony Bennett in 2006. Four years later, Joel added vocals to the evocative Jimmy Webb ballad 'Wichita Lineman' for the Oklahoma-born artist's 2010 album *Just Across the River.* As both songwriters are renowned for giving credence to the blue-collar experience through thoughtful lyrics and haunting melodies, they clicked. According to americansongwriter.com, after Joel described 'Wichita Lineman' as a 'simple song about an ordinary man thinking extraordinary thoughts,' Webb exclaimed, 'That got to me: it actually brought tears to my eyes.' (In 2019, Webb included 'Lullabye (Goodnight, My Angel)' on the 11-track *Slip Cover,* where he interpreted other artists' hits with acoustic piano.)

In 2010, Joel participated in the first of two nights designated for The 25th Anniversary Rock and Roll Hall of Fame Concerts. Predictably, he belted out the much-requested 'New York State Of Mind,' but with Garden-State rocker Bruce Springsteen at his side. The boss announced, 'Long Island is about to meet New Jersey on the neutral ground of New York City.' Joel boosted Springsteen's 'Born To Run' with husky vocals and piano comping. The two vamped on the coda 'Tramps like us/Baby, we were born to run.' Joel returned with other high-profile awardees, including Darlene Love, John Fogerty and Tom Morello for '(Your Love Keeps Lifting Me) Higher and Higher': A tribute to Jackie Wilson.

In 2013, Joel guested on the traditional ballad 'The Christmas Song ('Chestnuts Roasting On An Open Fire'), per the request of Johnny Mathis for *Sending You a Little Christmas*. The next year, Joel recorded with Barbra Streisand on the *Partners* album.

In 2014, he enthusiastically paid tribute to Paul McCartney by recording 'Live And Let Die' and 'Maybe I'm Amazed' for the album *The Art of Paul McCartney*. Perhaps Joel found himself reminiscing about McCartney's frenzied race through New York's busiest airport before a late-night appearance at that final Shea Stadium concert.

'Only the Good' Cover Billy Joel classics

In 1994 Tori Amos presented Billy Joel with *Billboard*'s Century Award in Sydney, Australia and reflected back on her time as a 13-year-old piano bar player. When taking requests, many international fans asked for Billy Joel songs. She recognized that, through his catalogue, Joel 'reached out to many different cultures.'

Joel told Amos: 'I'm glad to see that women artists are beginning to make some inroads into what has specifically been the male domain; specifically women piano players.'

The long-term admirer sang 'She's Always A Woman' at Teatro Arcimboldi, Milano on 17 September 2017. Her aria-like rendition imbued constantly moving chords and halting phrases.

The Blue Ridge Mountains-based acoustic quartet, Love Canon, put a foot-stomping spin on 'Prelude/Angry Young Man,' with mandolin, resonator guitar, banjo, standup bass and fiddle.

Finger-style guitarist Tommy Emmanuel recapitulated the simple elegance of 'And So It Goes.'

Melissa Etheridge underscored the reggae beat in 'Only The Good Die Young.'

While keeping intact the structure of 'Vienna,' Ariana Grande added a soulful dimension.

Hussalonia's 'Sometimes A Fantasy' blurs spoken word with technical ambience.

Alicia Keys stays mindful to the acoustic piano, but adds a swath of Joel's 'New York State of Mind' to her 'Empire State Of Mind.'

Beyonce Knowles – still with Destiny's Child in 2008 – served up a sincere version of 'Honesty' for *Matthew Knowles and Music World Present Volume 1: Love Destiny.*

Willie Nelson's 2019 'Just The Way You Are' from *Ride Me Back Home* conflates easy-listening blues harp with a spectrum of celebratory country flavors.

Dolly Parton's cover of 'Travelin' Prayer' eased in with a heartfelt violin solo before the legend grabbed the mic to mirror Joel's rapid-fire spiel. Parton garnered a Grammy nomination for Best Female Country Vocal Performance for her version. The bluegrass tune became Joel's second country crossover hit, on the heels of Garth Brooks' 1991 'Shameless.'

North Carolinian Lymon Roger remains hot on the trail of Brenda and Eddie in his electronic version of 'Scenes From An Italian Restaurant.'

Irvine, California's Soo Spice knocks 'Piano Man' out of the park by echoing the lounge piano introduction and singsong harmonica. She propels the saloon ballad forward with angelic vocals.

Calgary Alberta's power trio, Evidence, swap hypnotic keys for blistering guitar in their metal recast of 'Pressure.' The dramatic drum fills and warm harmonies superbly honor the original.

Touring Highlights ...

... courtesy of drummer Rhys Clark, who toured with Joel from 1971-1975

Billy's first live concert was at Ultrasonic Recording Studio, Hempstead, New York: a live 1971 concert with WLIR. Nervous excitement, you bet! We rocked with NY energy. Manhattan was the first road concert. Wow. Fun gig. America, here we come.

At Robin Trower, J. Geils Blues Band, when the word 'boogie' echoed towards the stage, Billy would reply (with middle finger in nostril), 'I got your 'boogie' right here,' then (seriously) launch into 'She's Got A Way.' It worked.

The Beach Boys, particularly Carl Wilson – told me at Farm Aid 1996 – made a request to their concert agency to have Billy Joel as an opener whenever available. It was a worthy leap for Billy, The Beach Boys and thousands of their fans!

The majority of Eastern U.S. audiences *got* Billy from the opening song (The Hassles, etc.), but the Midwest-West Coast took time to catch on. While playing major outlets up and down the Eastern Seaboards, we'd still be at The Troubadour in L.A. to 1973.

Meanwhile, Toronto, Vancouver, Memphis, St. Louis, Arkansas, Mississippi and New Orleans were *moving along with Billy* very quickly. Venues in cities went from club appearances to headlining (sold out) theaters and colleges and universities.

Joel also opened for Yes at the now-defunct Arie Crown Theater, Chicago, for a nice audience at a beautiful venue and later opened for Poco at a theater venue in the city center area to a nice response.

Bibliography

Books

Borowitz, H., *Billy Joel: The Life & Times of an Angry Young Man* (*Billboard* Book, New York, 2006)

Davis, C., DeCurtis, A., *The Soundtrack of My Life* (Simon and Schuster, New York, New York, 2012)

Davis, S., *The Craft of Lyric Writing* (Writer's Digest Books, Cincinnati, Ohio, 1985)

DeMain, B., *In Their Own Words: Songwriters Talk About The Creative Process* (Praeger, Westport, Connecticut, London, 2004)

DeVitto, L., *Life, Billy And The Pursuit of Happiness* (Hudson Music, 2020)

Duchan, J. S., *Billy Joel: America's Piano Man* (Rowman & Littlefield, Lanham, Maryland, 2017)

Eig, J., *Ali, A Life* (Mariner Books, NY, 2017)

Gavin, J., *Is That All There Is? The Strange Life of Peggy Lee* (Atria Books, 11 November 2014)

Ian, J., *Society's Child, My Autobiography* (Tarcher-Penguin, New York, 2008)

Purdie, B., *Let the Drums Speak!* (Pretty Media, LLC, Allenwood, NJ, 2014)

Ramone, P., Granata, C. L., *Making Records: The Scenes Behind the Music* (Hachette Books, New York, New York, 2007)

Schruers, F., *Billy Joel: The Definitive Biography* (Crown Publishing, New York, 2014)

Spears, R., *Dictionary of American Slang and Colloquial Expressions* (NTC, Chicago, Il. 1989)

Wards, E., Stokes, G., Tucker, K., *Rock of Ages, The History of Rock and Roll* (Rolling Stone Press, New York, New York, 1986)

Articles

'The Complete R.E.M., A Super-charged History with Peter Buck,' *Guitar World Magazine*, November 1996

'Behind This Song: Glen Campbell, 'Wichita Lineman,' *americansongwriter. com*, 2020

'Billy Joel Visits W10Q Philadelphia,' *Evening Magazine*, 1978

Chalyan, D., 'Why Did Billy Joel Destroy His Piano when Performing for Russians,' *rbth.com*, 12 August 2019.

Erlewine, S., 'Glass Houses,' *Allmusic Review*, March 1980

Finkle, D., 'Movin' Out,' *theatermania.com*, 25 May, 2005

Greene, A., 'Saxophonist Mark Rivera on His Years with Billy Joel, Ringo Starr, Foreigner, and More,' *Rolling Stone*: 'Unknown Legends' (yahoo.com, 29 September, 2020)

Harrington, R., 'Billy Joel's Midlife Confessions,' *washingtonpost.com*, 17 October 1993.

Lovece, F., 'Billy Joel song 'Zanzibar' goes viral on TikTok,' www.newsday.com, *Long Island Newsday*, 31 January, 2021

'Names In The News: Hit Confuses Younger Fans,' *Los Angeles Times*, Joel, 8 January 1990

Marsh, D., 'Billy Joel: 'The Miracle of 52nd Street,' 14 December 1978

McAlley, J., 'Storm Front,' *rollingstone.com*, 30 November, 1989

Moore, B., 'Story Behind The Song: Garth Brooks' Chart-Topping Billy Joel cover, 'Shameless,' wideopencountry.com

Moran, J., 'Billy Joel's Tribute Song to Troops in Middle East,' *Daily Telegraph*, 2008

Moran, J., 'Free Billy Joel Song,' *Daily Telegraph*, 13 December 2008

'New Billy Joel Vinyl Box Features Unearthed 1925 Concert,' *myradiolink.com*

O'Connor, L., McMahon, M., 'Goodnight Saigon Brings Recognition to U.S. Veterans,' vvmf.wordpress.com/2014/08/05, 5 August 2014

Orth, M., (It's A Wonderful Life), 'Split-Level Rock: Elliott Murphy and Billy Joel' (orig. *Newsweek*, p.67), maureenorth.com, 22 April 1974

'Why Did Billy Joel Cancel His Memoir?' *parade.com*, 4 April 2011

Sauter, M., 'Billy Joel Rocked the USSR in 1987,' 9 August 1996

Websites
americansongwriter.com
bethlehempaonline.com/steelgolden.html
billyjoel.com
blender.com
en.m.wikipedia
intheknow.com
myradiolink.com
newsday.com
onefinalserenade.com
parade.com
pennyblackmusic.co.uk
popspotnyc.com
rockhistorymusic.com
rollingstone.com
setlisting.com
songfacts.com
sputnikmusic.com
thelistenersclub.com
tiktok.com

Interviews
Beaudin, J., YouTube.com., Interview Elliott Murphy #4, 'Billy Joel: The Best Musician I Ever Met,' *rockhistorymusic.com*, 16 September 2018

Clark, R., interview with L Torem, December, 2021

Clark, R., The *Uncut* Interview, December-January 2021

Dassinger, G., interview with L. Torem, September 2021

DeVitto, L., interview with L. Torem, *www.pennyblackmusic.co.uk*, 2 August 2021

Douridas, C., interview with Leonard Cohen, *Morning Becomes Eclectic*, KCRW FM Studio, Los Angeles, 18 February 1997

Billy Joel interview, Library of Congress, 12 April 2017

'Billy Joel, Charlie Rose interview,' 19 October 2001, YouTube.com

'Billy Joel: River of Dreams,' YouTube.com, Dateline NBC, 1993

Dunaway, D., interview with L. Torem, 7 October 2021

Emerson, H., interview with L. Torem, 25 January 2022

Cavaliere, F., interview with L. Torem, pennyblackmusic.co.uk, 2 April 2022

Gourdine, A., interview with L. Torem, 15 September 2021

Gumbel, B., YouTube.com, 15 December 2016

Ian, J., interview with L. Torem, *pennyblackmusic.co.uk*, 5 November 2010

'Billy Joel Masterclass at CW Post,' YouTube.com, Long Island University, 1 February 1996

Murphy, E., interview with L. Torem, 18 December 2021

Nicolo, J., interview with L. Torem, 9 September 2021

Ramone, P., 'Stranger' Interview, YouTube, with Rob Prisament, 1998

Sciacky, E., interview, YouTube.com, 1978-1982

Stern, H., Joel, B., Master Class Town Hall on the Howard Stern program, SiriusXM, retrieved from *onefinalserenade.com*, 20 September 2021

Taliefero, C., NAMM video interview, 21 October 2019

Thoener, D., interview with L. Torem, 29 August 2021

Travers, M., interview with Billy Joel, YouTube, 1975

On Track series

Alan Parsons Project – Steve Swift 978-1-78952-154-2

Tori Amos – Lisa Torem 978-1-78952-142-9

Asia – Peter Braidis 978-1-78952-099-6

Badfinger – Robert Day-Webb 978-1-878952-176-4

Barclay James Harvest – Keith and Monica Domone 978-1-78952-067-5

The Beatles – Andrew Wild 978-1-78952-009-5

The Beatles Solo 1969-1980 – Andrew Wild 978-1-78952-030-9

Blue Oyster Cult – Jacob Holm-Lupo 978-1-78952-007-1

Blur – Matt Bishop – 978-178952-164-1

Marc Bolan and T.Rex – Peter Gallagher 978-1-78952-124-5

Kate Bush – Bill Thomas 978-1-78952-097-2

Camel – Hamish Kuzminski 978-1-78952-040-8

Caravan – Andy Boot 978-1-78952-127-6

Cardiacs – Eric Benac 978-1-78952-131-3

Eric Clapton Solo – Andrew Wild 978-1-78952-141-2

The Clash – Nick Assirati 978-1-78952-077-4

Crosby, Stills and Nash – Andrew Wild 978-1-78952-039-2

The Damned – Morgan Brown 978-1-78952-136-8

Deep Purple and Rainbow 1968-79 – Steve Pilkington 978-1-78952-002-6

Dire Straits – Andrew Wild 978-1-78952-044-6

The Doors – Tony Thompson 978-1-78952-137-5

Dream Theater – Jordan Blum 978-1-78952-050-7

Electric Light Orchestra – Barry Delve 978-1-78952-152-8

Elvis Costello and The Attractions – Georg Purvis 978-1-78952-129-0

Emerson Lake and Palmer – Mike Goode 978-1-78952-000-2

Fairport Convention – Kevan Furbank 978-1-78952-051-4

Peter Gabriel – Graeme Scarfe 978-1-78952-138-2

Genesis – Stuart MacFarlane 978-1-78952-005-7

Gentle Giant – Gary Steel 978-1-78952-058-3

Gong – Kevan Furbank 978-1-78952-082-8

Hall and Oates – Ian Abrahams 978-1-78952-167-2

Hawkwind – Duncan Harris 978-1-78952-052-1

Peter Hammill – Richard Rees Jones 978-1-78952-163-4

Roy Harper – Opher Goodwin 978-1-78952-130-6

Jimi Hendrix – Emma Stott 978-1-78952-175-7

The Hollies – Andrew Darlington 978-1-78952-159-7

Iron Maiden – Steve Pilkington 978-1-78952-061-3

Jefferson Airplane – Richard Butterworth 978-1-78952-143-6

Jethro Tull – Jordan Blum 978-1-78952-016-3

Elton John in the 1970s – Peter Kearns 978-1-78952-034-7

The Incredible String Band – Tim Moon 978-1-78952-107-8

Iron Maiden – Steve Pilkington 978-1-78952-061-3

Judas Priest – John Tucker 978-1-78952-018-7

Kansas – Kevin Cummings 978-1-78952-057-6

The Kinks – Martin Hutchinson 978-1-78952-172-6

Korn – Matt Karpe 978-1-78952-153-5

Led Zeppelin – Steve Pilkington 978-1-78952-151-1

Level 42 – Matt Philips 978-1-78952-102-3

Little Feat – 978-1-78952-168-9

Aimee Mann – Jez Rowden 978-1-78952-036-1

Joni Mitchell – Peter Kearns 978-1-78952-081-1

The Moody Blues – Geoffrey Feakes 978-1-78952-042-2

Motorhead – Duncan Harris 978-1-78952-173-3

Mike Oldfield – Ryan Yard 978-1-78952-060-6

Opeth – Jordan Blum 978-1-78-952-166-5

Tom Petty – Richard James 978-1-78952-128-3

Porcupine Tree – Nick Holmes 978-1-78952-144-3

Queen – Andrew Wild 978-1-78952-003-3

Radiohead – William Allen 978-1-78952-149-8

Renaissance – David Detmer 978-1-78952-062-0

The Rolling Stones 1963-80 – Steve Pilkington 978-1-78952-017-0

The Smiths and Morrissey – Tommy Gunnarsson 978-1-78952-140-5

Status Quo the Frantic Four Years – Richard James 978-1-78952-160-3

Steely Dan – Jez Rowden 978-1-78952-043-9

Steve Hackett – Geoffrey Feakes 978-1-78952-098-9

Thin Lizzy – Graeme Stroud 978-1-78952-064-4

Toto – Jacob Holm-Lupo 978-1-78952-019-4

U2 – Eoghan Lyng 978-1-78952-078-1

UFO – Richard James 978-1-78952-073-6

The Who – Geoffrey Feakes 978-1-78952-076-7

Roy Wood and the Move – James R Turner 978-1-78952-008-8

Van Der Graaf Generator – Dan Coffey 978-1-78952-031-6

Yes – Stephen Lambe 978-1-78952-001-9

Frank Zappa 1966 to 1979 – Eric Benac 978-1-78952-033-0

Warren Zevon – Peter Gallagher 978-1-78952-170-2

10CC – Peter Kearns 978-1-78952-054-5

Decades Series

The Bee Gees in the 1960s – Andrew Mon Hughes et al 978-1-78952-148-1
The Bee Gees in the 1970s – Andrew Mon Hughes et al 978-1-78952-179-5
Black Sabbath in the 1970s – Chris Sutton 978-1-78952-171-9
Britpop – Peter Richard Adams and Matt Pooler 978-1-78952-169-6
Alice Cooper in the 1970s – Chris Sutton 978-1-78952-104-7
Curved Air in the 1970s – Laura Shenton 978-1-78952-069-9
Bob Dylan in the 1980s – Don Klees 978-1-78952-157-3
Fleetwood Mac in the 1970s – Andrew Wild 978-1-78952-105-4
Focus in the 1970s – Stephen Lambe 978-1-78952-079-8
Free and Bad Company in the 1970s – John Van der Kiste 978-1-78952-178-8
Genesis in the 1970s – Bill Thomas 978178952-146-7
George Harrison in the 1970s – Eoghan Lyng 978-1-78952-174-0
Marillion in the 1980s – Nathaniel Webb 978-1-78952-065-1
Mott the Hoople and Ian Hunter in the 1970s – John Van der Kiste
978-1-78-952-162-7
Pink Floyd In The 1970s – Georg Purvis 978-1-78952-072-9
Tangerine Dream in the 1970s – Stephen Palmer 978-1-78952-161-0
The Sweet in the 1970s – Darren Johnson 978-1-78952-139-9
Uriah Heep in the 1970s – Steve Pilkington 978-1-78952-103-0
Yes in the 1980s – Stephen Lambe with David Watkinson 978-1-78952-125-2

On Screen series

Carry On… – Stephen Lambe 978-1-78952-004-0
David Cronenberg – Patrick Chapman 978-1-78952-071-2
Doctor Who: The David Tennant Years – Jamie Hailstone 978-1-78952-066-8
James Bond – Andrew Wild – 978-1-78952-010-1
Monty Python – Steve Pilkington 978-1-78952-047-7
Seinfeld Seasons 1 to 5 – Stephen Lambe 978-1-78952-012-5

Other Books

1967: A Year In Psychedelic Rock – Kevan Furbank 978-1-78952-155-9
1970: A Year In Rock – John Van der Kiste 978-1-78952-147-4
1973: The Golden Year of Progressive Rock 978-1-78952-165-8
Babysitting A Band On The Rocks – G.D. Praetorius 978-1-78952-106-1
Eric Clapton Sessions – Andrew Wild 978-1-78952-177-1
Derek Taylor: For Your Radioactive Children – Andrew Darlington
978-1-78952-038-5

The Golden Road: The Recording History of The Grateful Dead – John Kilbride 978-1-78952-156-6

Iggy and The Stooges On Stage 1967-1974 – Per Nilsen 978-1-78952-101-6

Jon Anderson and the Warriors – the road to Yes – David Watkinson 978-1-78952-059-0

Nu Metal: A Definitive Guide – Matt Karpe 978-1-78952-063-7

Tommy Bolin: In and Out of Deep Purple – Laura Shenton 978-1-78952-070-5

Maximum Darkness – Deke Leonard 978-1-78952-048-4

Maybe I Should've Stayed In Bed – Deke Leonard 978-1-78952-053-8

The Twang Dynasty – Deke Leonard 978-1-78952-049-1

and many more to come!

Would you like to write for Sonicbond Publishing?
We are mainly a music publisher, but we also occasionally publish in other genres including film and television. At Sonicbond Publishing we are always on the look-out for authors, particularly for our two main series, On Track and Decades.

Mixing fact with in depth analysis, the On Track series examines the entire recorded work of a particular musical artist or group. All genres are considered from easy listening and jazz to 60s soul to 90s pop, via rock and metal.

The Decades series singles out a particular decade in an artist or group's history and focuses on that decade in more detail than may be allowed in the On Track series.

While professional writing experience would, of course, be an advantage, the most important qualification is to have real enthusiasm and knowledge of your subject. First-time authors are welcomed, but the ability to write well in English is essential.

Sonicbond Publishing has distribution throughout Europe and North America, and all our books are also published in E-book form. Authors will be paid a royalty based on sales of their book. Further details about our books are available from www.sonicbondpublishing.com. To contact us, complete the contact form there or email info@sonicbondpublishing.co.uk